T0357837

TWO TRUTHS AND A LIONEL

ALSO BY BRIAN WASSON

Seven Minutes in Candyland

TWO TRUTHS AND A LIONEL

BRIAN WASSON

Quill Tree Books

An Imprint of HarperCollinsPublishers

Quill Tree Books is an imprint of HarperCollins Publishers.

Two Truths and a Lionel
Copyright © 2025 by Brian Wasson
All rights reserved. Manufactured in Harrisonburg, VA, United
States of America. No part of this book may be used or reproduced
in any manner whatsoever without written permission except in the
case of brief quotations embodied in critical articles and reviews. For
information, address HarperCollins Children's Books, a division of
HarperCollins Publishers, 195 Broadway, New York, NY 10007.
www.epicreads.com

Library of Congress Control Number: 2024950110
ISBN 978-0-06-326470-0

Typography by Molly Fehr
25 26 27 28 29 LBC 5 4 3 2 1
First Edition

TWO TRUTHS AND A LIONEL

1

MY NEIGHBOR AND LONGTIME RIVAL'S GOLDFISH JUST DIED.

It was delicious.

To clarify: I, Lionel Honeycutt, did not eat the goldfish. In fact, I remain in good standing with the marine life community.

It's my cat that's in the proverbial doghouse.

That fateful day—yesterday, to be exact—Michaela "Mickey" Kyle and I could only watch in shock and morbid fascination as my cat preyed upon its wriggly victim. Mickey gasped as my cat pounced and pinned the just-purchased fish to the asphalt of our street. She made this weird, high-pitched shriek as Harry chomped down, her demeanor deflating like a three-day-old balloon as we both watched the scaly, unliving mass slide down his gullet.

I blame bad reflexes. She blames the cat. And my existence.

Mickey had just returned home with the fish bag as I was trying to corral Harry back inside for his bath. The cat slipped away from me and ran across the road and into her driveway. This startled Mickey enough that she dropped the bag. It burst, and suddenly Harry was indulging in the feline version of street food.

"At least it didn't suffer," I offer meekly.

"The only way it could've suffered more is if it were fried into a filet, wrapped in a toasted bun, and sold alongside a McFlurry," Mickey replies.

And now I'm craving McDonald's.

We exit the city bus, Mickey plodding off and me barely squeezing out behind her as the door closes. Mickey soldiers onto the crosswalk and cuts right into the grass buffering the street from the mall parking lot.

"Slow down," I say, touching her shoulder. She heel-turns, her brown eyes somehow incandescent red.

"I'm gonna write a will someday," she declares. "And the first sentence will say 'I hate Lionel Honeycutt, and you must, too.' Because I want to make sure my loathing for you gets passed down for generations to come."

The Pet Emporium is on the far side of a mall on the far side of our town, Westlake. Both the mall and the town have seen better days. The mall is a relic of retail's golden years, having survived three recessions, two renovations, and a mass exodus of the local customer base to a bigger mall two towns away. The store is inexplicably placed next to the perfumery, so the whole wing reeks of dog hair and chlorine with a soft undercurrent of cherry-lavender flower bomb.

It's my favorite smell simply because it's attached to my favorite memory: buying cat toys and a carrier the day I adopted

Harry—or, as Mickey has dubbed him, "the Butcher of West-lake." He was a kitty then, and I, a kindergartner. So long ago that Mickey and I weren't even sworn enemies yet. We were friends, actually. Best friends.

I'm ten steps behind as Mickey barrels through the mall's side entrance. She makes no effort to hold the door open for me, and I almost trip squeezing through before it closes. Many of the same stores I remember from childhood line the corridor. The nail salon. The shoe place. The counterculture trinket store with the stylized neon sign.

The door chimes as she enters the pet store with me trailing her. A tall, thin rail of a guy behind the counter puts his phone down, scratches the stubble above his ring of neck tattoos, and cranks out a smile more laborious than his actual job. With a decidedly flat, unhelpful tone, he drawls out a "Hi, welcome to Pet Emporium. How may I help you?" The space above him is hazy, a wispy cloud of gray smoke yawning across the ceiling. *Is he seriously vaping?*

Mickey slowly glides over to the counter. "Yes," she replies. "I've got this pest problem I need eliminated."

"Fleas on the dog?" he asks.

Her head shakes. "Boy. Over the shoulder," she tells him with a slight nod. Leaning on the glass, her words shift into a low, conspiratorial mode: "Can you help me . . . *eliminate* this problem?"

"Uhhh," the poor guy says.

Mickey leaves him speechless as she barges toward the

aquariums, me following close behind. It's just us here, apart from a couple who look to be in their twenties. They're holding hands, spouting color names and compliments as they point to the more ostentatious fish. The antithesis of us. Mickey approaches a tank next to the one that the couple stopped in front of, examining each fish as a doctor would a patient. I wander to the couple's other side and peer into a different tank, figuring the more distance between Mickey and me, the better.

It's not long before one of the fish catches my attention. It has long whiskers like an elderly graybeard. It's sleek and unbothered by the others, and it doesn't swim so much as mosey through the water. It's mostly blue save a dorsal fin so wavy and silver that it looks like a feather cap.

While I watch it, a wave of sadness just barely touches me, as light and lingering as the prick of a thorn. Grandpa's feather hat. The one he wore in his first starring role, *Carnage at the Disco*. I loved that hat. He'd let me wear it around his house when I was younger, mimicking his famous strut that he so often broke into while walking into a brawl or away from a climactic explosion. I used to try so hard to be like him. It's weird thinking about how someone who once had so much life in him could have such a sullen and acidic ending.

In the last few weeks since it happened, completely random things—laundry detergent scents, snippets of old-school songs, and now this *fish*—have conjured feelings ranging from sad to celebratory. Looming over this swirl of emotions is the posthumous October premiere of what's hyped to be his most prestigious film. The one advance reviews have raved about and the streaming services are expected to fight a bidding war to carry. The one my parents and grandma are inexplicably unexcited about attending, despite it being only a month away.

"Hey, loser, you're gonna spook the fish," Mickey says. I snap to attention, just now realizing the couple has walked away. She's looking right at me. "Why were you staring anyway?" she asks.

I scramble for an answer. "Because it's blue" is the only thing I can come up with.

"What?"

"Well," I say, pointing to the aquarium in front of me, "they're called 'goldfish,' right? Shouldn't they all be gold?"

She shrugs, as if the answer is obvious. "They didn't start out gold." Her eyes settle back on her phone screen as it records the tank before her. I study Mickey as she studies her camera screen, capturing their movements with all the precision and perceptiveness of Spielberg. "It's genetics," she continues. "Goldfish derived from carp, which are kind of a dull greenish or olive color and—" She pauses, catching me staring her. "Well, you *asked*. . . ."

The doorbell chimes again. I look back toward the front and see the top of a kid's head bobbing along just beyond a high shelf. When he stops in front of a cage of chinchillas, I'm able to make out his face, slightly. I watch him for a while before turning my attention back to the blue fish. The Grandpa fish. But I can't help but keep Mickey in my periphery. She's so enthralled by the swarm of fish in her tank that after about a minute her phone and her nose are a few inches from the glass.

Why is she so into these things? They're just miniature swimming fish. You can't talk to them or take them for a walk. And the only time they're paying you the slightest bit of attention is when it's feeding time. I remember when I asked Dad for a goldfish in first grade. Grandpa happened to be there, and he scoffed at the request. "What's the use of a pet you can't even pet?" he asked. Then, turning to my dad, he said, "Them's for lightweights and lazy folks. Get that boy something with teeth." Despite my dad's audible groan, Grandpa was right. Never again did I ask for a pet I couldn't hold.

"Could you just pick a fish so we can go?" I ask.

"It's not that simple," Mickey says. She sidesteps, closing in on my tank. She starts snapping portrait-style photos of each fish before sifting through her work like she's viewing art at a gallery.

"So weird," I whisper, mostly to myself, but I also don't care if she hears. I suppose I should expect this by now. Her being so extra. This is, after all, the girl who openly bragged about her mom's documentary films on bird migration or the mating habits of tiger swallowtail butterflies, as if that were engaging lunchtime cafeteria conversation.

Even I, a simple six-year-old, knew she was a certified weirdo back then. She's always been that way. Ten years later, guys still stay away, even though she's grown to be what an objective observer would describe as cute—pretty, even, if you overlook the horns and forked tongue.

"I have my process" is all she says.

"Why does your process involve recording every fish you see?"

She doesn't answer, but not in a purposefully-ignoring-me way. It's more like she's flustered. She sucks in her cheeks and kind of angles away from me just a hair, the slight movement rustling up the vanilla scent at her neck.

A moment later, she points. "*That* one." I look at it. Nothing special. It's orange with a white dorsal fin and what appears to be an anvil-shaped birthmark just above its mouth. It curls around a lighthouse before darting into the underwater castle, peeking out at us from the throne room.

She beckons the clerk over, and he opens the top of the aquarium as Mickey directs him to the exact fish she wants.

"Okay, so. One more request," Mickey says, drawing my attention from the clerk. She shoves the phone into my chest. "Can you record this?"

"Record what?"

"The handoff." I squint, and she quickly adds, "Don't laugh."

My first thought, of course, is to bust out laughing, because *what*? How strange can she be? But I tamp down the instinct. For some otherworldly reason, this means something to her, so I gotta respect that.

I film as the clerk sets a clear plastic bag in the water and then dips a net into the tank. The fish easily dodges the first few swipes, making the clerk look quite incompetent trying to catch Mickey's chosen fish. It seems to be predicting his moves well in advance, like it's playing chess while the clerk is shoving the bishops up his nose. As the charade goes on, he gets more irritated, taking bigger swipes, grunting, even splashing water with his frantic thrusts. Mickey and I both grin as we watch.

And then we notice our shared grins and grin at *that*. A stark departure from our fates as archnemeses. So what if we share the same grim sense of humor?

Finally, the guy nets the fish and turns with a self-satisfied smile. "Got it." He thrusts the bag toward her, dripping water on my shoes.

"Wow! Bassmaster, fish tank level: Achieved!" Mickey says, clapping.

The guy gets all in a huff, defiantly declaring, "It's *carp*, actually."

Mickey simply curls a lip and pats his shoulder. "Never change, dude. Never change."

Actually, he *should* change. Both of us catch the smell of smoke from his clothes. Thin gray wisps float across my field of vision. But that can't be right. He couldn't have just vaped. He was just struggling to catch a freaking fish!

Mickey sniffs. "Dude, could you be a stoner *off* the clock, please?"

The guy starts to respond, but his words get entangled in a fit of coughing. He tries to wave away the smoke now descending like fog after a hard rain, but it's not working. It's covering the whole area.

"What is this?" Mickey coughs.

We get our answer a second later. A set of ceiling tiles collapses behind me, kicking up a cloud of dust. Each light pops as it goes out. Hot air singes our skin, and a hazy glow grows above us as tile after tile turns to peels of falling ash.

I point. "Fire!"

"No shit!" Mickey yells.

I hear shouting somewhere in the back. The couple. I turn to the store clerk. "There's people back there!"

"And I wish them the best!" he says. "Shit, I gotta get all these animals out."

A loud *crack* sounds out from above. I look up. A beam breaks. More smoke rushes down. The ceiling tiles are gone, and I can see the crisscross of struts and joists buckling. The fire is spiraling around an HVAC duct, with flames jumping off every which way and sparking new blazes. I spot a nearby display catch on fire.

I hear another crash from the back of the store. I put Mickey's phone atop a shelf and grab a pack of dog food. I hoist it over my head, thinking it might save me from falling debris.

We're barreling toward the exit when a woman's scream rings out. The *couple*. Why aren't they escaping with us? Instinctually, I make my dumbest move yet. I start trekking toward the back. When water splashes my ankles, I realize Mickey's following.

I glance over my shoulder, and she's *holding* an aquarium. I'm about to lose my effing mind. "Why are you holding that?" I yell.

Her eyes plead innocence. "For . . . dousing!"

It's obvious she's trying to save the fish.

When we turn the corner, it becomes apparent why the couple hasn't escaped. The man's legs are absolutely buried under a mound of grooming products, topped by a whole row of shelving. I drop the dog food and Mickey sets down the aquarium, and we rush over.

The guy groans. The woman is frantically pulling his arm, but I see the exhaustion in her eyes and the sweat beads streaming down her soot-covered face.

"What should we do?!" Mickey asks.

"Get the stuff off him!" I yell. Mickey grabs as many shampoo bottles as she can and hurls them. There's a huge whoosh of flame birthed by the chemicals. The blowback makes the area furnace-level hot. "Don't throw it in the fire!" I yell.

We start grabbing bottles and setting them gently but hastily on the carpet. When we uncover more of the guy's leg, I make the call to lift the shelf. I look to the woman still pulling him by the arm. "When we lift, you pull as hard and as far as you can!" I say to her.

Mickey and I crouch and try to grab the metal edge of the shelf before recoiling. It's too hot to touch. I take my shirt off and put the top half into Mickey's hands while holding the bottom in my palms. The metal's still hot but bearable, just barely.

"Lift!" I shout. The smoke thickens as we attempt to raise the structure. The man grunts as his significant other pulls, and I feel the guy's leg shift against my ankle that's firmly placed near the side of the shelf. It's working.

"I can't hold it much longer!" Mickey says.

"Keep going!" I reply, but I'm fighting my own battle. The metal's searing into my skin like a branding iron.

In the next instant, approximately a million thoughts crowd my head like bats in a cave. *What if we can't get this guy out? What if none of us make it?* The nerves in my body surge and tingle as adrenaline courses through me. Through dark smoke, I see the face of a woman who won't last ten more seconds, a girlfriend's desperate efforts to save her love. A man in the vise grip of death. The metal is like fire in my palm. Mickey yelps, then grunts as I let it go.

But I can't just let it go. I can be the hero here. Just like Grandpa.

My eyes shut. I try again. I grab the metal, tighter this time. It feels like pure hell. I crouch even more, like a loaded spring. My muscles coil as my mind counts down.

Three. Two. One.

I suppose, in retrospect, I should've stretched after PE earlier. Or drank more Gatorade. Whatever I've done that's bringing on my leg cramp during this harrowing moment, it couldn't have come at a worse time. My legs buckle, and I grab my calf. Mickey coughs out a "What the fuck?" as the woman screams and the guy cries out in agony under the dropped weight of metal shelving.

I start limp-crawling backward. Then everything goes black for who knows how long. Suddenly I wake, my eyes springing open, my lungs gasping for the "good air" driven low toward the carpet. Seconds later, someone who I suspect is Mickey staggers toward me, tripping *over* me. My hunch is confirmed when water from the aquarium she was carrying earlier splashes my face. Miraculously, I have the awareness to follow her, rolling onto my stomach and army-crawling toward the front of the store. Dozens of chinchillas and ferrets and guinea pigs stream out alongside me. Me, imploring Mickey not to drag a fish tank out with her. Her, of course, ignoring me. The nearby sound of sirens as we struggle into the fresher mall-corridor air beyond the threshold.

Dazed, I watch as firemen run toward the flames, and it takes a few seconds to register the two people they pass to get there. The couple. I look on as someone drapes a blanket over them and points toward us. They look our way, their nods tired but appreciative. I notice Mickey a few feet from me. She's bent over the lip of the fountain, splashing her face and wiping black ash from her cheeks. She sees me looking. Her expression softens. I think she's about to make a witty joke or even give a compliment. I let my guard down, a hesitant smile dawning on my lips. All she says is "You still owe me a fish."

2

TWO DAYS LATER, I STILL CAN'T PIECE TOGETHER EVERY-
thing that happened, but that doesn't stop my friend Theo from
filling in the details like spackle into wall cracks.

"I bet you it was some voodoo shit that started that fire. You
know that store is cursed, right?" he says as the bell rings.

My stare disengages from the poster I'm taping to the wall
and redirects on him. "No, I—wait, *what*?"

"Mm-hmm," Theo says, nodding. "Some of the clerks was
secretly hawking exotic Siamese kitten litters in the back of the
shop a couple years ago. God don't like liars or pet killers. Probably saw you and the clerk in there and went for a two-for-one
special."

I pivot until I'm square with him. The calmness in my voice
doesn't mask my agitation by a long shot. "For the last time: I
didn't kill Mickey's fish. My cat ate it."

"Yeah, and my dog ate my homework. Right," Theo says.
"Besides, you ain't gotta convince me. Convince God. He's the
one who tried to kill you."

I don't know about convincing God of anything, but my friend has officially convinced me that sniffing Sharpies to see if the colors smell different is not conducive to logical thinking. My eyes drift away from him to the other end of the hallway, where a pack of girls climbs the stairwell.

I wonder when my friend got so maddeningly opinionated. In retrospect, perhaps the first clue to fellow junior Theo James's descent was his decision to run for next year's student body president. He announced early. Like, *way* early. It's September now, and voting isn't till spring. He figures campaigning for months on end will win him more than strange looks and translate to actual votes. So he's done what any good guy with an astoundingly bad idea would do: He's roped his best friend into it. Me. I'm his campaign manager. Keeper of the poster-boards. Since we finished our history test early, Mr. Kendall let us leave to hang said campaign posters in the hallway. It feels weird hanging placards for an election that's several months away right beside advertisements for more immediate events, like the homecoming Fall Ball dance two weeks from now. But Theo's always been forward-thinking, I guess. The posters feature Theo dressed up as an eagle-eyed, stern-faced Uncle Sam, but instead of pointing, he's holding up a can of Axe body spray.

"Say no to B-O, vote for Theo!" he shouts at the incoming crowd. He nudges my shoulder. I call out listlessly as people pass. One of his campaign promises is to use excess funds to buy the school's freshmen two cans each of deodorant.

Most kids ignore me as they walk by. One gives a sort of

bemused glance you might give a street mime or a sidewalk magician. "A little more *oomph*," Theo critiques.

I repeat the slogan. Oomph-full this time. Still get ignored.

I look back down the hallway, my eyes tracking that same group of girls who just exited the stairwell onto our floor as I contemplate his long-shot campaign strategy to cater to the babies of the Westlake High family. *Freshmen.* I suppose it's admirable to care for the least of us. And that's the type of person Theo is. Kind. Charitable. Empathetic. All the adjectives that draw out soft smiles from friends' mothers and compel them to say well-intentioned but vaguely awful things like *I wish my kid were more like you.* But why center a campaign around freshmen? Why not puppies with three legs? The unhoused? That group of stoners who hang out under the oaks in the courtyard? *Any* group would be more sympathetic, really.

"You think our target message needs tweaking?" I ask.

He considers it for a moment as he takes a swig of his water bottle. His cheeks go all chipmunk as the water swishes around his mouth along with whatever thought he's chewing on. Before long, he shakes his head. All too earnestly, he says, "If we're gonna leave this school better than we found it, it starts with the youth. Feel me?"

No, actually, I don't. I want to leave this school, period. It's so *meh* here. Everything so humdrum, middle of the road. The Goldilocks zone of tedium. Much like its small southern name-sake town, there isn't much going on at Westlake High School. Other than a few good sports teams and a decent performing arts program, the school's been an endless hamster wheel of mediocre academics, churning out decades' worth of diplomas that might as well be tickets to work at one of the local mills.

"I understand," I lie.

My head swivels back to the approaching girls. I can feel Theo shaking his head.

"Come on, bro," he says. I know he sees what I'm seeing. *Who* I'm seeing. "I ain't witnessed anything this tragic since the Chastity Club's spring recruitment drive."

I can't help but smile at the allusion. I only know about this ordeal because Theo's actually in the Chastity Club. Not that he's chaste or anything—well, not voluntarily. This school is huge, so one thing it *does* have is a ton of clubs. And in order to drum up support for an impending campaign, Theo's been on a mission to make inroads with just about every single one. It's not uncommon nowadays for me to see him with random artifacts from various new endeavors. Recent sightings include Theo with a baguette and beret (French Club); Theo with knee-high socks, racket, and shuttlecock (Badminton Club); and Theo in goggles and a lab coat (Women in STEM). I never asked how he pulled that last one off.

Perhaps his most consequential club foray—to me at least—was his brief venture into Merengue Dance Club. He dragged me there once, and that's where I was first introduced to her. *Her* being Josefina Ramos. The girl I'm looking at right now. The girl I've been looking at from an acceptable, nonintrusive distance since freshman year. The girl who's damn near

16

impossible *not* to look at. Except if you're Theo, of course. He hasn't found a girl attractive since he saw Tom Holland in that Spider-Man bodysuit a few years back.

"She is beautiful, though. I'll give you that," he says.

I stand corrected.

Josefina's in the middle of a pack of girls who seem to orbit around her. It's fitting, though, as she's pretty much a star in the whole school's eyes. A walking grab bag of yearbook superlatives. She's classy and smart and kind. The kind of girl who spends summers volunteering at animal rescues.

I watch her walk toward a water fountain. The hallway lights don't so much shine on her as accentuate her beauty. They make the good parts glow. Thousand-watt smile. Long legs. Smooth brown skin. Hell, they're all good parts. And I'm not alone in thinking highly of her. Just ask her two million social media followers.

She stops at the fountain to refill her bottle. I feel secure in the knowledge that neither she nor her friends will look my way.

"I wonder what it feels like to be God's favorite," I mutter.

"A lot of pressure, honestly," Theo answers. I elbow him.

She takes a sip before closing the cap. And then something curious happens. She glances at me and waves. I don't wave back because it couldn't be directed toward me, right? I actually look around to see if anyone's near us. Nobody. Then, like a dumbass, I jab a finger into my chest as if to ask, "Who, me?"

She laughs. Several girls around her look up at me with

broad, expectant smiles, as if Josefina's gesture was some seal of approval.

In fact, I notice others, not in her pack, smiling as well. It seems everybody in the hallway is in on a secret that I'm not yet privy to. Well, everybody except Chase Wells. He's standing by his locker with his boys, a confused scowl painted across his face.

Chase is an all-American football linebacker and bully. It's debatable which pastime he's better at. While most would say football, having been the recipient of his expertly executed wedgies and leg whips throughout middle school, I'd have to go with the latter. It mostly tapered off in high school, primarily because there are enough buildings and obscure hall routes to avoid him. But the anxiety is still there. The tensing every time I see his smarmy smile or the knee-jerk flinch whenever his name is called.

In middle school, I tried standing up to him a couple times. It never ended well because, like my dad, I'm not much of an imposing force. To his everlasting chagrin, Grandpa didn't pass on the set of genes that had him dominating hurdles in college track and doing his own stunts well into his sixties. Of all the movie genres he acted in, action movies seemed like the most natural fit. To this day, professional daredevils try to mimic the double somersault he performed out of a skyscraper in *The Bad Don't Break Easy*.

Alas, I'd be lucky to pull off a double cartwheel. It just grinds my nerves to think of how it was possible for my dad to *not* inherit any of Grandpa's natural talent.

I don't get my answer as to why I'm on the receiving end of this extra attention today until right after third period.

I'm heading down the B-wing hallway with Theo to our calculus class. As we walk, everybody's eyes fall on us again. There's this mishmash of cheery grins, appreciative nods, and furtive whispers between friends. The atmosphere is so festive, in fact, that Theo has taken to finger-gunning, saluting, and fist-pumping while chanting "Yes, we can" like some sort of knock-off Barack Obama.

By the time we reach the water fountains, I notice current student body president Lori Chen approaching from the opposite direction, trailed by her entourage of student council members. She has raven-black pigtails hanging like braided ropes down her back, and a sprinter's body: short, tanned, and athletic. But her biggest wins have come in school rather than outside it.

My locker neighbor Kelly Isengard is beside her, transcribing Lori's edicts into the notebook in her hand. Lori looks none too pleased at Theo's antics. I shudder to think what she could do to him. From what I hear, she wants to run for reelection. Reportedly, she ran off a rival last year. And not just out of the campaign. Like, full-on out of the *state*. They don't call her "the Gavel" for nothing. But then she notices me right beside Theo, and something changes. Not like a smile or anything. More a barely perceptible acknowledgment of my existence. She whispers something into Kelly's ear, and Kelly furiously writes it down as they pass.

Only one person seems not to have changed their demeanor toward me. Mickey stands at the end of the hallway, eyes lasering in on me, her scowl as sharp as her elbows. She begins a deliberate, mechanical walk my way, like some Terminator in a plaid skirt and knee-highs. When she gets to me, she shoves her newly purchased phone in my face before I can react.

"Explain this," she demands.

Theo looks over my shoulder as we both watch. Although I've never seen the video, I immediately recognize it. It's the pet shop. Store footage. A bird's-eye view of fire spilling out from the ceiling. A shelf tumbling. A guy trapped. Me trying to lift it. I don't see Mickey, though. The angle must've cut her off. Confused, I nudge the phone to the side, my eyes meeting Mickey's glare.

"They had their live feed on," I say.

In an effort to drum up business, the Pet Emporium started a live feed of its store a couple years ago. Dozens of cameras perched high and low, aiming to capture any scintilla of stream-worthy content from the captive animals and insects.

She nods and spits out, "It's viral. Like an annoying communicable disease that just keeps resurfacing at the most inopportune times. Which is kinda fitting seeing as that's my long-standing perception of you. Keep watching."

I look back at the phone. The video cuts to a view of the grooming area hazed over by smoke. A dark silhouette runs past a smoke-filled screen. Was that me? I was never near that area. The screen switches back to a high angle. The man crawls away from the shelf, finally sitting upright. His girlfriend urges him on. Mickey staggers into the frame, though her shirt is lifted to cover her nose, so if you didn't know she was there that day, this footage doesn't exactly identify her. You can barely see me, too. Only my hand desperately waving through a hazy cloud trawling along the floor. Mickey stumbles right where the rest of my body should be.

"Bro, from what I can barely see of you, you looking like you're trapped in a weighted blanket. Why?" Theo asks.

"I had a calf cramp," I said. "Then I blacked out."

Once the video ends, Mickey jerks her phone back and starts swiping. She's breathing the same way I'd imagine a storybook dragon would. I look around as the warning bell for fourth period rings. Some kids in the thinning crowd are still looking from their phones to me, back to their phones.

"I can't believe it," I say, my words almost at a whisper. Is that why everyone's been treating me differently this morning? They think I saved that guy?

"They're even making dub-overs and memes about you," Mickey adds, shoving the phone back into my face.

I watch the screen again, but it's not the original. It's just a snippet, before the dark, heavy smoke started rolling in. A very *specific* snippet of shirtless me trying to lift the shelf pinning down the guy. I've got this determined action-hero grimace. Sweat drips from my skin like I've just stepped out of the shower. It's like a scene from one of Grandpa's movies.

Again, I notice Mickey's cut out of it altogether. If you

trusted the camera, you'd assume I lifted the shelf to save that guy *alone*, without Mickey. But that's the thing. I *don't* trust the camera. I remember us lifting it together. Me cramping and falling away during the second attempt. Blacking out.

This video is about twenty seconds, and it's overlayed with a bling filter that puts random starbursts and sparkles all over the screen. After it ends, Mickey swipes right. The next is of the exact same clip, cut off again right before the angle switches. There's no filter on this one, but instead it has a song overlayed. "My Hero" by the Foo Fighters. Mom got me into them years back. Heavy on the guitar riffs with drums hammering home the emotional resonance.

I look at the views. I nearly faint when I see the number. 20.4 million.

Mickey swipes again. This time it's the same clip but set in slo-mo to the *Chariots of Fire* theme song.

16.2 million.

Again, she swipes. Same footage, but this time there's only soft instrumental music with a woman's resolute voice soaring over it. It's a quote I've heard millions of times before: "Our deepest fear is not that we are inadequate. Our deepest fear is that we are powerful beyond measure."

38.8 million.

Mickey swipes out of the videos, and her iPhone goes back to the home screen. She's absolutely furious, cheeks puffed and red as a crayon.

"There's also one of you with the cute little mouse ears

and whiskers filter. And at least a dozen more with fire titled songs. Ed Sheeran, 'I See Fire.' Chaka Khan, 'Through the Fire.' Alicia Keys, 'Girl on Fire.'"

My eyebrow rises at that last song. Mickey shrugs. "I think some TikTokers were just trying to be ironic with that one. The *point* is, it's all a lie! Your 'heroics,'" she says, using air quotes, "are just a fictive creation of a social media culture obsessed with slick editing and mythmaking. And that's a shame."

"No, that's *awesome!*" Theo corrects. He swipes Mickey's phone and scrolls back through the videos, finding the Foo Fighters one. "These are Taylor Swift numbers!"

"Excuse me!" Mickey says, swiping it back. "Charli XCX at best."

By now, though, I'm smiling. This *is* awesome. The world thinks I'm a hero. And more important, the school does, too. I get out my phone and pull up my social media. I don't usually check—and I have all my notifications disabled—because what's the point when you average 1.5 likes per post? But if there ever was an accurate measure of the school's pulse, you'd find it online. Westlake is obsessed with socials. We even created our own hashtag, #WestlakeWhispers, the student body's own little trove of school gossip. Sure enough, I see the video over and over, along with shout-outs like "Fucking awesome, Lionel!" and "We stan a pet-loving king!" Imagine me, a nobody, getting this kind of attention. Goose bumps cover my body as I think of the possibilities. People inviting me to parties, passing me notes in class, asking me anything other than to borrow my pencil. I could get used to this.

"You have to fix this," Mickey demands. "There's already a Reddit thread calling you 'Achilles of the Animal Kingdom.'" Confusion creases my brow, so she explains the commonalities. "You know, Achilles? Famed Greek hero?" I squint, still not getting it. She persists. "Disregarding your own life to save others. Propensity to be caught shirtless in moments of high drama . . ." She cuts her eyes at Theo and then back at me. "Best friend is gay. . . ."

Theo offers a *You got me*–type shrug before adding, "And both befallen by ill-timed leg injuries."

"So you *have* to fix this!" she reiterates.

"Fix what?" I ask, a big smile framing my quiet laughter.

"Fix the fact that all these people think you're some Superman who did this all on your own. I was there, lest we forget!"

"I didn't forget," I reply, realizing only afterward how doubtful that claim might be. By definition, "blacking out" means *not* remembering. There's a black hole of drama in between me cramping up and Mickey tripping over me, and I couldn't tell you a thing about it.

"I saw it all," Mickey says.

"Did you, though?" Theo asks. We both look at him, equally skeptical. "I mean, there was so much smoke in the video. Smoke can mess with your head." My gaze returns to Mickey. I can almost see the uncertainty creeping into her brain.

"But I *felt* the shelf get heavier when this ignoramus fell over," she says. "Then, a few seconds later, it got lighter, and I could lift it again."

"And there was more smoke, I presume?" Theo asks.

"Yes."

"So, he could've gotten back up and helped."

Mickey's eyes laser in on me. "Did you?" she asks. Her question is high-pitched, almost panicked.

I close my eyes, forcing myself back to the scene. Feeling the burning metal dig into my hands. The strain on my biceps. The knotting of a calf that still feels tight today. Falling into smoke. Swooning and almost drowning in it. Fighting it . . .

And then I'm crawling toward the exit.

I'm now acutely aware of my shirt collar rubbing at my neck. I fight the urge to pull at it because it'll make me look guilty. *But guilty of what, exactly? Lying? No. Misremembering?* Would having holes in your memory big enough to drive a semi through be a crime? It was a traumatic event. I escaped with my life. Maybe it's too much to ask of me to escape with my mind fully intact, too.

"I can't say for sure," I answer.

"I *knew* it!" Mickey nearly shouts, the words drawing the attention of the few passersby left in the hallway.

"But you can't say, either," I continue. "You don't know what I did, do you?" I ask. She opens her mouth but hesitates before responding.

"You saved the whole fucking pet shop!" a voice calls out.

The three of us turn, and there's Josefina. She walks over

with three of her girls, a slight head tilt flipping her long curls. Ceiling light looms over her shoulder in an almost-ethereal, fluorescent way—like the hallway wanted to make a personal halo for her but on a public-school budget.

"Congratulations . . . hero," she says.

"You rock, Lionel!" Stacy Lawrence parrots. Meg Martin follows up with "What you did was so hot," and Jocelyn Marx concludes with "Four-legged rizz god." I don't respond.

"So what was it like going viral for the first time?" Josefina asks. Again, I say nothing. It's like my mouth's been clamped shut. "You're practically famous now. Like me." She must read my silence as much more than just being starstruck because her eyes pinch with concern. "You good?" After waiting a few more quiet seconds, Josefina glances up at Theo. "Is he, like, mute?"

I feel Theo's slap to my back, and it's like my brain remembers to breathe again. Air and spit shoot out, almost landing on Josefina's feet. Theo's grip on my shirt keeps me from collapsing as I drop to a knee. I'm gasping. Josefina's freaking out. Mickey's just standing there watching me, dumbfounded.

As I catch my breath, Theo reaches high up in the lie closet for even the flimsiest of excuses, finally coming down with "Smoke inhalation. Doctors said he may never fully recover."

Josefina crouches, getting eye level with me. The expression on her face is that of a pedestrian stopping to console a stray puppy.

"Oh, you poor thing," she says. "I completely understand being overwhelmed after such a traumatic event."

She takes out her phone and lifts it up so that it's angled down at us. I see both our faces on-screen just before she takes a pic. "What are you doing?" I ask hoarsely.

She doesn't answer, but by the way she holds her phone, I'm able to see her thumbs gliding across the keyboard.

She types out a caption: **Props to our local hero. Still dealing with the fallout, but shining nonetheless.** She punctuates it with three praying hands emojis, **#WestlakeWhispers**, and **#FinaFam**, her clarion call for her loyal followers.

I look back up at her. "Thanks," I say, the word practically jumping from my lips. "I mean, for the shout-out."

She shrugs. "Hey, us influencers gotta stick together. Maybe we should hang out sometime. Talk brand synergy."

"Sure."

No doubt she means posting duets and reciprocal tagging, but I can't help but think of another kind of synergy. Her on my arm at my grandfather's movie premiere next month. Us posing in front of the cameras, our giddy faces streamed to millions.

We exchange contacts. She holds the camera in front of us again, this time switching to record mode. Like a seasoned news anchor, she warms to the camera. "What up, Fina Fam? Be sure to check out our favorite hero—and one of my favorite guys—at . . ."

She angles the phone at me. I barely manage to croak out my handle, "LBoog321."

"Parting words?" she asks.

"Ummm . . ." I draw a blank for God knows how many

seconds before noticing Theo and Mickey above me, looking on as they, too, wonder what I'll say. For lack of anything better, I spout out, "Vote for Theo James. Westlake SBP!"

Jo's look is one of mild bemusement. She tilts the phone back toward her. "And there you have it," she says. A tongue out and deuces sign follow her quick "Peace out."

Before I can even process what happened, she's up. Slowly, I rise with her. By the time I think to ask to see our post, she's walking away with the real-life version of the Fina Fam. "How'd it look?" I call after her.

"I'll send you a link," she says, giving me the same deuces as she goes.

The three of us stand there for a while, with Theo googling Josefina's number to make sure it's not just spam. Mickey is fuming, face looking like a literal cartoon teapot. It's all I can manage to just play it cool and not moonwalk right in front of her.

"You can't go on with this! I demand you come clean!" she says, stamping her foot.

"You can't demand anything," I say.

"I'll expose you!"

"With what? You saw the video footage. It's inconclusive at best. I have a foggy memory. You're not positive."

"Not positive," she mocks. "We're not talking pregnancy tests, Lionel! We're talking real life. . . ."

She turns and paces toward the other side of the hallway, continuing her rant as Theo drifts away and heads to class. I'm about to do the same when something makes me freeze. Rather, someone.

He's a thin kid. A babyish countenance. His glasses look like a prop from a *Harry Potter* movie, and he seems like he took a wrong turn on the way to middle school and somehow ended up here.

But as lost as he looks, I can place his face perfectly. Just not *here*.

I'm immediately transported back to the pet store, smoke-filled memories barreling back in flashes. It's the kid who entered the pet store after us. The glimpses of his face as he looked at the caged chinchillas are clear to me. Even as I was crawling out, I still saw him through the smoke. I remember how he dragged himself and two ferret cages out from the next aisle over. Ashen and sweaty, writhing with coughs.

Where did this memory just appear from?

My breathing shallows as I approach, my heart drumming against my chest. What the hell am I even doing, coming up to him like this? Before my brain can register my actions, I'm ten feet away. He's looking at two slips of paper. The first is powder blue. I recognize it as a class schedule. But getting confused about your schedule in the middle of September, when we started back in August? *Is he new?*

"You okay?" I ask. He doesn't speak. Examining him more closely, I soon figure out why. He looks down at the second paper, a map of the school. I notice he's holding it upside down. Taking it from his hands, I rotate it and hand it back.

"Here," I say. "Does that help?"

He nods, only glancing at me. He gets an inhaler out of his pocket and takes a long drag. As he exhales, I ask his name. He looks at me with a heavy dose of skepticism. His shoulders draw in as the papers crinkle in his hands.

He studies me once more before opening his mouth. "Jimmy," he wheezes. "Jimmy Palladino."

There's something in his voice that makes me sure he's not from around here. A subtle but punchy snap to his words, like they've got somewhere to be. An accent you'd hear in *Goodfellas* or *A Bronx Tale*, except more PG-13.

"I'm Lionel." I put my hand out to shake. He flinches. It's the nervous kind that signals I've gotten too far into his personal space. But then his expression changes, his nerves congealing into something more akin to mild embarrassment. "Where you from, Jimmy?"

"Yonkers." He must read my confusion, because he quickly elaborates. "Near New York City."

"What brought you here?"

He shrugs and reaches down for his bookbag. "Dad got a new job this summer." The last word comes out like "suhmah," and I have to bury a smile. And they talk about *our* accents. "So not much of a choice, I guess," he says.

"You like it here?" He doesn't say anything, but the face he makes isn't exactly a ringing endorsement. I fake a laugh. "Dude, it's not that bad. The girls are pretty cute. And nice, too. They even got their own song named after them."

Jimmy squints up at me as I hum the opening melody to the oldies pop hit "Carolina Girls." It's around the seventh note that I realize why I'm making a complete ass of myself in front of a boy who looks like he should have a chaperone. Every question, every silly joke I make is just me dancing around what I really want to know. The *only* thing I want to know: *What did you see at the pet store?*

My humming trails off as he rises with his book bag and slips a strap onto his shoulder.

"Hey, umm, you were at the pet store, right? During the fire?"

Jimmy flinches. His nod is barely perceptible and quickly trailed by a stammering "I—I, umm, gotta get to class." Without even waiting for my response, he takes off up the nearest stairwell. He's at the top landing before I call out to him.

"Wait."

He pauses and turns as voices and footsteps sound out from above him. Hesitantly, I say, "What did you . . . ?" But I can't get the words out because I'm suddenly distracted by the commotion gathering at his back. That moment is enough to trigger a disaster.

Taking my silence as a cue, Jimmy turns again, unaware of the athletes stepping right onto the landing from above. Chase Wells is backpedaling as he jokes with his friends. He and Jimmy collide.

Both go tumbling halfway down the bottom set of steps in an awkward tangle. I hurry toward them.

"Dude, watch it!" Chase says.

"Sorry," Jimmy sputters.

Several hands reach down, all for Chase. The star line-backer swats them away. In a grand showing of indignity, Chase plants his massive palm right on Jimmy's chest to prop himself up, pinning the boy down. The other players have a good laugh at that.

Chase lords over Jimmy, his eyes appraising and angry.

"Didn't you see me?" Chase asks. Jimmy doesn't speak, which only makes Chase angrier. "You a freshman?" Jimmy nods. After what seems like an eternity of stony silence, surprisingly, Chase's face relaxes. He even extends a hand, which Jimmy hesitantly takes. I tense, sensing a trap. Chase pulls Jimmy's arm, rag-dolling him upright, then lifts him, shifting himself and Jimmy toward the railing. Jimmy's arms and legs flail as he dangles over the railing that lines the landing between the first and second floors.

"Westlake Eagles, boys! Fly, baby, fly!" Chase shouts.

Jimmy lets out a screech, gasping for breath as something falls from his pocket and rolls down the steps. Chase is still holding him over the railing as his friends erupt in riotous laughter. I finally breathe when Chase lets the kid down.

Chase then bumps into me as he resumes his walk down the steps, his friends following like supersized lemmings.

Coughing violently, Jimmy sinks down to the ground, his back against the railing but angled in a precarious and unnatural way.

When I kneel at his side, I can see he's woozy, cheeks flushed, and each breath comes out ragged, broken up by hacking coughs. He looks bad.

"Jimmy!" I try shaking him as more footsteps sound out from above.

He can barely look up at me. I cup my hand to his shoulder. My heartbeat pounds at my chest like a snare drum.

"What do you need?" I ask.

He can only wheeze, and his face has taken on a ghostly bluish hue.

"Help!" I yell out, and almost miss Jimmy's head nodding in the direction of something out of reach. I look down and see it just steps below us. The thing that fell from his pocket. His inhaler!

I reach down the three steps to grab it and jam it up against his lips. We make the briefest of eye contact as I firmly and clearly say, "Don't give up on me, Jimmy."

And that's all Jimmy needs. He nods and takes in a deep, laborious breath. Seconds pass and I remove the inhaler. His trembling hand grasps my wrist as he wills himself to look at me again. His gaze is tearful but appreciative.

His breath steadies as the panic resides. Finally, he manages the verve to whisper, "You did it."

"*We* did it," I correct.

The next thing I hear is applause from several students up above.

3

NOT ONE TO LET A BRANDING OPPORTUNITY PASS, LIONEL
Honeycutt Sr. took to calling the days immediately following
a premiere the "Honeymoon." To Grandpa, it was a time of
breathing easy and basking in his own success. A time to celebrate and be celebrated. A time to have some iteration of his
name slapped onto another product, building project, or festive
occasion.

There's Honeycutt Hams ("A Real Man's Ham").

There's Honeycutt Auto Mall, down on Westchester Ave.
("Where the Rides Are Sweet and the Prices Won't Sting").

And who could forget Honeycutt Honey, which, instead of
a bear, was packaged into an eight-inch-tall likeness of grandpa
doing his famous Ghost Chop pose from his first hit film,
Shadeheart 1: Taj Mahal Takedown. Incidentally, the film was
also where he got his nickname, Papa Shades, after the signature sunglasses he'd wear on set.

Dad always said he liked the honey most, because it kept
a piece of his father home with him during the months he was

away filming. And while a miniature plastic likeness of Grandpa could never replace the legend himself, it was a reasonable substitute when you think about it. Even for me, it's always been great that I could just open a kitchen cabinet and be reminded of how cool Papa Shades was. How cool *others* thought he was. What the product reminds me of most, though, is the level of sacrifice it takes. What he had to give of himself to adequately care for his family.

With the release of the pet store videos taking off, today has felt like the start of a Honeymoon for me. With each successive period, I get more and more smiles and glances paired with random hallway shout-outs and fist bumps. Totally unprompted, Daisy Flanagan said I had nice eyebrows in French class. Two seniors from the PETA Peers Club bear-hug me in the science hallway, thanking me for my heroism. Turns out, every single animal, with the unfortunate exception of two chinchillas, made it out alive. And when I picked up the Starburst that Graydon Carter dropped in Honors English, he simply tossed his hair back and said in that *Baywatch* reboot voice of his, "Dude. Keep it. You deserve it." I could understand being that magnanimous for a yellow, but this was *pink*. The real deal.

Everybody thinks I did something heroic at the pet store. And who's to say they're wrong? Certainly not me. Yes, I blanked from the moment I was victimized by a leg cramp onward, but I'm sure I staggered back up and helped lift the shelf. Otherwise, that guy never would've made it. Mickey's an absolute twig, and I don't envision the significant other winning any

Ironman contests anytime soon. So of course I was the hero. I *had* to be.

"I'm giving you one more chance to confess that it wasn't you," I hear as I walk out into the school's front portico after last period ends. Mickey's voice is strained and pitchy, biting at me like a mosquito that won't leave me alone. "Are you gonna come clean?" she asks.

"What is there to come clean about?"

Mickey draws in a deep breath and shouts, "Lionel Honeycutt isn't the hero you think—"

Her words muffle as I clasp a hand to her mouth. More than a few people watch us with vague suspicion as I pull her behind one of the huge white columns.

"Why are you out to get me?" I ask. Her eyes flit down to my hand as more muffled words come out. I remove it, slowly, ready to clamp it back on at the first sign of revolt.

"You can't tell me that it's even the least bit fair that you're getting all the credit when I did at least half the rescuing."

She's not wrong. Whether I had a hand in saving the guy or not, there's no doubt that Mickey was a hero. If the store hadn't been so dark with smoke, the world would know that, too.

"Okay, so I'll just make another video with Jo and give you props."

The look she gives me is both incredulous and disgusted. "That's the *last* thing I want."

"So you really just wanna sabotage me, then?"

"I didn't say that," she answers.

36

"But you don't think I saved that guy, so . . ."

"I didn't say that, either." I huff. She must recognize my growing frustration because her expression softens. She closes her eyes, takes a breath, and opens them. "I honestly don't know whether you saved that guy or not. It was smoky. We tried lifting. The shelf got super heavy when you fell away with that cramp. Then, seconds later, it got lighter again. Could it have been you helping me again? Who knows? But what I *do* know is that you were on the floor before the shelf lifted off that guy, and you were on the floor afterward."

My hands slap against my waist. "Okay, so you don't know for sure, either. Grab an oar because we're in the same boat."

Her lips press tight, and the muscles lining her jaw edge toward the surface. It's the same face she used to make every time we played two square in our cul-de-sac, and I'd spike the ball so hard it'd roll down the street. She glances at the people still streaming out of the school. Then suddenly, she grabs my hand, pulling me along. I almost trip down the first step, she's so forceful with it.

"Where are we going?" I ask, barely keeping up as her arm strains mine.

"Somewhere private."

I don't protest. I figure I at least owe her that, after not even having tried to share the glory. So I just walk. We cross the street and clear two blocks before we pass Westlake Elementary School. I watch her curiously as we cut through the Turner's Grill parking lot. I know where we're going. We used to take this route to downtown and back home every Tuesday during the summer for the special at Hot Dog Palace. At the far edge of the lot, there's a chain-link fence that was damaged during a storm a decade ago. The fencing is rolled back like the top of a sardine can. We slip through and stalk into the woods alongside a creek with the flow of a leaky faucet.

It's another quarter mile before we reach our destination: a pond surrounded by massive oaks, willows, and magnolias. Loving Pond. It's a crescent-shaped body of water next to a clearing, kind of like an oversized Pac-Man. There's a trail that leads there. Once wide and welcoming, it's hardly visible today because nature eventually claws back what isn't ours to begin with. Everything is still and picturesque and very Zen, just like it's always been. Something you'd see on a screen saver.

"I haven't been here in years," I say.

"Not missing out on much," Mickey replies.

"You still come?"

She shrugs. "Sometimes."

I get tight-lipped suddenly, my stomach swelling with regret as I remember that I wasn't the only person who liked to frequent this pond with Mickey. This place was her mother's favorite, too. How many times has Mickey been out here in the two years since her mom died? Alone. Without anyone to share what her mom used to call "the perfect place."

I'm silent as we walk down a small slope toward the bank of the pond, and I hear all the nature sounds that a hurried world tends to take for granted. The whistle of wind through branches. Tree leaves crinkling underfoot. Crickets and katy-dids starting their evening calls. After taking in a sight we've shared countless times, Mickey doubles back to where the creek feeds into the pond. I figure out where she's going—the grassy knoll near a huge old oak we called Big Bertha. We used to lie there and talk and play silly games, like the one where we'd point out clouds that looked like celebrities.

Our favorite, though, was Two Truths and a Lie, the get-to-know-you game where you hide a lie among two fascinating details about your life. My most interesting ones always involved celebrities I'd met through Grandpa. However, Mickey almost always had my lies figured out. It was unnerving the way she knew me. She could read me like a tarot card. There's so much we know about each other thanks to that game, from my fear of falling from high places to the heart-shaped birthmark on her right thigh.

I beat her to our spot, sitting on the best patch, the place undisturbed by roots protruding from the ground. She rolls her eyes and sits next to me.

The quiet meets us here, folding around us like a blanket. I try to distract myself by watching a seed from a nearby maple floating down like a helicopter, and then I look out at the panorama of the pond. This place was a staging ground for all kinds of elementary school high jinks for the neighborhood kids. An old pier juts out from the far end. Perfect for diving. Enough rusted pieces of metal are scattered around to outfit an army of pretend knights. For a few years, a thick climbing rope even hung from the branch of a towering oak, until an adult happened upon it and cut it down. Everything that made that pond a parent's nightmare made it our own prepubescent oasis.

When I'm done scanning the grounds, I realize Mickey's staring at me.

"So," she says.

"So," I parrot. It's obvious our congenial moment from just a few seconds ago drowned in the shallows of the creek.

"Since it seems like you're dead set on gaslighting the school, I've concluded that it'd be uncouth of me to stand in your way. So I won't."

"Good," I reply.

"But as the closest witness, I'm entitled to certain demands for my silence."

I go bug-eyed for a moment before catching myself. "Okay, demand, then."

My patience with this escapade is beginning to dissolve like a mouthful of cotton candy. I brace myself for whatever concession she might try to extract from me. Season pass to the aquarium. Weekly goldfish stipend. Anything more than that and I won't give in. I refuse to be blackmailed. For once, people at this school aren't treating me as an afterthought. They're taking me seriously. And you know what? I deserve that.

Besides, I know a thing or two about demands. I'm Lionel freaking Honeycutt III. The name itself demands deference. If Papa Shades were here to see his progeny being treated like a cast-off fast-food wrapper, he'd stroll into the school and kick the ass of any student whose breath so much as smelled of McDonald's. Then he'd kick my ass for letting it happen.

Grandpa gave demands. He never accepted them. It's about time I followed suit.

My mouth opens, and I prepare an absolute right hook of a refusal when her next words knock me back like a sucker punch.

"I need you to help me make a documentary," she says.

I look straight at her, squinting. "You sure?"

I watch Mickey's eyes right then for any hint of falsity. But all I see is the same earnest, soulful look that spilled from her mother's deep brown wells. Mickey's mother, Serena Kyle, was one of the best documentarians to pick up a camera. The type of person who could see our world in ways others could only dream of. It's not totally out of left field. Mickey's always had a knack for this, even since first grade. Capturing people and places in their most photogenic, natural states. In fact, she *loved* it, until her mom died of cancer two years ago. And then she just . . . didn't.

According to Theo, Mickey stuffed her brand-new Canon in the recesses of her closet right after the funeral and hasn't taken it back out since. She confided in him that it was too hard doing something so dear to her mother. I wasn't aware that she'd quit filming because we'd already had our falling-out two years prior to this, when we were twelve. All I'd done when Mrs. Kyle died was send a sympathy card. Mickey never responded. Our estrangement stemmed from a massive blowup Serena had with Papa Shades, the details of which were never quite clear to me. What made things more perplexing was that they had been such good friends, with Serena inviting him to documentary screenings and even giving him directorial pointers whenever he'd visit from Calabasas. When they fell out, I naturally sided with Grandpa, and Mickey understandably had her mom's back.

So why pick up the hobby now?

"I'm sure," she says, nodding stiffly, but I can hear it. The small hairline fracture of a crack in her voice. Barely noticeable but still there. She's not sure at all about this.

"Why'd you bring me here to tell me this?" I ask.

"Because I want to shoot it here."

"Shoot what?"

"The golden eagle."

My eyes become slits as creases form at my brow. Mickey explains that her mother's first film was on the migratory patterns of these rare birds. Serena Kyle once told Mickey she camped out for days at the pond to catch sight of it. Mickey wanted to do kind of a sequel to the documentary, where she recorded and tracked the same bird. To Mickey, revisiting her mother's debut would be an ultimate honor.

"Who all's gonna see it?" I ask.

She just shrugs.

I don't press the issue because I'm sure she's thinking about entering it into those amateur filmmaking contests, the overachiever that she is. Plus, I'm too busy trying to process the craziness of it all to follow up. Shooting a film with my archnemesis. Having to spend more than five minutes together without acting on my inclination to dive headfirst into the pond just to get away from her voice.

Mistaking my silence for interest, Mickey begins explaining the ins and outs of eagle migration like she's Bindi Irwin with baby hairs. It's annoying how much more she knows about outdoorsy stuff than me. Grandpa loved the outdoors. He always looked in his element when wrestling anacondas or staring down jaguars. *Southsider in the Serengeti* was the most fun he'd ever had on set he told an interviewer once.

In his later years, Papa Shades had been batting around different ideas for various artsy films. Said it'd be a way to help cement his legacy. His most notable project is the documentary set to premiere next month. Apparently, years ago, Grandpa got wind of a reclusive set of families living in the most remote part of the North Carolina Outer Banks. Roughing it. Shunning society. Real *Where the Crawdads Sing* vibes. He said all the shots just came to him in a dream somehow.

He spent months out in those marshes, living off the land so he could film them in their element. By the time Hollywood heard about the project, everybody wanted in. Tom Hanks even offered to narrate it for free. The distributor and marketers are pulling out all the stops for the October 12 premiere. A-list celebrity guests. A big gala and feast. A *This Is Your Life*–type highlight reel. Even though it's being held in Charlotte—at Papa Shades's insistence—it's the hottest ticket in Hollywood. This fact makes it all the more frustrating that my family is so unenthused about going.

I'm noticeably less excited about the other event on everybody's radar: the homecoming game and dance on Friday, October 4. My indifference mostly stems from not having a date for it. I'd normally tag along with Theo, but I'm sure he'll take his boyfriend, Jordy.

The way Mickey gets into describing the possible lighting angles and lifespans and mating habits of these birds, the more of her mother I see in her. The woman who made me snow cones on hot summer days or ran foot races with me down the block just because. She was that kind of person. Full of life and wonder and whimsy. Mickey used to be that kind of girl, too. To me, at least. We were as close to soulmates as eleven-year-olds could be. She was my best friend for a huge part of my childhood. And then she became my worst enemy.

Mickey snaps her fingers, bringing my mind back to the present. She's got this smirk like the Grinch after pulling a heist on Whoville. "Why not just document the thing yourself?" I ask.

"Because I need star power. And a narrator. And you have one of those low, serious voices, like your bottom jaw just went on strike for low pay."

"Jesus, Mickey. You can't expect someone to go along with your scheme right after you've essentially blackmailed them."

I spring up from the grass. She follows, sheepishly apologizing. "Okay, sorry," she says, catching me. "*There*, I said it. Sorry." The words sound forced, like they've spoiled on her tongue, and she has to spit them out. "Look, who better to be a part of this documentary than Pet Store Jesus?" she adds. I'm not convinced. She must read it on my face because she sighs, adding, "And despite my superior witticisms and overall charming mien, you might be surprised to learn that I'm not that well-liked."

"The mystery of our time," I say dryly.

Her hands slap against her waist. "I know, right?" she responds without a hint of self-awareness. "Probably jealousy, but the reasons are unimportant. However, I will accept the fact that, try as I might, sometimes I can be a little grating, socially. And while God and a very skilled in-network therapist aren't through with me yet, unfortunately this documentary can't wait. I want it done by mid-October."

"Papa Shades would've loved narrating something like this," I mutter, not even realizing I've praised her idea aloud until I see the cross look on Mickey's face. Her lips press together, sealing in whatever choice words she has for the man.

After a long while, she simply says, "Can you please help? It's not even full-length. Just a ten-minute short."

I'm tempted to say no, just to spite her. I'm not sure of the repercussions of that route, though. Whether Mickey could or would actually spread the word that I'm not quite the hero I've made myself out to be.

But what I do know is that you were on the floor before the shelf lifted off that guy, and you were on the floor afterward.

Yikes. Just thinking about Mickey's account of the rescue pricks at my conscious. Even if she couldn't prove that I didn't help save that guy, her recollection is damning enough. At least to me, it is.

When I look at Mickey to give my answer, the sunlight hits her face just right, and I see her mom. The woman I grieved for when she died. Even if there wasn't the vague threat of blackmail, I resolve right then to do it for her.

"No more insults," I say.

"How about a four-per-day limit like they do with Tylenol?" The look I give her forces a quick retreat. "I'll try," she mutters.

"Promise?"

"Promise."

As if to solidify the bargain, she sticks out a pinkie and sheepishly grins. I take it with mine, and we do a pinkie-pull, double-palm slap, elbow-touch jump turn. Our secret shake. It's been years. Like digging up a fossil. We're both surprised we still know it. We try to hide our smiles, but the amusement shows despite our best efforts.

4

WALKING HOME, I CUT THE SAME BACKWOODS PATH MICKEY
and I used all those years ago. The trees stretch upward in bends
and tangles, creating a biome full of still air and bird calls. Oak
leaves fall like confetti, only to be crushed underfoot with every
step. I think about how familiar this all is. How we'd pretend
different parts of the thicket were rival kingdoms.

I look skyward, the echoes of childhood memories playing
in my head. The feelings of childhood come, too. The carefree
sense of being untethered to reality. Mickey and I, alone in this
small world of our creation, where our primary antagonists were
dragons, sorcerers, and the setting sun.

No, I think, shaking my head. I can't get pulled back into
memories. Just like I can't bring Papa Shades back, I can't bring
our friendship back, either. Some things are better left buried.
This little project we're doing? It's a transaction. Nothing more.

Just as I clear my mind of the good times, I step into my
front yard and see my dad. I immediately get annoyed by the
sight of him squatting by the hydrangea bushes that mark the

property line. He's wearing the same blue gloves doctors use in hospitals. I groan. Seeing him here, like this, is so routine by now, I could set a calendar around it.

Routine. That's an apt way to describe the person my birth certificate and various other legal documents claim is my dad. Lionel Honeycutt Jr. is maddeningly, embarrassingly routine. The *Cream of Wheat with no sugar every morning*–type routine. The *walk to the mailbox in his black robe and Carolina Panthers T-shirt on days off*–type routine. The *can't help but talk about his yearlong 1969 Chevy Camaro restoration project anytime anyone demonstrates the slightest awareness of how a carburetor functions*–type routine.

He pauses when he hears my feet padding across the yard. Then he straightens himself, making that low, guttural noise that adults of a certain age make every time they get up or sit down. He does an abbreviated machine-wash spine stretch before saying, "Here comes the hero! Hey, son." The smile is there, like always, but tired, like always, too.

I give him the same punchless "Hey, Dad" I offer up most days after school.

"How was school today?" he asks.

"Fine."

"Tell me one thing that made you laugh."

My shoulders slump, almost dragging the bag down with them. This again. Recently, he's been doing this thing where he's been asking random questions about my feelings to try to spark some conversation or something. It's so contrived, like he learned it on one of those midday self-help talk shows that double as paternity test reveals. He actually watches those things. Papa Shades would *never.*

Before I can bat the thought down, it *does* cross my mind that several things made me laugh today, the foremost being the videos Mickey showed me. More specifically, getting a kick out of how mad they made Mickey. It would be too much of a thing to tell Dad, though. So I say, "Nothing, really."

"Well, okay." The smile stays but disappears a little, too.

"Honey?"

I look to the porch and see Mom. She's leaning on the railing, long hair neatly gathered in a silken blue head wrap. She waves as if I've returned from active duty rather than just school. She pinches a hem in her dress and lifts it enough that I can see the birthmark over her ankle as she moves down the steps to the front yard. Then she strolls barefoot, brown toes buried in browning grass.

Dad and I edge away from each other as Mom approaches. It's for her convenience and our protection: Paulina Rice Honeycutt's natural state these days is in between us. I wonder if she cares that she's a kind of refractory device come to life, bending light and working whatever dark magic exists in her to keep the tension down.

Was this the role she'd envisioned when she quit her job two years ago to take on two elderly in-laws, Grandma and Grandpa? To become not only a homemaker but a peacemaker? If that wasn't the plan, she hasn't let on. In a warped way, with all that's happened, it's good knowing there's at least one dog-matic optimist in the family.

She touches a hand to my cheeks. There's no cutesy "hero" quip or any boasting about my apparently well-known exploits. She just says, "How's my love today?"

"Fine."

She kisses my cheek and tells me to get started on home-work because dinner will be ready soon. It's amazing how little Monday's incident has affected her perception of me. Sure, she was proud when the news got out. But she was much more con-cerned for my well-being. And now that she knows I'm good, it's back to regular old Mom things: "Is your collar straight? Are you washing your face at night? Are you eating enough?"

She kisses Dad, too, imploring him to take a break soon. Dad blushes as much as a Black man can when she compli-ments her "handsome, sweaty, sexy guy." I cringe. She excuses herself by saying she's gotta get back to packing the last of Papa Shades's memorabilia. Then she walks back toward the house. When she reaches the porch, she calls out, "Save some for me, okay?"

"Sure thing," Dad says sarcastically.

As he bends down with that same old-person groan, I think about asking what I've asked no less than five times in the past two weeks. The question that's become more of a nag than any-thing. But if Grandpa taught me one thing, it's to never give up on the really important things. I open my mouth to speak as Dad rises. The stench of what he's now holding hits me well before I see it. My mouth clamps shut again at the sight of dog poop. A huge, damp brown clump of it. He holds it up in his gloved hands as if he's a waiter showing a featured dish. "Right here," he announces.

From the porch, Mom claps appreciatively, like her beau's just found the Holy Grail. I lurch back as he brings it closer to me. No real awareness that the contents of his hand could be considered hazmat material at all US health care facilities. All he says is "Great fertilizer. Mom's tomatoes'll really love this."

Forget about asking him my question. It's all I can do not to slap his hand away. That and breathe . . . reluctantly.

When he finally bags it, he crouches back down to the hedges. Mom blows me a kiss and walks in. Then I look at my dad, who's grabbing more clumps of dog poop from the ground.

"Why not just confront him about it?" I ask.

"I did," he answers.

"And?"

"And Mr. Laramie can only do so much. He's seventy years old."

Mr. Laramie's dog has been Houdini-ing his way out of his backyard fence for a couple years now, using our hedges as his personal commode. And Dad's been patiently grinning and bearing and cleaning it for the same amount of time. Every once in a while, Dad will catch our neighbor outside and extract feeble promises of fence repair and potty training and better overall citizenship, only to see the same smelly surprises just a week or two later.

"When you get that old, you start to forget things," Dad says, nodding back to Mr. Laramie's house. "Besides, you can only do so much with bad knees on a fixed income."

"He hasn't done *anything*," I protest.

Talking to Dad, you'd think Old Man Laramie was so weak he couldn't lift an eyebrow. But there is precedent for being over retirement age and a fully functioning adult. Just look at Grandpa, up until right around his seventy-fifth birthday three years ago. Sure, he couldn't fly fighter jets or jump from tall buildings at that age. But he could still ably fire a rifle and take the S-turns pushing eighty mph down Mount Yeager. He could spend two months camping in coastal marshes to film what will likely become his most renowned work of art.

"Just give him time," Dad says weakly.

"He's older than space travel. He might not have that much left."

"All the better reason not to rush him," Dad quips.

I imagine how Papa Shades would handle this situation. It'd likely involve some R-rated words and a few threats that'd make even Homeland Security blush. Lionel Sr. was more willing to step on toes than me or Dad ever were. And not just step on them. Break them. Grind them to a pulp and feed them to the crocodiles he kept out back of his second home on the outskirts of the Everglades.

"Whatever," I say, raising my hands in mock resignation as I turn and trudge across the yard.

I go inside, glad to be trading poop-perfumed air for the

conditioned kind. The living room fan is on high, spinning currents with new scents down on me. Lilac and alcohol. The rubbing kind and the drinking kind. My grandmother Mae Ella Jamison, or "J-Maw" as she's affectionately called, sits in her favorite chair in the far corner, her feet precariously propped up on a step stool that's cushioned with a decorative pillow. Mom's protestations notwithstanding, J-Maw says this configuration is the only way to keep her arthritis in check.

I drop my book bag near the door and mutter a "Hey, J-Maw" as I walk across the hardwood floor. I bend low and hear the peppermint rattle against her teeth as I kiss her on the cheek. Mom exits the back room carrying an empty cardboard box. She rubs my head as she passes, disappearing into another hallway.

"You have a good day today?" I ask.

"The stories are messy, and the scotch is neat," she replies. "I'd say it's been a fine one."

I look at the mounted TV. On-screen is her favorite soap opera, *All My Grandchildren*. An old guy lies in a hospital bed surrounded by loved ones. Tremulous riffs from an organ play as he dramatically points to several of them who are, in fact, *not* his biological children and therefore disinherited from the will. Each, in turn, sling their flowers, Hallmark cards, teddy bears across the room as they storm out. One particularly aggrieved *not*-son even lunges to choke out the man. Messy, indeed.

"Looks like it," I say.

I make my way to the kitchen and study the fridge's

contents. As I browse the selection, I hear the unspooling of packing tape coming from what was just weeks ago Grandpa's room. I get sad and a twinge angry thinking how the sum of his life will be reduced to a couple dozen boxes collecting dust in a storage garage. Sure, his movies will always be out in the world. But the personal stuff. The stuff salvaged from past moments like stolen artifacts from memories. Those will be gone as soon as Dad rents the U-Haul. I close the refrigerator and gaze at a picture on the door. It's old, washed out in color, a white line down the center marking a deep fold. Grandma and Grandpa. She's smiling lovingly, hanging off his shoulder with her leg back-heeled above her stocking line like a starlet doing a foot-pop pose. He's the opposite. Upright. Lips straight as a ruler. Mustache too thick for his thin, twentysomething frame.

According to Dad, my grandmother and grandfather were opposites. She was the warm one. He was frigid to the touch. Her soft-spoken, him hardscrabble. Magnetized by their differences, they became an unexpected whirlwind of a couple. But the same curiosities that attracted them, as time passed, turned them into a walking, talking fission reaction. I didn't really grow up experiencing the love as much as the bickering. My grade-school science teacher once showed the class how magnets weaken over time. While my classmates were enthralled, I'd learned that lesson a long time ago watching my grandparents.

I remember the day they moved back here just over two years ago. Grandma had been pushing the idea of them coming to live with us, bowing to the reality that aging was overtaking their abilities to live independently. Grandpa was dead set against it. And boy, had they fought over it. This may have been the only argument J-Maw ever won with him. Not surprisingly, he'd sulked and complained about it right up to his deathbed six weeks ago.

I always wondered how they ended up like that. How do you stay with someone with whom arguing is as habitual as biting your nails? I assumed it was misplaced passion. A love that can't quite express itself, so instead of leaching out, it explodes.

I asked J-Maw about it once, but she told me to stay out of grown folks' business. She prefers not to talk about her past exploits with him. About *him*, really, ever since he passed. She'll watch his movies a lot, looking blankly at the screen as he ropes both cattle and crooks in his first Western, *A Colt Called La-Marcus*. Or she'll mouth the lines to her personal favorite—his only noir romance—*Sin on the Seine*. She's memorized everything right up to that climactic line from the famous kiss scene with Aida von Pelt in front of the Eiffel Tower: "Damn girl, I love you sum'thin fierce."

But whenever I pull out old photo albums to look through with her, she gently demurs, saying "I prefer the big-screen version," whatever that means.

Being around her now, I feel kinda bad for her. I *know*. People grow old. They die. But still, to lose someone so special must cut deep. And to add to that, Papa Shades had lived a life beyond the reach of most people's wildest dreams. Starring in blockbuster movies. Jet-setting around the globe. Meeting foreign dignitaries who asked *him* for autographs.

How do you live with someone larger than life? And alternatively, how do you keep living when they're gone?

Papa Shades's outsized qualities make it all the more vexing that my family isn't treating his final premiere as a bigger deal—as his last hurrah. Why wouldn't you want to celebrate the film that critics say will sweep through awards season, especially when its creator—our patriarch—can't do it himself?

I feel pulled to ask as I head back to the living room. J-Maw is still fixated on the soap opera.

"Grandma?"

"Umm?" Her eyes stay glued to the TV.

"You still watch Grandpa's old movies, right?"

"Sometimes."

"Why?"

She sighs deeply and brings a hand to her face as the show cuts to a commercial. Closing her eyes, she rubs the spot at her nose where her glasses rest. When she opens them again, they drift toward me. "Nostalgia, I guess. Watching him at his best."

"You know, Grandma, critics say this new film *is* his best."

We're silent for a moment, but her gaze remains fixed on me, the crow's feet deepening at her eyes. Finally, she says, "I done buried that man. Now I just wish y'all would."

I slink out and head to my room. My eyes immediately travel to the "Shade Wall," where I retape a curled poster edge of Papa Shades jumping out of a moving freight train. After the blemish is fixed, I step back and take in the whole wall adorned with posters of Grandpa's action hero feats. A year ago, I actually had *two* walls filled, but when Harry slipped in here one day and clawed his way through at least a dozen posters, I had to rearrange and consolidate.

I spend some time smoothing out any bubbles between the paper and wall before heading to my desk. At first, I sift through my social apps and notice dozens of Jo's followers have started following me. Seems it all started right after that video she posted of us. Just being *near* her is making me more popular.

I then trade minutes of the next hour between homework and typing new campaign slogans into a shared Google Doc. Theo's in the doc, too, and each suggestion is met with a veto, along with comment bubbles that hold some variation of "Not subversive enough," to which I inevitably reply with different variations of "You're running for school president, not fomenting a coup."

I play the teenage version of a groundhog, only coming out when I'm sure dinner's ready. Meat loaf, greens, and corn bread. Comfort food inhaled in an uncomfortable silence, broken only by the clanging of utensils against dishware. I finish my food and rise from the table when Mom clears her throat, glancing awkwardly at Dad. Their eyes speak a language I can't understand and J-Maw doesn't care to. Then Dad dabs a napkin to his lips before plastering on the thinnest of smiles. I stand still, knowing something's about to come.

"Well, hero," he starts. "Seems like your story's made it to the big leagues."

I lower my dish to the table, not quite understanding. "What?"

"*Good Morning Charlotte* got in contact with us this morning. They, ummm . . ."

There's a stilted silence where words should obviously be. I stand there waiting, but it's like he can't bring himself to finish his thought. When the silence gets long enough that it starts to tiptoe from curious to unpleasant, Mom fortunately jumps in.

"They want to interview you," she spouts, trailing her reveal with a golf clap. The sound tapers pretty quickly when she realizes nobody else is going to join in. The surge of dopamine is late-coming, but eventually it hits me with the force of a Mack truck. Despite me wanting to play it cool, a wide smile crests at my lips. The big shots. Actual news entities want to talk to me. To tell my story. Who am I kidding? This is *major*! I open my mouth, about to acknowledge as much, when I realize it's only me and Mom who seem genuinely excited. Dad's pushing greens around with his fork, and J-Maw's just staring at Mom, mouth half-open, a question propped at her tongue. As Mom relays the details of the interview request—how it will likely take a few days for them to firm up the details, and how they'll simultaneously be reaching out to my school as well for possible backdrop shoots—my grandma interrupts. In the most J-Maw way possible, she says, "*Good Morning Charlotte*? Them's the anchors who got caught having relations, wasn't it?"

"*Good Morning* America," Mom corrects.

"Oh, I know them two was having some good mornings," she quips, laughing as she slaps a knee. "Good evenings and good nights, too."

"Mom," Dad says.

"Hope they got good divorce lawyers," she cackles.

"*Mother.*"

"Oh, hush up!" J-Maw says, waving his unease away. "One of those good mornings was how you got into this world."

"*Okay, now,*" Mom says. The clanking of her fork to her dish punctuating her interjection. "Who wants dessert?"

Well, I *did.* . . .

I excuse myself seconds later, sacrificing dessert for my sanity. In my room, I study for my Spanish quiz until boredom gets the best of me. My mind trudges back over the day like footsteps along a beaten path. To the pond, where somehow Mickey—of all people—netted me into a scheme to help narrate her documentary. To school, where I'm suddenly Mr. Popular. To Josefina, whose simple smile made me feel absolutely seen, vibrantly colored in and brought to life. As traumatic as that fire was, if this ordeal brings us together, it'll have been well worth it.

I retrace just about everything up to that dinnertime conversation. My mood sours as I analyze how it went sideways. I guess that's the way things are around here, though. When Grandpa and Grandma first moved in with us, Papa Shades would grouse nonstop about how nobody in the family treated him seriously. How he was constantly disrespected with restrictions like early bedtimes, no cigars, and salads instead of steaks for dinner. I chalked it up at the time as the limitations that came with being old. Now I'm not so sure. Not one person in the family is making as big a deal of my heroism as the average kid at Westlake. It's obvious, and it sucks.

I check my texts again, an act that's become as habitual as cracking my knuckles. My spirit deflates when I see that Jo hasn't texted. Eventually, my thoughts stray, lost-puppy-like, to Jimmy. My stomach grows heavy, like something else is in there, much harder to digest than my meal. Guilt, maybe? Even if it's unclear as to whether I rescued the guy, I'm certain I didn't rescue any of the animals. Almost all of them made it out, apparently, even the fish. When the firefighters came, two tanks were just sitting right outside the entrance. No way that Mickey and the store clerk pulled that off by themselves. *Did Jimmy do it?* And if Jimmy could manage to save a bunch of animals . . . what else could he have saved? Or . . . *who?* The thought turns my stomach to brick.

My mood downshifts as my thoughts wander again to our recently departed. I'm drawn to the photo of Papa Shades wedged into the frame of my vanity that's attached to my desk. He's wearing his trademark black newsboy cap and tinted aviators. He's not smiling. He never did for photos. Or elsewhere, really. His cheeks have tiny scars and craters all over, like someone threw shrapnel at a brown canvas. I know it's from decades of sun exposure. He believed lotion was for wusses. But those kinds of things are what make him so authentic. He was himself, always. Strong. Brave. Without regrets. The things I wish I could be. Or maybe—just maybe—things that I now am.

I open my laptop and notice the News Alert bulletin at the right of my screen. While I usually ignore them, this time something catches my eye. My name. Or rather, *our* name.

Acting legend's grandson the newest action hero?

I click the link, and it pulls up a video segment from Entertainment Global TV network's flagship show *Hollywood Hangout*. During the clip, the grainy pet store footage shows as co-anchors Braxton Nance and Justina Carlson tag-team to narrate the ordeal. How a fire caused by a faulty HVAC system blanketed the store with smoke and flames, forcing me to spring into action and save a trapped patron and countless pets. Braxton then connects my heroism to Grandpa's movie legacy. I'm awestruck and a little disturbed that the news of this has gotten so big, so soon.

After the clip is finished, I go to YouTube. There, I watch countless video compilations of Grandpa and read even more adoring comments. Most have been there for a while, but ever since his death, thousands more have been pouring in. They run the gamut. Shock at individual feats. Reverence at the overall body of work. Commemoration of a life well lived.

Sometime near midnight, I drift off thinking that—for the first time—I've done something that would make him notice me. Even if it's from the beyond. That he's looking down at me. Still not smiling, but proud nonetheless.

5

THE WEIRDEST THING ABOUT BEING—IN MICKEY'S WORDS—
"Pet Store Jesus" is how naturally I acclimate to the fame. By
Friday morning, the buzz surrounding me has become background noise. The hype machine has been gearing up to a roar,
but my response to it is leveling off.

When I get to school, there's a gauntlet of kids lining each
side of the hallway. I'm surprised but also *not* surprised, in a
way. Classmates have been doing fun stuff like this for me
since the videos dropped on Wednesday. Their hands are outstretched and expectant, and they whoop and cheer as I walk
through, high-fiving each one. It's only about twenty kids, and
most are from the Spirit Club and the PETA Peers, but it's
still insane.

At the end of the line is Theo, holding a wide, neon green
poster and an even wider smile. The edges of the paper are festooned by lilacs that have been flattened and glued, and glittery
block letters spell out "America's MVP" with the words "and
Theo's BFF" scrawled not much smaller right underneath. At

the very bottom edge of the poster are the words "Vote for Theo!"

My own smile collapses as recognition dawns. I stop in front of him. "Is that my poster board?" I ask.

He nods. "Yep."

"How'd you get it out of my locker?"

He makes a face like, "Duh." "I know your locker combination."

"How do you—"

"Same as your laptop code," he answers. I make a mental note to talk with him about boundaries later. "Theo, I needed that for a science project." I tell him. "And besides, I paid for it. With my *own* money."

"Dude, chill. Don't worry so much. I gave you full credit for the in-kind contribution. Can't have a school hero and future student body president brought down by a campaign finance scandal, can we?"

He points to the right corner. Sure enough, I see "Paid for by Friends of Theo Super PAC" in tiny disclaimer type.

"Now, technically it's just a PAC," he says, "but you are pretty 'super' in my book."

I lurch over and jam my hand into his pockets, rooting around despite Theo's protestations of "What are you doing?" and "*Help!*" and "This is hallway robbery!"

Undeterred, I pull out his wallet and extract two dollars. We continue down the hall, but I can't go ten steps without a random shout-out and a catcall or two. Even Harper Thompson smiles and winks. She was my middle school crush. Theo used to call her Harpoon, because boy, I was *hooked*. My, how the tables have turned. I coyly but confidently wink back.

This is probably my life now, I think. Smiling, glad-handing, getting cheek-kissed while posing for selfies. Give me a Skeletor jaw and an accent aigu because I'm Westlake's version of Timothée Chalamet. Can't say I mind the idea of it. I've heard Chalamet is the Chala-*man* with the ladies.

But honestly, I've only got eyes for one girl. Josefina. I see her at her locker, her usual entourage of future sorority pledges gaggled around her. She's wearing a sky blue minidress and a heart necklace that sparkles when the light hits just right.

I watch as she takes one of those sky selfies with her phone, way up in the air, her friends jockeying to get in the frame. I'm sure it'll be on Instagram soon, the #FinaFam swimming to the comments section like sharks to chum. The only thing that breaks my stare is hearing someone shout "Watch out!" about two seconds too late. I hear a *clank* paired with multiple gasps as I run into a bank of lockers, my head wrenching back.

Stunned, I tent my hands above my nose, feeling for any damage. Theo comes around to face me. I smell copper and run a finger above my lip. No visible blood, thank God.

"You okay, dude?"

I nod, shutting my eyes tight. Somebody laughs—hard. I recognize it. It's Chase. Mentally, I shrink into the shriveled heap of a boy I was in middle school. He must be loving my downfall. My eyes remain closed as I wait for others to join in the mockery.

But seconds pass, and the ripple dies out.

When I peek through squinted eyelids, even Chase isn't laughing anymore, just standing there awkwardly, looking from passersby back to me, wondering if they witnessed the same cataclysmic collision that he did. But if they did, everybody's doing a heck of a job pretending they didn't notice.

Right then, it clicks for me. They *are* pretending. I've seen similar versions of this exact same phenomenon play out before. Whenever a cool person does something decidedly uncool, everybody else mysteriously develops a case of situational cataracts. They go totally blind.

Now they're ignoring my screwup. So I guess that means . . . *I'm cool?*

"Hey, are you all right?"

Both Theo and I shift our focus toward Mickey, who's looking quite concerned as she approaches us. A bemused expression crosses Theo's face. Then, scoffing, he says, "Girl, why do you care? You have a vision board of ways you wish to see Lionel embarrassed."

The statement jolts Mickey, as if she's suddenly remembering she's supposed to hate me. She replies all too defensively: "Just, like, unzipped flies and incontinence. Not real, physical harm."

"He might actually wet his pants if things kick off with him and you-know-who," Theo says.

"Who?" Mickey asks.

"Josefina," Theo says. "They're gonna hang out sometime,

'talk brand synergy,'" he adds with air quotes, parroting Jo's own words to Mickey.

I watch Mickey closely, scrutinizing her expression for any hint of disdain. She doesn't disappoint. Her stare pivots from Theo to me. "Jeggings Barbie?"

"She's wearing a *dress*, actually," I correct, not realizing until the words roll from my tongue that the Barbie part was the supposed insult.

Somehow, Theo's more offended by Mickey's statement than I am. He jumps in with "Girl, hush your mouth. Now, I like Jo, but my girl Margot is my top Barbie."

"Funny thing," a voice drifts in from behind us, "I met Margot Robbie this past summer." The three of us turn to see Josefina, having appeared like mist at dawn. "I landed an internship in Studio City. We took a lot tour one day, and she was filming some new psychological thriller."

"Damn" slips out of me.

"Yeah," Jo replies, nodding all too earnestly. "We really clicked, actually. Bonded over our roots in foreign countries. She's an Aussie, you know."

"My girl got a new movie coming? What's it called?" Theo asks.

"*Trial by Fire.*"

Not one to miss a chance to be The Most, Theo dons an Australian accent about as well as an ill-fitting coat and quips, "I guess they're finna put Barbie on the barbie, mate." I cut my eyes at him. Mickey groans. Jo, however, giggles.

"So we both know celebrities," I say.

Jo nods and asks, "How about you, Mickey? Met anybody famous? Any celebs in your family?"

Mickey gets flustered, red in the face, eyes drifting downward as a gaggle of sounds come out of her mouth, none of which I can make sense of. I take this grand opportunity to add some clarity. "Aren't you related to that Real Housewife?" I ask. "The one convicted of embezzlement?"

Mickey's fingernails rake against one another as she says, "Aunt Tia."

"And also, wasn't the Christmas Tree Killer a distant relative?"

"Great-Uncle Bob, yeah." Voice trailing, she adds, "But not so great, obviously. Because of the murders and all."

"And I vaguely remember a cult leader. . . ."

Mickey's eyes flash up at me. "Okay, we get it," she says.

Mercifully for Mickey, Jo redirects the attention back to me: "Sorry about not texting you the other night. I just got caught up with homework, and then my friend Megan called because she broke up with her boyfriend, Riley, and that was a whole thing. Wait, do you know Megan and the girls?" She motions behind her as she checks her phone. I see girls smiling and pointing like they're whale-spotting on an ocean tour. I meekly wave back.

"I don't know them," I lie. Everybody knows Josefina's friends. They blanket the student body's social feeds like wallpaper. The kind of girls who play starring roles in pubescent teens' dreams.

"You up for McSweeney's this afternoon? We can talk collabs."

I love McSweeney's. It's the ice cream parlor Mickey and I used to go to whenever we could scrounge up the money as kids. "Uh, *sure*," I reply.

"Awesome! I'll meet you out front after my volleyball practice."

With that, she retreats back to her group, which collapses in on her like a pack of hungry jackals until we don't see her anymore. Mickey walks off in a huff. I turn to Theo, who's looking surprisingly annoyed, too.

"Really?" he says as we start walking. "You didn't talk up my campaign again. We gotta keep the momentum."

I feign remorse. "My bad, dude," I say, shaking my head.

"Bruh, you know how much it'd boost my run to get Josefina and crew in my coalition? Right now, it's just you, Mickey, Hunter, some soccer teammates, and the three dudes from the Norse Mythology Club, and only because I convinced them I have Scandinavian ancestry."

As we stop in front of Theo's locker, I look him up and down. "But you're like . . . *Black*."

"Obviously, but let's keep that between you, me, and Odin for now. I need everybody I can get. And Josefina is, like, a force multiplier for popularity. I get her firmly in my camp, I get the upper-class girls, I peel off some jocks, and suddenly I'm a front-runner."

Incumbent president Lori Chen would have something to

say about that. Don't let the diminutive frame fool you. I'm not sure she can ride all the rides at Carowinds, but I'm absolutely certain she'd shiv a rival to get to the front of the line. Because if you believe the rumors, that's exactly what she did with Grayson Haverford. He ran against then-VP Lori two years ago on a reform-minded campaign, promising to rid StuGov of its long-suspected corruption. Siphoning funds from candy sales, price-gouging dance tickets, instituting an underground fresh-man fight club—that sort of stuff. By all accounts, Grayson was set to win big. However, two days before the vote, he shockingly withdrew himself from the race. A week after that, he withdrew from the school altogether. Deleted all his socials. Ghosted his friends. To hear the school tell it, he'd spirited to Zihuantanejo, Mexico, and began a new life working ocean boat tours.

Honestly, I know that's not true, though, because LaTasha Marx said she saw him two months ago at a Quik-E Mart in Hillsville a county over. Said when she brought up his cam-paign against Lori, he got this pressed look and just started muttering. If Lori did that to a veteran reformer like Grayson, what could she possibly do to a neophyte like Theo?

The warning bell rings, and Theo and I dap each other up. "I'll catch you later," he says.

I need to find a way to kill time before Jo's practice ends, so I ask, "Wanna hang right after school?"

He shakes his head. "Can't. Norse Club goes till late tonight. It's Sea Shanty Week, so things get kinda wild."

He starts beating time, palm to thigh in a repetitive 4/4.

Soon, lyrics pour from him amid the din of hallway noise, a soulful alto belting out like it's punching air. He's actually singing in the middle of a hallway. Worse yet, a *sea shanty*.

Faces full of amusement turn with his every step. I'm amazed that a person can be so oblivious to the yawning gap between his perceived social status and reality. It's like there's a multiverse out there where Theo's popular—one of those time-warpy crossover episodes where his popularity exists in all dimensions.

The few times I brought Theo around to meet Grandpa, they never hit it off. But in this one specific, egocentric way, they're both dead ringers for each other. Except Papa Shades's dream actually was a reality.

Unlike most others, the man was obsessively driven to achieve those goals that others couldn't fathom: "Not going after your dreams is like pissin' in a champagne glass," he would always say. "Pretty to look at, but ain't gonna taste that good."

I suspect it was Papa Shades's desire to see *my* dreams come to fruition—paired with a general disdain for Theo—that led him to drive me to my breaking point on a hot summer day two years ago. That day, on our neighborhood street, was a watershed occasion for several reasons. For starters, it was the only other day I've ever blacked out. Secondly, it was the day that cemented Serena Kyle's hatred for my grandfather. And, perhaps most consequentially, it was the angriest I'd ever seen my dad. I don't remember everything, but I remember what Dad did wounded Papa Shades on some core level that he never quite recovered from.

I watch Theo as he melts into the crowd, my secondhand embarrassment for him only made palatable by a parallel sense of admiration. He's got a certain stick-to-it-iveness to him. It's how he went from being just all right at soccer as a kid to becoming varsity captain this year. He's persistent like that. Whatever he puts his mind to, he can do. But still, count me skeptical as far as this SBP runs goes.

When the bell rings, I realize I've been loitering far too long. I need to get to class. The hallway thins around me as I scramble to wheel the numbers on my locker. I yank out my textbook and take off on the kind of walk that's more like a jog. When I'm by the water fountain, I hear my name called behind me. A voice—deep, foreboding. Nervously I turn and see Principal Weyrich.

I gulp. "Yes, sir?"

A tall guy with perpetually flushed skin, Principal Weyrich gets taller and redder as he gets closer. He's clutching the pink detention slip pad he usually carries. I extend an open palm, mentally preparing myself for one to be jammed into it for being tardy. Instead, he reaches out his other hand, taking mine, and clenching it tight. Shaking the life right out of it.

"You did good, son," he grits out. The words are as firm as the handshake. "Your grandfather—*the* Lionel Honeycutt, right?"

I nod as he lets go. "Yes, sir." I slide my hand behind my waist so it can slowly die in peace.

"Guess that sort of courage runs in the family." I nod again.

"I've been meaning to say something sooner, but let me be clear: at Westlake, what he's done and, more important, what you've done . . . Well, those types of things don't go unnoticed."

He points to a gold plaque on the hallway wall engraved with a large H. I know the smaller text inscribed below it by heart. Named in honor of the charitable contributions of famed alum Lionel Honeycutt. Funny thing, this school has seven wings: The A, B, C, D, E, F, and . . . H wings. The last used to be G, until Papa Shades gifted the school a cool $50K upon the promise of having one renamed in his honor.

Principal Weyrich continues: "We want the broader community to take notice, too. To really see what a Westlake man is. How, here, we don't just mold minds. We mold people."

I'm not totally getting why this chat is turning into an army recruitment ad, but I nod yet again. I figure if I just "Uh-huh" and "Yes, sir" in all the right places, this conversation will be over soon enough.

"Son, *Good Morning Charlotte* contacted us, asking if they could interview some of your teachers. Well, we got to talking and figured out they could do the interview right here, with dozens of schoolmates cheering you on. I spoke to your parents already, and I know *GMC* reached out to them first, but I just wanted to make sure we're all set."

"I, ummm . . . sure," I say.

I blink as his hands come together in a thunderclap. "*Great.* Glad to have you on board." He tears a pink slip out of his booklet and presses it against the wall, scrawling. He hands the slip to me, his face now grim. I read the messy writing, only exhaling when I finish the signature line.

Lionel Honeycutt late to class. Please excuse. —P. Weyrich

Weyrich leans in, his voice diving down to conspiratorial mode. "I didn't put the time or period, so feel free to mosey into the rest of your classes, too." He winks. "Today only." He clicks his tongue and pats my shoulder, harder than I think he meant to, because I can feel a bruise coming on.

I take full advantage of my pass and go the long, roundabout way to class, thinking about how this could be the breeziest high school career in history.

6

DURING SECOND-PERIOD CLASS CHANGE, I SPOT JIMMY
again. It's crowded, so despite trailing for an entire hallway, I
can't reach him before he ducks into his class. Something about
seeing him again sets me on edge. I can't focus on anything else
during my morning periods. I can't revel in the pats on my back,
and all the kudos become white noise. All I really want right
now is to get the truth. And if he was there that day, maybe he
could help me with it.

But I have to wait for it. *Lori Chen* makes me wait.

When the lunch bell rings, I rush out of my fourth-period
class and head straight to the cafeteria. Standing beside one set
of double doors is the student body VP, a senior named Paige
Wellington. She's flanked by two huge, mop-haired, chin-
acned guys who I only recognize because of their full-page
state-championship wrestling spread in last year's yearbook.
Heavyweight Todd Lovelace and 220-pounder JaQuan Bige-
low, or—as the undefeated duo has come to be called—Lovey
and Big.

They're looking right at me as I approach, causing my anxiety to dangle that much farther off a cliff's edge. When I move for the door, Lovey and Big block me. My steps freeze as I look at them, stunned.

"Could you . . . ?" I start, making a move to squeeze past. But it's no use. Their bodies are like two sides of a narrow canyon. Immovable. I give them my own stare-down eyes, but neither guy betrays any emotion. Exasperated, I look right at Paige. She's stone-faced as well.

"Lionel," she says.

"Yes?"

"Lori would like to speak with you."

I nod meekly, and she motions for me to come with. We wordlessly walk away from the cafeteria, Paige's heels clacking steps ahead, Lovey and Big on each side of me. Students cast curious glances our way as we head against the flow of traffic, toward the quieter, less chaotic domain of the Career and Technical Education department.

When we get to the end of the tech hallway, Paige opens the last classroom door. Lovey and Big post up at opposite ends of the door frame, standing like Roman sentinels.

I whisper in Paige's ear, "Is this where student council always meets?"

"We prefer to just go by 'The Council,'" she answers.

Hesitantly, I step past the threshold. The lights are dimmed, giving plenty of latitude to the red and orange glows emanating from lava screen savers on the desktops lining the room.

Everything about the setup has this vaguely hellish feel to it. Well, everything except *one* thing: the aroma. It smells like someone just baked cinnamon rolls. Several students are gathered at one long, makeshift table crafted by individual desks that have been pushed together. At the center is a silver platter topped with . . . *pastries?*

The students lean into each other and whisper as I creep closer to them. At the head sits the smallish Lori, who looks like the world's most unassuming mob boss. She relocates both pigtails from her shoulders to her back. Then she holds up a finger, and the whispers die out. Slowly, she hooks that finger into a come-hither motion. I take the cue to sit at the opposite end of the table, the legs of my chair scraping the floor. As my bottom touches the seat, the door shuts and a lock clicks. My anxiety is on a Stairmaster right now.

Paige positions herself behind Lori. Then Paige clears her throat before announcing, "This meeting of the Council is called to order. Participants may not speak unless clarifying Council rules for the benefit of all, or unless recognized by the chair." Paige folds her arms. A loud *clack* sounds out and redirects my attention back to Lori. She's holding a gavel she's seemingly produced from thin air.

It all feels so very *Avengers Assemble*, except instead of Avengers, it's just a roomful of overachieving type-A students. I look around. Besides Lori and Paige, there are six students total, three on either side of me. I only personally know Kelly Isengard, my locker neighbor. Beside her is Sarah Wake, the head cheerleader and StuGov treasurer. And Mason Vance, the secretary, sits across from both, typing on his MacBook. They're all expressionless.

Lori lays a palm out, gesturing toward the pastries. Without a word, all the others take one. I watch them all as they dutifully, if quite robotically, take a bite. They give discerning nods while chewing. Lori's eyes zero in on me. Something about the length of the table makes her an imposing figure, even though she'd be lucky to hit five foot two on her tiptoes.

"Éclair?" she says gently.

"What?" I ask.

Paige harrumphs. "You must be recognized by the president or VP to speak."

My eyes fall back on Lori. She flicks her wrist and says, "Thus recognized."

"Who's Claire?" I ask.

"An *é-clair* is a French choux pastry, Lionel. The last couple years, I've taken up baking as a stress reliever of sorts. From time to time, I've enlisted my cabinet members to be my loyal test subjects, hence the array of confections."

I'm skeptical of the offer until the scent of caramelized sugar hits my nose. That stuff's like cocaine for my taste buds. I reach across and grab one. Her thin line of a mouth twitches upward ever so slightly as I take a huge bite.

As I chew, she continues: "I've been experimenting lately with a new recipe that substitutes shortening and olive oil for butter. I've found the resultant taste to be earthy but . . .

compelling. You see, in baking, as in life, it's best to be receptive to change. And that's why I brought you here today."

"Really?" I ask. The word comes out garbled because my mouth is stuffed.

Paige clears her throat. "You must be rec—"

"Thus recognized," Lori interrupts. "Lionel, we won't take much of your time. Are you familiar with Ralph Waldo Emerson's famous quote on heroism?"

I gulp down my food and ask, "What quote?"

"Emerson. On heroism."

I squint. "'Heroes get remembered, but legends never die'?"

"I believe that's from *The Sandlot*," Lori corrects. "Emerson said, 'A hero is no braver than an ordinary man, but he is brave five minutes longer.'"

"Oh."

"Lionel, you find yourself today at the intersection of acclaim and commonality. You are the everyday man who's become a hero. The inspiration of the student body. The school would be remiss not to capitalize on such an asset."

"Capitalize?"

"I would like to offer you the opportunity to endorse me."

"Excuse me?" I reply, the words coming out squeaky as my brain tries to compute what she just said.

"Endorse me," she repeats. "And next year, when I win, I'll take you on as my chief of staff."

"Why me?"

Lori's lips break just barely, conveying annoyance at the

question. She removes her glasses, shuts her eyes, and sighs as she rubs her fingers across the bridge of her nose. When she opens them again, she says, "While any objective observer would judge my reign to be beyond reproach, my term has nonetheless been marred by recent allegations of corruption and graft."

Kelly tentatively raises her hand. Lori casts the briefest of glances her way. "Thus recognized."

Kelly looks right at me, grin Sharpied on her face. "All *false*, of course," she says, nervous laughter ribboning through her words. "Lori Chen is the kindest, warmest, most wonderful—"

The gavel slams the tabletop once more, and Kelly shuts up, pinning herself to the back of her chair. Lori gives her a thin-lipped smile as she sets the gavel down. "Thank you, Kelly," she says, in a dry, thankless tone. Then she turns to me again. "With these allegations abounding, I think it best to boost my public relations appeal. You could help me do that." I open my mouth to speak but pause, remembering Paige's previous reprimands. Lori flicks her wrist again. "Thus recognized, now and henceforth."

"First of all, what about my friend Theo? He's running. Why not choose him?"

To this, Lori simply says the word "file." Moments later, a girl to her left slides a manila envelope across the table. As Lori holds it up, I see the words "Oppo Research: T. James" stamped in huge red font. She gives the first page a cursory glance and says, "B student. Civic-minded. Receptive to criticism. Are those *really* the qualities we want in a leader?"

I want to scream "yes," but I know no matter how loud I say it, she won't listen.

Lori takes my silence as an opportunity to give her own credentials. "As a second-gen Taiwanese American, every year I've been in school here, I've endured the sharp sting of stereotypes, racial 'othering,' and taunts. I vowed to take the presidency because I wanted the power to enact change. To make things more equal. To foster social and global awareness. And that's exactly what I've done, Lionel. I've fought. And I've won. And with your help, I can vanquish my enemies again."

The way she seamlessly transitions from just talking about "change" to beating her enemies doesn't quite sit right with me. It's kind of like that saying about absolute power corrupting people. And that says nothing of my unwillingness to betray Theo like that. That's a nonstarter. I shake my head, weakly offering, "I can't." I could never do this to Theo. Just rip away something he's dreamed of since he'd somehow convinced his parents to let him watch *House of Cards* at the impressionable age of nine. I clear my throat, scrounging up some bass for my voice as I say, "I'm sorry, but I just—"

Lori holds up a hand and cuts me off. "The decision doesn't need to be made today, so take some time to ponder the implications. But I urge you, Lionel, to consider what mark you'd like to leave on this school. Think about your legacy."

There's something about the way she intones "legacy" that sears it into my consciousness. Like the word doesn't so much suggest an opportunity as it does an ultimatum.

Lori raises an eyebrow. I can feel the dryness in my throat as I scrape out, "I'll think about it."

I won't, of course. Never would I betray Theo like this. But the concession is a painless ticket out of this room. I can think of a definite way to say no later.

Lori gavels the meeting to an end, and slowly everyone but me files out. As Paige passes me, she leans in and whispers, "Personally, I preferred the *Sandlot* quote, too."

7

I ENTER THE NEXT WEEK OF SCHOOL WITH SUCH EASE THAT
it feels like the days have been put on a conveyor belt. Monday's
Good Morning Charlotte interview goes perfectly, and within
an hour after it airs, I've gained 2,000 followers on Instagram
and 500 on TikTok. The crazy thing is, I've only posted three
TikToks total. People are actively *searching* for me on these platforms. On Tuesday, Chase barely bats an eyelash whenever I
see him in the halls, and the concessions lady at Theo's soccer
game Wednesday slides me a hot cocoa "on the house" as I pay
for my Snickers.

Harper even flagged me down as I walked by her locker
this morning, implying she didn't have a date for the homecoming dance coming up in early October. Whereas a month ago, I
wouldn't have hesitated to ask her, today I held back. I'm pretty
sure Jo and I could begin something special real soon, and I
don't want to complicate things.

The great fortune extends beyond the school grounds. Yesterday, I got news that the town intends to honor me with the

Order of the Eagle Award. Mayor Kirk himself penned the invitation. Said I was the bright light this town needed. I was touched, honestly. Papa Shades received the award twenty years ago, so it'll be a nice full-circle moment. The only downside is it's at next month's Marin County Fair, which I hated going to even in those years I went with Mickey. But to honor Grandpa's legacy—and to make myself available to be celebrated by a town that desperately needs something to celebrate—it's the least I can do.

I guess there's something about saving someone's life that gives you a karmic boost—a feeling that nothing can go wrong. And that's exactly the attitude I need to have going into this afternoon's date with Jo. We were supposed to meet last Friday, but she's already postponed three times for various semi-coherent reasons, the last of which being "Some stupid Chads are swarming my menchies again, so the FinaFam's trying to get them yeeted off the platform. I've gotta coordinate." So today, Thursday, is the big day. Jo promised she won't postpone again.

I sit in my seat in the second-to-last row of long tables on the left side of the cafeteria. Theo's still in line, but I've got my food already: the school's lasagna (surprisingly good), fries (meh), and green beans (not even green). I'm two spoonfuls of lasagna and three fries in when a tray slams down across from me. I nearly choke at the sight of Mickey sidling up to Theo's seat. She points. "Dude, where'd you get carrots? I totally missed them."

"They're green beans," I say.

"Oh."

She starts eating her lasagna as if it's the most normal thing in the world for sworn enemies to break bread together. I look over her shoulder, trying to spot Theo, but getting annoyed when I don't.

"What are you doing?"

"What?" she asks. The word is muffled because her mouth is still plenty full.

"Sitting here," I say.

She chews some more and makes an elaborate production of swallowing, clearing her throat, and dabbing a napkin at the corners of her lips before speaking. "I figured we could plan out the logistics of how exactly to do this documentary. We can start this afternoon. I'm thinking one of our shots could be in the middle of Loving Pond since the eagles have been spotted there before. We could wade in to get a high-up shot of an eagle gliding in. Maybe even a Dutch tilt as it swoops down. But, fair warning, there was a new invasive frog species just discovered there a couple years back that emits a slightly poisonous skin secretion when agitated, so we'll need waders and gloves."

"No."

"Well, okay, then, but don't go blaming me if it burns when you pee, because I warned—"

"I mean no, I'm busy this afternoon," I say.

"Tomorrow?"

"Campaign stuff with Theo."

"Well, when we gonna start?"

"As quickly as possible so you'll be out of my life."

Mickey huffs. "Hate to go all *Pitch Perfect* 'Cups' song on your ass, but you're gonna miss me when I'm gone."

I lean over the table, a smirk dawning on my lips. "So, (a) You didn't hate that. That's like your favorite movie. And (b), I definitely will not miss you."

"Okay, (a) *was* my favorite. Everybody has an a cappella summer. Mine just lasted a few years. And (b) I'm surprised you remember."

"Why wouldn't I? You wore a neck scarf for two straight years."

"Flight-attendant chic was the style back then."

I look dead at her. "You also insisted everybody call you Bella."

Mickey laughs. A high, abrupt, tinny sound, like someone stepped on a rubber bath toy. I realize I haven't heard that sound in years. I can't help but smirk. Not at her but at the memory. "So I picked up a habit or two. Besides, it wasn't any worse than the year you discovered *Dirty Dancing*."

"Stop."

"The black leather jacket. Dragging me to Loving Pond so you could practice dancing on that log. The *hair gel!*" she exclaims, pointing right at me, her eyes going wide like she's just spotted a distant memory.

"*Stop*," I say louder. But she doesn't. And part of me doesn't even want her to.

"To this day, I'll never understand how your Black ass thought you could turn a high-top fade into a Patrick Swayze swoosh curl."

I can't help but laugh. For a moment, we revel in the merriment of remembrance, holding that past moment like a treasured souvenir. As the giggling dies out, I wave the recollection away, saying, "It was a confusing time."

Right then, I hear a "Yo!" ahead of me. Mickey looks back and sees Theo approaching. He stops at her side. She smiles wide.

"Hey, Theo! Come join us!" she says, as if Theo and I don't sit together every single day.

Theo sits down beside her, daps her up, and says, "Sis, what it do?" before downing a fry.

"Strategy sesh," Mickey answers. "What's up with you?"

"Same ol', same ol'. Campaign draining me. AP Bio still kickin my ass. Norse Club pretty lit, though. You should come out. Everybody's excited about Valhalla Fest next Saturday."

"Y'all doing anything special for it?" Mickey asks.

"Sea Shanty Showcase."

I fully expect Mickey to look as confused as I did, but instead she goes, "Cool. You heard that new one from Dem Longship Boyz?"

I squint. *Dem Longship Boyz?*

"'Sailors Never Die'?" Theo answers, sitting down. "From *Ragnarok Volume 2*? *Pssshh*. Girl, I've been on that."

Both recognize my confusion, but Mickey's the one to put

my mind at ease. "There's a hip-hop/sea-shanty fusion movement going on in Scandinavia. It's a whole thing."

Theo looks at me and says, "You should come out, though. I'm lead alto, and Lars Guntherson's pretty legit with the bars. If we place, we get to sing at the Marin County Fair next month."

Without thinking, I say, "Sure." I'll be there anyway to receive the town's Order of the Eagle Award, so it won't be a problem. And besides, as many times as he's come to my boring-ass cross country meets, I figure I owe him one. Besides, it does sound mildly interesting. At my acceptance, Theo gets genuinely excited, smiles wide and toothy as he gives me the details. Mickey pilfers some of Theo's fries as they talk about songs and school and life. After a while, Theo yanks the subject back to the original topic of interest.

"So what was y'all talking about before I came?" he asks.

"We're filming a documentary," I mutter. He looks unsure of what he just heard. "Long story," I add.

"Oh, I'm good for long stories," Theo says. He looks at Mickey. "Tell me about it."

My mouth shoots open as I try to give the blink-and-you'll-miss-it version, but Mickey beats me. I groan as she starts. Throughout Mickey's childhood, she was known to go on and on about anything film related, especially if it involved her mom. And it wasn't that Mrs. Kyle didn't deserve the praise. She *did*. Her awards sprawled from all kinds of exciting and exotic places throughout the world: Thessaloniki, Marseille, Toronto. But it's just that Mickey's tales tend to go overboard.

As I'm reminiscing about Mrs. Kyle, Mickey transitions from talking about her current project to her magnum opus idea of creating a film linking cruelty-free makeup to third-wave feminism. I'm just sitting there wishing this was a cruelty-free conversation. Suddenly, Theo very purposefully digs his fork into his tray until it snaps. Mickey pauses as he holds up a jagged piece.

"Damn," he says. "Gotta get a new one."

And he's off and away, like an escapee from prison. Mickey resumes talking. Oblivious. I watch Theo disappearing into the crowd as I plan my own escape. It's when his walk veers toward the restroom that I notice Jimmy. He's sitting alone in the sparsely trafficked corner of the cafeteria near StuGov's canned-food donation box and a stack of unused chairs. He's doing that thing kids with no seat mates do where they pretend there's something remarkably interesting about their food and they just look at it for long periods of time. I smile and half wave, but he doesn't notice. Too busy navel-gazing. Literally just looking at an orange.

Two small objects fly into my field of vision, one landing in front of Jimmy's tray and the other hitting him square on the shoulder. He flinches, but otherwise doesn't look up from his tray. I look left, and sure enough, three tables over, Chase and his stupid friends are snickering as they steal glances at the lowly freshman. Chase holds a half-torn roll in his hand. No doubt the other half is on Jimmy's table.

My heart sinks. I feel so bad for him. Like if I just called an

800 number and donated twenty-three cents a day, I could save his life like on one of those abused puppy commercials. At that moment, I see myself at Jimmy's table, braving the taunts and food items lobbed in from long distance. I don't know what gets into me, but I stand up and start walking over, leaving Mickey hanging mid-sentence. I decide right then and there that I *can* help him—again. I *have* to help. As a newly popular person with a good heart, I feel it's my duty to give back, like Grandpa would. In his later days, between all the cursing and complaining, Grandpa used to say it was always important to give back. His biggest philanthropic achievement was setting up an acting school that provided scholarships for needy kids. The "Lionel Elites" and the "Honeys" would even put on this mash-up of all Papa Shades's greatest performances at the end of each year. He'd drag the fam to those shows. They were boring as hell, honestly, but one thing that stuck out was how appreciative those kids were.

Maybe if I take Jimmy under my wing, some of my swag will rub off on him. The jocks will stop bothering him. He might get invited to a party. Hell, who knows? By the end of the year, a girl or two could be interested in him. He could be my own little "Lionel Elite."

Beyond all that, there's still the knowledge that he could be the key that unlocks the whole pet store mystery. Now might be my best chance to pry into his memory for info. I go over to his table and make small talk. Among other things, he does acknowledge he was at the pet store when the fire occurred.

Says his parents felt guilty over the move and let Jimmy shop for possible pets to help make the transition easier. His parents were in the food court when it all went down.

After a couple minutes of the back-and-forth, I invite him to sit with us. Initially, he refuses, but at my insistence, he reluctantly agrees.

When we return to my table, Mickey looks pissed. But as she watches Jimmy sit down beside me, her demeanor shifts from caustic to curious. After introductions, Mickey commences with the annoying game of asking a person from a different region all kinds of random questions like "'Soda' or 'pop'?" ("Soda," Jimmy answers), "Subway or taxi?" ("Cah"), and "So, New York-style pizza. Why such big slices? It's like I'm eating a freaking Yield sign" (?????).

After that last one, I can see Jimmy is getting a little overwhelmed, so I step in.

"Jimmy here is a freshman," I say.

"Fresh meat, huh?"

"Yep. You wanna know what else is kind of interesting about him?"

"What?"

"He was at the pet store," I say. *During the fire.*

Mickey drops the fry she'd just picked up from Theo's plate. "No shit! *Finally*, someone who can relate to my struggles. Can you believe that everyone thinks this arrogant jawn's the one who saved that guy, and yet, coincidentally, nobody's seen any clear proof of it?" Jimmy narrows his eyes at her. "What? You guys don't use 'jawn'?"

I lean over the table, my words at a whisper. "'Jawn' is more a Philly word . . . and almost exclusively a *Black* word."

Mickey looks at Jimmy. "What do you guys call dumbasses?"

"Schmucks."

Pointing at me again, she asks, "Can you believe what this arrogant schmuck's been doing?"

"What's he been doing?" Theo's reappeared again behind Mickey's shoulder.

"Being fake," Mickey says.

"Have not," I reply.

"Unfortunate," Theo says, sitting down beside Mickey. He picks up one of his now-cold fries and starts gnawing at it. As he chews, he asks, "Who's the white dude?" with the casualness of a dinner guest asking to pass the rolls.

"*Surprise*, we adopted," Mickey deadpans.

"They are cute, aren't they," Theo says. "I love it when their hair does that twisty thing at the top." He looks at Jimmy, his face brimming with sincerity. Pointing a fry right at the kid, Theo says, "And congrats to you, little fella. You're gonna love seasoning."

It's right about now that I feel really bad for what I've gotten Jimmy into. My friends will eat him alive. But I need him around. I need to know exactly what happened.

"Jimmy, they're idiots," I say. "Don't you worry about them.

Speaking of worries, do you ever worry there's things you can't remember about that day at the store?"

Jimmy's eyes go wide. "You blacked out, too?" he asks.

Christ. *Too?!* Anxiety spikes in me, tensing my shoulders. If he blacked out, that might eliminate him as Mickey's counterpart in saving the guy. But on the contrary, the fact that he did makes his memory as suspect as mine.

I'm about to ask what's the last thing he remembers, when Theo jumps in. Holding a fry at his lips, he says, "I learned about this in psychology class. Certain traumas we block out because our brains aren't equipped to handle them." He then details a litany of incidents involving Chase doing embarrassing things to me throughout middle school, with each example punctuated by Theo asking, "You remember that one?" To the ones I say no to, Theo mechanically replies, "See? Trauma."

I decide to give up my search for the truth for now. I tune Theo out and reach over to pat Jimmy's shoulder. "Hey, man, you need anything—*anything*—you just shout me out, okay?" His nod is almost imperceptible. "In fact, as of right now, consider yourself under my wing. I'll show you the ropes around here." He nods again, still weakly, but there's a little more life to it. "And you know what else? Feel free to sit here anytime, okay? Till you find your people."

"Bro, we *are* his people," Theo spouts. He plucks a business card from his pocket and slides it across the table. Jimmy reads it. *Say No to B-O. Vote for Theo.* "There's no better ally for your kind than me." Mickey stops chewing and gives Theo the side eye, to which he quickly adds. *"Freshmen.* Not white people. I mean, not that I don't love white people, too, but—"

"Just stop," Mickey interjects. Fortunately, Theo does, and we whittle away the remainder of lunch talking about the highlights and lowlights of southern living, and dispensing sage advice on how to survive being a freshman in high school. By the end of lunch, Jimmy does look more upbeat, less pale. And that, in turn, makes me feel good. Like I don't need to save someone's life to be a hero. I can just be their friend.

Jimmy goes his own way after dumping whatever's left on his tray as lunch comes to a close, and Theo busies himself taping "Hope" flyers along the cafeteria walls, with his picture in place of Barack Obama's. As Mickey and I get in line to bus our trays, Josefina splits off from her girls and hurries toward us.

"Oh shit!" she says, "You're going viral again!" Mickey is forced to step back as Jo wedges between us and holds her phone up to me. I see bird's-eye-view footage of me in the stairwell stooped over Jimmy. I distinctly hear myself saying, "Don't give up on me, Jimmy!" as I shove his inhaler into his mouth.

Jo sets her eyes on me, giddy with excitement as the video ends and loops again. "Did you save a freshman's life?"

"You gotta be fucking kidding me," Mickey says, looking away. But her words and the slap of her hands against her waist is just background noise. I *did* save Jimmy's life. And I *am* an influencer. People seem to be watching my every move and—so far—loving what they see.

Something else catches my attention. I squint at the caption of the video. "What's with the hashtag?"

"Ohhhh! Hashtag Lionheart! It's the number three trending hashtag on Twitter!"

"Oh Christ!" Mickey snarks. I ignore it. Still, I can't help but notice, despite her obvious irritation, she's inching closer, peering over my shoulder at Jo's phone.

I look at Jo. "But this was last week."

"Yeah," Jo says, "like, technically, Dylan Jacobson was the original poster, and he has, like, ten followers total. But Foster Meehan found it and *reposted* it a few hours ago, and the rest is history."

My brows knit together, confused. "Why . . . Lionheart?"

"It's your new nickname. Cool, huh?"

Lionheart . . .

Actually, it is kind of cool. Better than "Lionel," that's for sure. If my name wasn't part of the family legacy, I'd have ditched it with the Tuesday-morning trash years ago. But who came up with it? And why?

Again, I glance at Mickey. I can tell she's pissed because her lips are tight and she's breathing like she just did a gym circuit. She's doing her level best to hide it. Raking her fingernails.

"How'd that happen?" I ask.

"From what I heard, it started locally," Jo says. "A few seniors were talking about it this morning. I guess it just kinda blew up. We should capitalize on this. This afternoon, we'll talk scalability and market penetration."

"You bet," I say. *You bet.* I replay my response in my head.

Calm, relaxed, rolling right off the tongue. That's good—at least for me. When I was younger and Papa Shades would occasionally take me around celeb friends of his, he'd laugh every time I tripped over my words of adulation. As I grew, I noticed the laughs took on a different tenor—more aggrieved than good-natured. I couldn't figure out why, and I never really got the chance to. A few years before he died, I came to the realization that he hadn't been taking me around his celebrity friends at all anymore.

"Great," Jo says.

Mickey steps into my view like an insistent toddler with a question that just can't wait. "Hold up. *She's* your afternoon plans?"

Before I can say anything, Jo says, "Yeah, we're getting ice cream at McSweeney's."

Mickey winces at the word "McSweeney's," like it's a sucker punch.

For years, Mickey and I have considered ourselves ice cream connoisseurs. Long before we settled on our favorites, we'd come to McSweeney's together whenever we had extra money to try the different flavors. We'd sit across from each other at one of the small tables near the windows and feel the goose bumps rise with every lick of our cones and draft of cold air from the AC. We'd talk about ice cream—old flavors we wanted to try again, new ones we'd invent if we had our own shop. Just two kids without worry, escaping to a sugary-sweet world.

"You're going for ice cream?" Mickey asks. The shock is

ablaze in her eyes as she looks at me dead-on.

"Yeah," I answer, guilt pinching at my side.

"Have you been?" Jo asks. "Their butterscotch is to die for!"

For a moment, the place seems as quiet and vacuous as a Robert Frost poem. Then Mickey cautiously breaks the silence with a lonely question: "In a . . . waffle cone?"

Jo shakes her head. "I always get a cup."

Butterscotch. In a cup. Wow.

"You know, Title IX gave us options," Mickey says. "It doesn't have to be this way." But Jo just gives a quizzical look in return, and the conversation stumbles into awkward territory until Jo, sensing the unease, says a hasty goodbye. As she and her groupies exit the cafeteria, Mickey cuts her eyes at me. "Butterscotch?" she asks. "They give that shit out with wooden spoons and laxatives at retirement homes. Why on earth would you pay for it?"

My eyes flit up to the ceiling, the walls, anywhere for a believable excuse. "Maybe it's like a retro thing," I finally say. "A throwback to a simpler time."

"The Great Depression?"

"Nobody's perfect, okay?"

"You're defending her just because she's being nice to you," she complains. "You *know* I'm right."

"Trust me on this," I say. "She's good people."

Mickey's face is a marriage of skepticism and annoyance. My lips purse as she opens her mouth to speak. I'm ready to spike back whatever insult she tries to volley Jo's way.

But instead of an insult, she simply says, "Yeah, whatever. Just be careful around her." She dumps her tray. "Girls like that don't hang out with guys like you unless there's something else they want."

"She *wants* to know more about me," I respond. My words are authoritative enough to almost convince me they're 100 percent true.

Mickey doesn't say much else as we leave the cafeteria. She's always been this way. Moody. Barbed. Kind of jealous. That's definitely where this is coming from. Maybe if she wanted some accolades of her own, she could save a pet shop, too. Or just be a nicer person in general.

8

ON THE SHORT WALK FROM THE SCHOOL TO THE ICE CREAM
parlor to meet Jo, I play back some of my day. Aside from the
irritating moments with Mickey in the cafeteria, it's been a
good day. Actually, a great one. I pulled a B on my French quiz,
and at the end of seventh, that arrogant prick Jordan Ericks bet
I couldn't down five Warheads in a row, proclaiming, "The pet
store is child's play compared to how intense this will be." I sure
showed him. By the fifth one, every student in class was pounding on their desk chanting, "Lionheart! Lionheart!" When he
lost, he had to give me the entire bag. Since I couldn't actually
taste anything anymore, I passed them around the class.

I've noticed that about myself lately. Sacrificing myself for
the benefit of others. It's just in my nature, I suppose. And me
being me is finally paying off in some amazing ways. Tripp
Newsom, a varsity quarterback, risked a full-on detention when
he declared, "This dude's the fucking man!" And Brynn Coo-
per, the Fires for Christ president, even said that I have the

spirit of David in me. Which . . . cool, I guess.

The weather is like my mood right now. Warm. Sunny. Chill. Good ice cream weather. I spend much of the walk thinking of and rehearsing filler lines to make sure my conversation with Jo doesn't lull.

You have such a lovely smile.

Your skin really glows. Do you sweat a lot?

Complimentary but not too flirtatious. I want to signal my interest but leave some wiggle room for deniability in case she's not into me.

When I get there, I spend another five minutes fake-texting at a table so I don't look like a loser. Finally, Jo arrives, smiling wide as she approaches the table and announces, "Your Barbie has arrived."

She winks. Despite my embarrassment at having said it, I chuckle as well. I think we have our first inside joke. We exchange niceties, but then I panic when the conversation stalls within a few seconds and my mind blanks. I get all fidgety and even start tearing a napkin into shreds as the silence blankets the table. However, I mercifully regain my footing when she mentions how it's awesome that my granddad was a movie star. Turns out, she's a huge fan. I can almost see the twinkle in her eyes when she recites lines from his blockbuster action-adventure franchise *Arizona Jenkins*. And we share a tender moment recounting the climactic death scene in Papa Shades's coming-of-age film about an inner-city beekeeper who took in two underprivileged kids being menaced by local gangs. Turns out, *Beez in the Hood* is both Jo's and my comfort movie.

I sit there absolutely enthralled as she talks about how his performances have inspired her to make a run at Hollywood. And her backstory is a casting director's dream. I learn that she's the granddaughter of immigrants who traveled thousands of miles from Bogotá to Brownsville, Texas, while fleeing the Colombian civil war. Her parents endured hardscrabble lives— her mom as a seamstress and her father as a mill worker—just so their kids could have a better life. Jo, like the good-hearted person she is, vowed to buy them a house when she makes it big. And honestly, she's basically there now. Two million followers across all platforms.

Jo takes out her iPhone and shows me her various accounts. Embarrassment wells up in my stomach when I admit I've barely done *anything* to cultivate a following. "No time like today," she reassures me. Then she snaps a picture of us cheek to cheek, captioning it No better place to chill #icecream #newbestie #FinaFam. She tags me, adds our location, and presses send. Within seconds, I've got twelve new followers.

Wow. She's like a clout magnet. I look up at her, amazed. "I just got a dozen new followers."

Her eyes pinch. She looks genuinely concerned. "That all?" she asks.

Jesus. That all?

"How many follows do you get a day?"

She shakes her head. "I don't call them follows. I call them *fellows.*" My head tilts, and I squint just so. She must read my confusion because she adds, "Fellow travelers in this crazy journey we call life."

Somehow that sounds both totally off the wall and right on target for what I'd expect an influencer to say. But the way she says it so earnestly makes me appreciate her humility that much more.

"I love that."

She nods. "Yeah, me too. I feel with my position, I have a responsibility to promote an atmosphere of togetherness, just like your grandpa."

"How do you figure?" I ask.

Jo doesn't answer right away. She just positions her phone in front of me as she explains: "Remember COVID? When everybody was quarantining? A bunch of celebrities did that iPhone supercut singing lyrics from John Lennon's 'Imagine'? Remember that?"

Barely. I never actually saw the video, but I vaguely remember hearing about the backlash.

Jo presses the play button on a YouTube video, and sure enough I see Gal Gadot staring wistfully at the screen as the melody begins. Jo dreamily sighs as the clip cycles through a who's who of celebrities singing lyrics. And there, sandwiched between Natalie Portman and Zoë Kravitz, is Papa Shades. He's shirtless, lounging poolside while donning his trademark sunglasses. He croons a line in his unmistakable tenor.

Jo hits the pause button and draws her shoulders tight. "I

still get chills seeing that. Don't you just love seeing famous people doing good in the world? I mean, I would *kill* to get an invite to participate in something like that."

The word "invite" sounds out like a clarion call. My throat goes dry as I realize this is the perfect time to make a move. I imagine what Papa Shades would say.

Them scrawny arms ain't gonna get no bigger unless you keep something hanging off 'em. That something might as well be a pretty girl.

Clearing my throat, I will my eyes to meet Jo's. "Hey, would you, umm, like to go to my granddad's premiere next month? I mean, like, with me?"

Her eyes go wide. It's as if Jo's face has its own sunrise, her lips curving into an ebullient grin. "The one with the tree name?"

"Yep. *Beyond the Bald Cypress.*"

I always feel awkward saying the title. It's not catchy or alliterative. Just vague and vaguely pretentious. But I suppose that's how these "prestige projects" tend to be.

"Oh my God! I'd love to come! Thank you!"

Without warning, she bear-hugs me, practically falling into my lap. Once Jo regains her footing, she squeal-claps, looking at me like I'm her hero. My body warms all over.

The way Jo's eyes light up, you'd think I told her she won the lottery. I'm feeling the same way, too, actually. The premiere is Saturday, October 12, just a couple weeks away. What was already gonna be a celebratory affair will be that much cooler with her by my side. And who knows—if everything goes well before then, I might even convince her to attend the homecoming dance with me.

Jo suggests we decide on ice cream. She insists we order through her app so she can get points. I give her my order. One cup Neapolitan, chocolate chips on the chocolate side, strawberry chunks on the strawberry side, with a spumoni twist in the middle.

"Spumoni?" she asks.

"Pistachio shavings," I clarify. "In the 'Notes' field, just tell them you want 'The Lionel.' They know me."

She punches in the order and heads to the counter. I wonder if she actually got butterscotch. I can imagine Mickey griping about it if she were here. I know Mickey's order so well by now that I can mouth the words right as she spouts them: two scoops Rocky Road, with sprinkles, but in a separate small cup. Mickey's got this thing about proportional allocation of sprinkles. She won't so much as lick the cone unless all sprinkles are evenly distributed, because, in her words, "Why make the road even rockier?"

As I wait, I check out Jo's TikTok profile. Her latest video was taken half an hour ago. It's one of those choreographed dances set to the latest trending sound. She's doing it with her volleyball teammates.

I shove the phone in my pocket when I see her walking back.

"Mmm, yummy," Jo says, setting the treats on the table. "Napoleon for you."

"Neapolitan," I quietly correct.

"Let's take another selfie." She smiles. Before I can even say "Yes," she's leaning over the table with the camera in my face, her cup cheersing my ice cream cone in a toast.

She studies the picture like it's art at a museum. As far as I can see, it looks perfect, but she makes a face like she just ate bad sushi. "One more," she says.

I plaster on a smile but have to wait as she bends down to grab lip balm from her bag. Once ready, she snaps another one, which she finds acceptable. Just seconds after she posts it, scores of people like it, with dozens more commenting with exclamation points and "OMGOMGGGGG" and heart-eye emojis. I check my phone and have twenty-eight more follow—er—*fellows*.

Soon afterward, the subject turns back to me and my "heroic roots." I talk about life following Grandpa's footsteps, and for the first time in a long time, I don't feel all that intimidated comparing myself to him, talking about the memories that made him such an influential person in my life.

I tell Jo about a time I remember really clearly, when I was around ten years old. Our family was visiting Papa Shades and J-Maw in California. On that particular day, Grandpa, my dad, and I went on one of those Entertainment Global interview show sets so he could teach me the ins and outs of the business while publicizing his most recent flick, *Come at Me, Bro*. It was one of those mega-blockbuster ensemble cast deals where a ginormous space rock would destroy Earth if a disparate band of washed-up scientists and retired fighter pilots couldn't rocket into space and destroy it first. Huge budget. Lots of Oscar buzz. It was supposed to launch him into the company of the most bankable stars of all time, right up there with DiCaprio and Clooney.

The entrance to the studio was a set of those big metal double doors with the bars you have to push to open. Going in, I tried to push through them but was too weak, and Papa Shades just stood there watching me struggle through his dark sunglasses, his long shadow lording over me. Didn't matter that the door was rusted and sticking. He refused to help. Even when my dad tried to intervene, Grandpa swatted his hand away, saying, "The boy's gotta learn. Ain't nobody opening no doors for him in life." With each failed attempt, I could feel him getting more and more frustrated. Sighs heavier. Fist pounding into palm more incessantly. Eventually, he removed his sunglasses, and I saw his fiery eyes taking in my failures in 4K. He squatted beside me and spat out, "Opportunities are for the strong, not weak."

Then my dad said, *"Enough,"* and basically punched the door open.

Grandpa simply put his sunglasses back on, straightened his hat, and strolled right in. Dad was furious, and I was so embarrassed.

But that wasn't everything. The worst of it came toward the end of the interview. The journalist segued into Papa Shades's family life, as she noticed that he had guests with him. On a whim, the lady asked me to join them in front of the camera, despite Grandpa's obvious discomfort. She even beckoned me to sit on his lap, something I never remember him having done. He awkwardly shifted as I tried to balance on his knee like a bull rider on a recalcitrant steer. I remember shying my eyes away from the bright glare of stage lights as she asked what I wanted to be when I grew up. I looked for my dad but couldn't find him. Then I looked right at the lady and said, "A hero. Just like him," nodding back at my idol.

The laugh I heard was garbled at first, as if Grandpa had choked on it as it came out. But then he coughed through it and cackled so violently that I almost fell off his knee. Right after the interview, Dad and Papa Shades had a heated argument in the parking lot as I sat in a running car just steps away. Dad never attended another interview or premiere or showing again. Grandpa didn't really care. Nobody ever told me what was so funny about what I said.

This time was well before my training day catastrophe, when Papa Shades had me nearly dying in the street before Dad intervened. While I don't remember all the details of that day, or how their relationship became broken beyond repair, I don't need to. I can put two and two together just fine. When Dad and Grandpa fight, it's usually because of me. How I don't measure up. How I'm more like my dad in that way than either Papa Shades or I would like for me to be.

There's a moment when I realize I've been droning on and on, talking way too long. I get antsy suddenly, stumbling over my words. But seeing Jo listening intently and reacting to my every voice inflection gives me comfort. Jo reminds me a lot of that lady who interviewed Grandpa. Beautiful, disarming, quick-witted. She could put a rattlesnake at ease.

After the story is over, Jo's lips twist to the side a bit as lines form at her brow.

"He seems kind of harsh," she says.

"Really?" I wasn't expecting that, but her quick nod tells me the characterization was fully cemented in her mind before the anecdote had ended. I add, "He just knew how to motivate people."

"Laughing at someone is motivating?"

"If it gets them to be better," I say without thinking. But the statement rings quite awkward as it echoes in my mind, like a discordant key on a grand piano.

Jo simply shrugs at this and says, "To each their own, I guess."

A few minutes later, we finish our ice cream and leave. For the next two hours, she takes me on a blissful, whirlwind trip through the town of Westlake. We sneak into the downtown clock tower and turn the big hand so that it's five minutes early. We take the ghost pepper challenge at Ralph's Bakes and Brew. And right around twilight, we paint the school's spirit rock so that it says "Love Is Love." Through it all, Jo documents everything with her phone.

By the end of the date, we're both exhausted but exhilarated. Tired but pumped somehow, too.

I love every minute of it. I'm living life to the fullest.

We somehow end our evening strolling the lamplit promenade along Pikes River. Jo gushes about the romantic scenery as we approach "Proposal Point" between the water fountain and the gazebo. On a whim, I drop to a knee and shoot my shot, asking her to the dance. The moment she says yes, I'm so excited, I feel like climbing the fountain. When I divulge this to Jo, her eyes go wide as she suggests we rerecord the whole scene with me doing just that. She scrambles back to her car to get the tripod and portable ring light. We endure seven takes and countless curious stares till we get it right, but I swear each time feels just as thrilling as the last.

When I tell Jo our escapades remind me of Papa Shades's one wild-night rom-com *Sleepless in Motown*, she tells me I'm "stepping into his legacy." After a few seconds of thinking, I nod. Honestly, it feels good to be here. Feels like it's exactly where I belong.

9

WHEN I FINALLY GET TO MY HOUSE, I STOP AT THE TOP STEP
of the front porch and look across the street. At Mickey's house.
The light is on in her room and the curtains are drawn. I think
about all the times when we were kids and I had "big news" that
I just *had* to share with her, and I feel a twitch in me to text her,
to tell her about my date with Jo. But I beat back the impulse.
No use trying to conjure a distant past.

A spark of excitement rockets down my spine at the thought
of Jo and me getting serious. Who'd have thought it? Me, just
wrapping up an hours-long date with the most popular girl in
school? From dodging swirlies in eighth grade to dating an
influencer at sixteen, this is a comeback story on par with the
Rocky movies.

I guess it's not impossible when I think about Dad getting
with Mom. To this day, I have no idea how he pulled that one
off. The prototypical nerd snagging a girl who no doubt had
suitors lining up at her door. Apparently, Papa Shades had the
same reservations, too. Dad told me about the time he first

brought Mom home. J-Maw had to repeatedly elbow Grandpa because the man couldn't stop snickering at the odd pairing. After a couple gin and tonics, Grandpa even implied Mom was a gold digger, sniping, "Boy, you'd better always hold her hand, because if you let it go, it'll slide right in your pocket."

To her credit, by all accounts, Mom held it together for hours longer than most would suffer through his ribbings. It was only when Grandpa got what he deemed his "Next Big Movie Idea" that Mom decided to walk out. Everybody thought he was being genuine at first. He gathered them on the couch to present his idea, and they nodded and listened as he described a new twist on an old fairy tale, weirdly inspired by the lovely new couple. In Dad's retelling, Papa Shades held up both hands as if presenting a movie marquee as he looked right at his son. And my dad kept it together even a few seconds after revealing the title: *Beauty and the Least.*

I asked Mom about this incident years back while she was clipping hedges. She wouldn't talk about it. Nor would she say anything bad about her father-in-law. But it didn't take a press release, or any words, really, to see that they never got along. I get it. Grandpa can rub people the wrong way sometimes. That's how stars are. You gotta take the good with the bad.

That same conversation, I also asked about why she got with Dad. Her explanation was as unsatisfying as it was short. The clipping stopped as she turned toward me, her face shaded by a huge sunhat. She wiped the sweat from her brow and simply said, "He was a nice guy. Funny, too, in his own goofy way" before going back to clipping.

That couldn't have been the only thing, right? That's a rom-com thing, not a real-life thing. For the life of me, I haven't been able to figure out what's so special about Dad. He's super smart, yeah, but any high school nerd'll tell you that gets you about as far as a poorly molded spit wad. He's all right looking, but not much better. Slightly above average height. Thin face. Hair graying at temples. Recently, he's been getting more of a dad bod, which, to Mom's unending, giggly amusement, he insists on everybody calling a "father figure."

Okay, so he *is* kind of funny. But that's it.

I go inside the house and mumble a greeting to J-Maw, who's sitting like a terra-cotta statue in front of the TV again.

I immediately recognize the movie she's watching. It's the famous breakup scene in Papa Shades's noir film *Last Tango in Tulsa*. I watch the screen as he looks deep into Sofia Gustafson's blue eyes and says, "Baby girl, I'm a tornado. Good to look at from a distance, but a nasty motherfucka to get caught up in." In my periphery, I can see J-Maw mindlessly mouthing the words. She only notices I'm there when the movie cuts to another shot. She takes precisely two seconds to pause the TV, study me, mutter a greeting, and then unpause it. Harry meows from his perch right beside her, but otherwise they're uncurious and likely pretty ambivalent as to my existence at the moment.

I go to my room and start on my homework but can't really concentrate. It's literally impossible with all the hype. Theo said yesterday I should start doing new TikToks to build my brand. It doesn't even look like I need to. Every fifteen seconds I'm getting a notification for a new follower. I even get tagged in posts by students mentioning my heroics. The distraction is almost unbearable.

I check my email and see Theo's sent me yet another draft of his SBP acceptance speech. This one's labeled "T James Acceptance_Edit_Final_Final 2_Revised." I laugh at the fact that this is all months premature. But I admire the go-getter attitude. A far cry from Lori, actually. The Gavel, huh? Tough on the outside but squishy as Play-Doh when the pressure's on. As calm as she was at the Council meeting, her wanting my endorsement absolutely reeks of desperation. Right after school, she even cornered me with her goons in the PE wing, offering to sweeten the deal by giving me a 5 percent cut of next year's Candygram sales. Like I'm for sale or something. Theo must've spooked her. I chuckle even harder at this.

As I'm reading, I hear a knock at my door. The sound pattern tips me off as to who it is before I even open the door. Dad's got this *tap tap tap soft-pound* thing that he's been doing ever since I can remember. Pleasant if inconvenient. Wholly unobtrusive. A far cry from Papa Shades, who was somewhat of a knocking extremist. *Pound pound pound POUND.* He'd repeat that until you either answered or a door hinge broke, whichever came first.

"Yeah, Dad?" I call out.

"Wanna play *Galaxy Defenders*? I heard there's a new mod we could try."

"No thanks," I say.

My brow furrows as I eye the closed door. It's been at least two years since we last played together, but he's been asking every week since Grandpa died almost two months ago. This used to be one of the few things we'd managed to bond over. We'd feast on chips and soda while tackling role-playing games for hours until Mom forced us both to bed. Somehow, somewhere we grew out of it all.

"Can I come in?" he asks. His voice is muffled by the door, but the easygoing tenor comes through clear.

"I guess," I say. And then "It's your house" under my breath.

I hear the knob turn as I face back toward my computer. He enters, and from the corner of my eye, I see him studying the room. He ignores the Shade Wall in favor of the others. Takes in posters of tricked-out roadsters worth more than most houses. Stops at a picture of an Aston Martin, touching a hand to a bottom edge that has curled upward.

"You know AR is the next step in these babies, right?"

The words draw my attention back to him. "Augmented reality?" I ask. He nods.

"Nothing faster than the speed of light. But tech scientists these days are close." He gives off this self-satisfied smile at what I'm sure was a joke he'd just thought up in his head.

The carpet groans underneath Dad's feet. I hear the bed squeak behind me as he lowers himself to sit at its foot. "You know, your grandfather never trusted any of the new car tech when it came out." He laughs and adds, "Heck, it took him till the early 2000s before he'd even switch from stick shift to an automatic."

Grandpa showed me a stick shift once. Let me sit in the driver's seat of his '67 Chevy Impala and explained to me how a gear shift helps to shift the car's gears. After I commented on how hard it'd be to remember the steps, he yanked me out and said, "Real men do hard things, boy." Then he ordered me to the passenger's side and took me for a ninety-five mph sprint down Interstate 47. It was the scariest, most fun ride I'd ever been on. Sitting here now, I can't imagine Dad ever taking me on a joyride that intense.

"Of all the things your grandpa was, adaptable to change was not one of them," he continues.

I nod. That's been true my whole life. Grandpa nearly had a fit when the family forced him and Grandma to move here from his hillside Calabasas retreat two years ago. He'd broken a hip and a collarbone in successive falls but still insisted, "I survived two months in the Mojave Desert. I can damn well manage a set of steps." Didn't matter that he stayed in a highly specialized, air-conditioned yurt during that "survival" stint. Or that it was the *Gobi* Desert, not the Mojave, one of the many memory mix-ups he'd been making at the time. Grandpa wanted things his way, and he usually got it. When he realized he wouldn't win this battle, he gave the family the silent treatment for two weeks.

It was a homecoming of sorts. He grew up in Westlake. Met a nice preacher's daughter and married her here. They put down roots. At the beginning of his career, he could count on a wave or friendly tip of the hat for every block he walked on his trips downtown. But as his popularity shot up, he decided he needed an address more befitting his status. J-Maw reluctantly went along with him, but she always said this was her home.

"Don't really need to be adaptable when everybody bends over backward for you," Dad says.

I know Dad means this as a subtle way to praise the virtue of flexibility, but it doesn't come off like that to me.

"Grandpa cut his own path," I say quietly. "Can't fault that."

"Very true," Dad replies. "You've got a tiny bit of him in you that way." I grimace at the remark. *A tiny bit?* The man is my idol. Dad saying that is basically like him saying we're barely even related. After a while, I just can't take it anymore. I do a half turn in my chair and ask, "Was there something you needed, Dad? I've got homework."

Dad seems struck at first, sputtering for a response. "I did have some news, actually. PetWorld, the big chain? They contacted us about a possible sponsorship opportunity." He delivers the news with all the cheeriness of someone giving a eulogy at a funeral.

"How much they talking?" I ask.

I catch his reflection in the mirror as he holds up a hand. "Whoa, now. It's not that simple. You need to be very careful when people and companies come around offering this quick money. They'll take you for a ride quick, and I'm not talking about Aston Martins anymore." He runs his hand across his face. "Honestly, we may want to consider a blanket no-deal policy, at least until you've cleared high school."

Huh?

I swivel around in my chair, shock written all over my face. "Then why'd you even tell me?"

"To let you know."

"Just so you can then let me down? And besides that, why aren't you excited about the good things that are happening to me?"

I can see he's taken aback, his expression a mix of confusion and hurt. "I *am* excited for you."

I shake my head. "Not when Mom had to tell me about *Good Morning Charlotte* because you couldn't even get the words out of your mouth. Not with this sponsorship deal."

Dad gets up from the bed. Two steps have him hovering above my left shoulder. I see him breathing hard, his cheeks puffed, as if he can't wait to say the words he's about to spit out. He points at me. "I've seen what fame does to people. How it messes with their head."

"You've seen *one* example! How Grandpa had to sacrifice everything for us."

"I *was* the sacrifice, Lionel!" he nearly yells. He catches himself, bringing his voice down for his next words. "I didn't have a father and your grandmother didn't have a spouse. For most of our lives, we had a stream of income, and that's it."

The way he points, just jabbing his finger so deliberately, sears my anger like meat touching the grates of a grill. He doesn't deserve to be so authoritative. What has he done to earn the right to lord over this house? Everything he got, he owes to Papa Shades, the man who made sure Dad had a secure childhood and put him through college. Dad wouldn't be *half* the man he is without Grandpa's foundation. At that moment, I resolve to accept the PetWorld sponsorship, with or without Dad's blessing. A small act of defiance, but a needed one. I am my own person. My own *man*. He needs to know that.

I get up from my chair and straighten. We're almost the same height. He's got about an inch on me, but I'll catch him soon enough. He won't have much longer to look down on me. Grandpa was six foot five, so Dad never could with him. At least not until the man was six feet under.

I shake my head and say, "You can't stop people from becoming who they're destined to be," I say. I'm going to be a success, whether Dad likes it or not.

The next half hour passes with the haste and opacity of a summer storm. Dad "explodes" at me in his usual understated way. Lots of tut-tutting and "Son, you need to listen"-ing, and a tone as firm as a scrap of plywood. My mom's able to calm him by making the case that with the fire and Grandpa's death, I've been going through a lot. We settle into an uneasy truce for the night, with them slinking away to the back porch to stargaze over a bottle of wine, leaving me and J-Maw inside in front of the TV again.

We start watching *Law & Order* until the obligatory dead

body scene about two minutes in. It clicks in her brain that there's an impressionable young mind in the room, and she quickly turns it off, muttering, "Can't give the devil a foothold."

"J-Maw, you could barely see the body," I reply.

"You could see enough to know it was dead. Lord knows, I can't go to the Pearly Gates and have Saint Peter asking me why I was okay with my grandson watching smut."

For Grandma, "smut" is a catchall term to describe anything you'd be too embarrassed to mention in church. Dead bodies definitely fall in that category.

She flips channels until she finds a *Jeopardy!* rerun before resting the remote on the arm of her chair. A bearded guy starts the round with a science-y category. Right on cue, Harry skulks into the room, purring and curling up right beside her, maneuvering under her hand until it's squarely at petting position on his back.

I gaze at her and the glow of the TV touching her face. She's enchanted by the rapid-fire Q&A, although she knows none of the answers. Not that she isn't smart or anything. It's just she sacrificed a ton when she chose to be with Grandpa. A chance at college was one of those things. In a way, even though she's traveled the world, she's less worldly for having spent her life with him. For the second time in two weeks, I attempt to question J-Maw about Papa Shades. To see how she's been dealing with all of this.

"Grandma?" I ask.

"Yeah . . ."

"You never really talk about Grandpa anymore. . . . What is quantum mechanics?" I answer.

The show announcer deems the theoretical physics term the correct answer.

"Ain't that much to say," she replies.

"But isn't keeping his memory alive a way to honor him? What is Bletchley Park?"

She squints as she looks at me. I know she's wondering how I got so smart. It's not hard to answer. Dad gifted me his knack for all things science.

"That man's got enough honors to last this life and the next," she says. "Don't need any more from me."

We watch the rest of the category, with me answering two of the other three questions correctly. J-Maw switches channels at a commercial break. I blink as she surfs past one of those Hollywood news channels. I glimpse Papa Shades's face.

"Could you go back a sec?" I ask.

She does, and I catch the end scene of *A Colt Called La-Marcus*. Grandpa petting the sick horse's mane one last time before having to put it down. I'd recognize that clip anywhere. *Anyone* my age would. It was the *Bambi* of our time.

J-Maw gets up to go to the bathroom as I keep watching. I figure the segment is about Grandpa's premiere, and they're using old clips of his as an emotional hook. Classic Hollywood tactic. Abruptly, the montage cuts off, showing two anchors in a studio. A Breaking News graphic blares in the middle of the screen.

I hear the voices of Entertainment Global TV's *Hollywood Hangout* anchor Braxton Nance as he gravely intones, "New information has come to light in the Westlake pet shop saga, casting doubt on the deeds of a teenage kid gone viral."

Air catches in my throat. The grainy pet shop video is pinned to the top-right corner as Braxton and co-anchor Justine Carlson stand before a large, curved desk outlined with neon lighting. A chyron ribbons across the bottom of the screen, reading "Pet Store Hero a Fake?" Justine chimes in: "Did Lionel Honeycutt, grandson of the famed namesake actor, actually save lives? Or is his story just another tale fit for Hollywood? We have a witness who can shed some light on the subject. Story coming Sunday."

Witness?

I can't help but think that my reputation, not unlike the pet store, is about to go up in smoke.

10

MY THOUGHTS ARE LOUD AND PANICKY. WHAT DOES THIS
new witness have on me? Firsthand testimony? Unseen footage? Will it show I'm not a hero? Will the whole school think
I've been lying to them this entire time? Will I be an internet
laughingstock?

I spring up from the couch so quickly that Harry jumps
from his spot and hisses. I scramble to my room, collapse on my
bed, and take deep, labored breaths. I look up at the ceiling. My
heart rate steadies as I let myself sink into the mattress. Once I
calm down, I mentally process what I just saw on the TV.

The bad news is there's a witness willing to speak out on
what really happened. What makes this info especially discon-
certing is that I can't prepare for it because I don't know what
they'll say.

The good news? The anchors' words were just a promo.
The interview with the mystery witness is set for Sunday, and
it's Thursday, so I still have time. Time to do what, exactly? I
have no idea. Move to Colombia and change my identity and

just start over? Perhaps Jo can show me around. She has family there.

Jo! My phone!

I haven't checked my phone for hours. She could've texted me. I lunge for my phone on the nightstand next to my bed. I have three voicemails. Each a variation of "Hi, Lionel, this is the *Hollywood Hangout* show. We've recently come across some new information that contradicts the prevailing narrative of what happened during the pet store fire. Could you call us back so we could confirm your accounting of events?" I delete all three.

I also see dozens of social media notifications and two text messages. Both from Jo.

Luckily, the timestamps for both were from just minutes ago. I open and check, a rush of excitement pulsing through my body like a shock wave.

The first says **Just thinking about our time together** with a smiley-face emoji.

The second, which came in a minute later, says, **btw, did you hear about the mystery witness?**

I drop the phone. All my hysterical thoughts and insecurities come rushing back like water from a breached dam. If *anybody* from school knows about the interview, then that means *everybody* will know soon enough. My mind cycles through the list of possible suspects.

One primary suspect rises from the ashes. My eyes narrow as I get a visual of Mickey enviously standing on the sidelines as

I revel in all the attention. Motive. Insider knowledge. Opportunity. It's her. It must be.

I rise from my bed, breathing hard again, and do a Terminator walk to my window, where I push back the curtain. I can see directly across the street to her house. It sits small and lonely under the dark of night. A soft orange burn outlines the shutters of her window. She's in there, probably plotting my demise as we speak. I don't even put my shoes on. I just open my window and raise a leg to climb over.

Her window is at the far-right, street-facing corner of the ranch home she shares with her dad. Back when we were friends, we spent many an afternoon there playing Scrabble or PlayStation or plotting our next adventure at the pond. I liked the imaginary dragon hunts, and she favored the daring escapes from remote CIA black sites. Those memories are a far cry from this moment, where I'm trying my best to figure out how to confront Mickey on her betrayal. I snake my way beneath her windowsill, determined to finish the rivalry we started four years ago.

The window is cracked open. Through it, I can make out an empty room. Scents of basil and garlic catch my nose. Pesto Friday. Fond memories accompany the scent. Sometimes, during the summer months, we'd plan "night ops" at the pond for the dwindling hours of evening, when the sun seemed to be tucking itself in just past the treetops. Since being out so late was a no-no for both sets of parents, Mickey would invite me over for pesto, and afterward, we'd pretend we were playing

Uno in her room before sneaking out through the window. Something about the twilight made us fight imaginary villains harder, run faster. In those moments, I really did think I could be just like Papa Shades. Those times with Mickey were some of the best nights I've ever had. Happy and untouched by the worries of the world, slaying monsters and mosquitos with reckless abandon.

I hear Mickey's voice as she bounds into her room, bringing me back to the present. Here's my chance.

I knock at the window. She looks up, squinting at first, before making out my silhouette beyond the glass. She drops her phone. Her scream is loud and short, like that of a puppy with its tail caught in a door.

"Mick? You okay?" her dad calls out.

"It's me!" I hiss. She glances back at the door before her eyes settle on me again. I can see confusion turn to distress. Before she can get a word out, I whisper-yell, "Let me in!"

It's as if instinct kicks in for her. She rushes toward me, pulling the window open about eight inches. She tugs at my shoulders as I slither into her room, falling face-first onto old brown carpet so roughly that it burns my cheek. I manage to maneuver myself upright.

"Mick?"

She doesn't answer her dad. She just mouths, *What are you doing here?* with all the venom of a cobra. Now it's my turn to not answer, because what, exactly, *am* I doing here? She places both hands to hips and mouths, *Well?*

I shrug and mouth, *Confronting you!* It's only then that I fully take her in. She's got these red-and-black pajamas on with one of those hideous, cannibal-flower-looking Demogorgons springing from her chest with the words "Strangest Thing" stylized in red horror font across her collarbone.

Her eyes grow big as our unspoken conversation evolves into a fusillade of heated whispers. "Over what?"

"You're ratting me out!" I reply.

"No, I'm not!"

"Mick?"

My breath catches and her body goes rigid. Jamar Kyle's words are much closer now. We listen silently and, soon enough, hear footsteps nearing her door from the hallway.

Go! she mouths.

Where?

She points, and I turn to the open window. I try diving out but severely misjudge the angle in my haste, smacking my head against the lift at the bottom. She gasps as I stagger back, falling to the carpet again. I see her face above me, both hands tented over her lips and chin.

There's a knock at the door. "Michaela?"

Shoot! I put a hand to my own head as I writhe on the floor.

On top of the all-consuming headache I've just given myself, another pain comes shooting in. I wince at the steady blows of Mickey's foot to my torso. She points toward the direction of her kicks, and I realize she's herding me under her bed. I roll over and army-crawl until I'm blanketed by shadow. The door creaks open just as I drag my feet beneath the frame.

Even against carpet, Mr. Kyle's footsteps are heavy. I watch as his feet slowly, methodically move around the bed. He asks if Mickey's okay. She sputters out a yes. Other questions follow—ones meant to take up space and air as he inspects the room for any hazards or harms that could befall his little girl. Mickey answers all the questions dutifully.

The window creaks shut as he chides her for not closing it at night. She protests that it's Pesto Friday and she was airing out her room, but he's insistent she leave it closed, his tone bordering on obsessive. I guess that's the natural way of things when a loved one prematurely dies. You hold on that much tighter to the ones still here.

Mattress springs whine above me as he sits. He takes a deep breath and I can hear him pat the bed space beside him. She sits, too, and I see both their feet planted inches in front of my face.

"How've you been? Since the, you know . . ."

I assume he means the pet store fire, and I feel guilty for listening closer. I do want to hear what she's told him, though. There's no way she'd have agreed to a TV interview without keying him in on it.

"I'm fine," she answers.

It's silent for a long moment, as if her dad wants her to say more. When she doesn't, he just says, "Well, I'm here if you need to talk."

I can almost feel the bed lifting above me as they rise.

"Fish are looking great," he says. "I know you had your heart set on a new one. Tell you what. This weekend, we'll drive to the pet shop in that new mall over in Millington."

"Sure," she says.

Mr. Kyle walks toward the door as I crawl precious inches closer to the edge of the bed. I hear the handle turn but then a pause. He turns back abruptly, hustling toward her. From what I can hear, it sounds like the embrace of a man who genuinely fears this hug could be his last.

His words are muffled, half spoken into the fabric of her pajamas, but I can make out what he said quite clearly.

"I'm so glad you didn't step foot into that pet store."

What?

Right after the door clicks shut, Mickey drops to all fours and claws at the carpet to get to me. She bends her head to the floor and gets so close I can smell the mint of her shampoo. Her eyes are fanatical.

"What the hell, man?!" she says.

"Okay! Could you just . . . ?" I snap my fingers, and she takes my hand. As I struggle out, I can feel her nails cutting the skin of my wrist and forearm. I'm pretty sure gripping me that hard isn't necessary, but I guess I deserve it.

Once standing, I dust myself off. From what, I don't exactly know. But I feel like I should be doing something as she waits, head cocked, foot-tappingly impatient, for an explanation.

"I told you already," I say. "I came to confront you for ratting me out to EGTV."

"And *I* told *you* I had nothing to do with that," she says.

"Well, who did?" I ask.

She presses her hands to each side of her head, but no words come. The way she looks at me, there's no need. She knows it's impossible I got this far without at least considering an entire suspect list. Her hands drop. Instead of answering, she asks a question of her own. "Why'd you assume it was me?"

"Because we *hate* each other." *Isn't it obvious?*

Her lips part and she draws in a breath. But again, she doesn't speak. Something about her changes, though. Her face clouds with disappointment. But it can't be that. Maybe she's just tired.

Her shoulders slump as she plops down on the bed, the fanatical look long gone. In its place is a blank stare at a wall adorned with K-pop posters and strings of Christmas lights. I get uncomfortable lording over her, so I sit down next to her. Maybe "hate" is too strong a word, especially this late at night.

She asks to see the interview promo. I go to the channel's website and see it's the number one trending video there. I play the clip, despair washing over me as we watch. Ugh, this is gonna be so bad when it gets out. When the clip is over, she simply says, "You sure it wasn't the idiot pet store guy?"

"Why would he?"

"For credit. He had security footage access. He watches the tape, catches something new, and drops a bombshell on whatever TV station will have him. Boom. Eight minutes of fame."

"It's fifteen minutes," I correct.

"Pretty sure he can't count that high."

I laugh and nod, glad for the momentary reprieve from the sinking feeling that's settled in my stomach. For all her annoying qualities, Mickey's always been great at well-timed jokes.

I get this inexplicable urge to put an arm around her shoulder to rope her back in. So strong that I have to ball my hand into a fist to stop it. To distract myself, I look around the room. It's nearly just as I remember it the last time I was here. If the K-pop posters were still photos of Misty Copeland and Simone Biles, it would've felt like we were nine years old again.

"I see you've redecorated," I say.

She shrugs, looking around with me. "Yeah, had to switch it up a little. It's still missing something, though."

I get up, pacing methodically, studying each corner like a museum curator. I touch a blank strip of wall beside the TV. "Maybe some stick-on 3D butterflies or flowers over here."

"What are we, in elementary school?"

I ignore her, making my way to the next wall. My arms go wide. "Maybe one of those quote decals over your bed. 'Carpe diem'? 'To thine own self be true'?" I hear an audible grimace behind me.

"Wall quotes are so tacky, though," she says.

I turn around. "They're *profound*."

"They look trashy. They're like the tramp stamps of home decor."

I roll my eyes but continue my walk. No way to convince Mickey of something when her mind's made up, but I push a little further just to annoy her. I meander toward her nightstand and pick up a framed photo of Mickey flanked by her mother and father. I'm getting early middle-school vibes. Mickey with rubber-band braces and a scrunchie was by far the funniest looking Mickey. I position myself so that I can see her reaction from the corner of my eye.

"Well, whenever you decide to level up your room, just let me know," I offer. "I usually charge, but for you? A small discount."

Mickey scoffs. "Like I'd ever take interior design advice from a guy who had a plushie wall."

"Plushie *corner*," I correct. "And it was tastefully done."

"Wall," she insists.

"You're exaggerating."

"I have photographic proof." I do a double take as she whips out her phone and starts thumbing through the screens. Within seconds, she sidles up to me and shows me a chaotic collage of fur and color taking up at least half the wall space in my room. I squint at the picture, incredulous. There must be eighty stuffed animals stacked into the world's most comfortable dogpile. "Do you still have this?" she asks, a laugh braided into her question.

I shake my head. "Spilled orange juice on it in eighth grade."

It was for the best, honestly. Once Grandpa saw it after he moved in, he wouldn't let it go. Kept calling it "the softest thing I've ever seen since Charmin came out with three-ply." Papa Shades's "shade" got so unbearable that it was a relief to get rid of it.

"Oh my God, that's so sad. I *loved* Plushieville!" she says. "I remember for my birthday one year you gave me the mayor."

"Mr. Jiggles. And he was *deputy* mayor. Why were you taking secret blackmail pictures of my room, anyway?"

Her eyes go wide as she kicks at my calf. "You *sent* me that pic! Remember?! You were so proud!" She snatches her phone away to study the photograph once more.

"I sent you that?" I ask.

"Yeah. When you first created it. I was so confused, too. Like, *Why am I getting an empath's version of a thirst trap?*"

Ouch. I bury a smile, pretending to ignore the comment as I make my way to the huge fish tank pedestaled at the corner of her room opposite the door. My eyes follow the fish swimming without care or cause. I feel her watching me as I crouch, my nose coming close to glass. This used to be one of my favorite things about her room. Marveling as the fish move about, fins like brilliantly colored ribbons feathering through water. Mentally, I try to insert the fish Harry had eaten into the visual, but I can't.

"I'm sorry," I say.

"Don't be. They're only fish."

I know she doesn't mean it. She's trying to make me feel better. They were never just fish to her.

"May I ask why?" I say.

"Why what?"

"Why do you have so many?"

"It's a thing my mom and I used to do." I turn to look at her, and her focus shifts from me to her nails. The playful tone she had had moments ago has blinked out like an old streetlight. "Each time one of us had a birthday, we'd go buy a fish to celebrate. The day I bought the fish was . . ."

"Your mom's birthday."

The revelation is a gut punch. I want to slither right back out that window, never to return. She didn't react the way she did just because her fish had died or because she had lingering beef with me. She reacted that way because of what the fish meant.

The worst part is, I should've known. Mrs. Kyle's birthday parties were neighborhood affairs. I've been over to celebrate several times, always in the backyard under the stars and to the silky tunes of Motown oldies. Serena Kyle was truly a bright spot on our street, a sparkler on a hot July night. I'm sure it was the same in her family, too.

But her magnanimity didn't just limit itself to the neighborhood. She was cool with everybody. Whenever Papa Shades would be home to visit, Mrs. Kyle would always make a point to stop by and say hey. It didn't hurt that they shared a love of filmmaking and the outdoors. Before their falling-out, she and Grandpa joked and bantered and seemed to get along like two old friends.

Mickey rises from the bed without a word and shuffles toward the dresser. She blithely repeats "Just a fish," but there's a hitch in her voice that suggests she's pinning some deeper feelings to the back of her throat. She grabs the remote. Next thing I know, the mounted TV screen comes to life with what looks like a beautiful ocean screen saver, except I can see the Netflix logo tucked into a bottom corner.

"You want me to go?" I ask, standing up. I sure would want me to. Can't feel good having someone come into your house and dredge up memories of a deceased loved one.

"If you want," she replies.

I don't move. Something's unspoken here. Undone. Like quitting your homework on the second-to-last problem.

After a moment, I ask, "What are you watching?"

"Just some documentary," she answers. She hits the Play from Beginning button. Airy music floats above the sound of rippling water as a snorkeler cuts through an ocean's surface to explore the shallows beyond an empty beach.

I look closer, recognition sparking in me. "Is that the one about the South African guy who learns how to reconnect with his family by swimming with an octopus?"

"*My Octopus Teacher*? No," she replies. "It's along those lines, though. It's about a woman who learns to love herself again after a tumultuous divorce by exploring the life cycle of a Caspian Sea fish."

"What's the title?" I ask.

"*My Koi Professor*," she says.

Figures. The screen goes dark before birthing into extravagant blues and greens, with a sleek red fish swimming at a distance. We both sit on her bed and listen as a female narrator self-importantly intones: "When I followed a man, I found a

133

dog. When I followed a fish, I found myself."

The visuals hook me within the first few frames. We're fixated on the screen, me asking questions about the reef and sea life, Mickey pointing out the different koi species and their idiosyncrasies, both of us captivated by the woman's story. As Mickey comments on the nuanced camera angles and the editing choices, it becomes clear that the documentary Mickey wants me to help her with is her way of carrying her mother's torch. I can relate to this. It's not easy living in someone's shadow.

Countless minutes pass. By the time Mickey's dad yells about the hand soap needing a refill in the bathroom, we're both sprawled out beside each other on the bed. I keep having to turn away from her to shoulder-wipe tears from my face. The documentary is just that good. I look at her, and a question as light as a feather floats into my mind.

"Why'd you tell your dad you weren't in the pet store?" I ask.

Her eyes remain fixed on the screen. "Stuff worries him now. Now that . . ." She doesn't have to finish what she's saying. "So I just avoid doing that, when I can."

"But he doesn't know you're a hero," I say.

Something that's really bothered me about everybody calling me a hero is nobody's giving that same credit to Mickey. If there's anything 100 percent true about that moment, it's that *Mickey* stepped up. She braved whatever heat or smoke or chaos swirled around her to do the impossible. She saved that man's life even if, perhaps, I didn't. But she's never highjacked any of my conversations with Jo or Jimmy or any of my admirers to say this.

"He knows I'm alive, and that I'd never risk that," she says. "And that's enough for us."

The to-the-point way she replies tells me I shouldn't push the subject, so I don't.

"You think maybe Jimmy could've set up the interview?" I ask.

"No."

"Like, no possible way?"

"Only one way to find out," she says. "Get him alone. Get him on your side. He'll talk."

As if it were that simple. I accept her response without protest and lie back, reveling in the comforts of the moment while keeping an ear out for her dad. Just like the old days.

Except it's not like the old days. Not *exactly*, at least. Her eyes are locked on the screen, but mine can't help drifting toward her. I feel like a voyeur, stealing precious moments to take in her features. The stillness of her deep brown eyes. The gentle curves of her cheekbones, chin, and nose. The delicate skin of her face, given a faint blue hue by the light of the screen. The features I'd long ago committed to memory. But tonight, I'm noticing them in a different way. A way that burns me on the inside and makes my fingers itch to the touch. The screen fades to black before birthing again into brilliant orange, and she tilts her head toward me. Her smile is sleepy and amused, half of it shrouded by bedcover.

"What?" she asks, the word twined with laughter like ivy on fence posts.

"You just look . . ." Something catches in my throat. I can't possibly be thinking what I was about to say.

"Look what?" It's quiet for a moment as Mickey waits for me to finish. When I don't—can't—her face turns serious. "What's wrong?"

"Nothing," I reply. And that's just it. There's absolutely nothing wrong with this moment. But shouldn't this moment be with Jo? Or anybody, really, besides Mickey?

Silence settles in again. Mickey gulps, a knot slowly, subtly working its way down her throat. That's the first inkling that she's feeling what I may be feeling.

She tries to play it off with a smirk, teasing, "You're being weird," as she reaches out to swat at my shoulder. I catch her hand. It's soft with the scent of cocoa butter. I hold it like I would a flower petal, running my thumb over her palm. She keeps it there. I bring it close to my cheek. And I bring myself closer to her.

People say the best kisses are full of sparks or fireworks or some other spectacle. But I think that's wrong. The best ones— like this one—are less combustion but more compulsion. I feel *compelled* to kiss her, like she's a force of nature. Gravity. Inertia. Magnetism. The pull of my lips to hers. The press of her hand to the nape of my neck, urging me closer still. But funny thing about forces of nature. They're so natural that nothing about them seems forced. Neither does this. Kissing Mickey is as easy as watching a sunset or breathing. The way we graft onto each other, rolling above the tangle of bedsheets, it's like we're meant to be this way, to live in this moment for years longer than the minutes we have.

Muffled laughter spills from both of us as we roll right off the bed, landing on my back. Fingers pressed to each other's lips, we shush each other as Mickey's dad calls out.

By the time he reenters, I'm back under the bed, thinking about how this is Mickey. How it can't be. How *we* can't be.

11

ABOUT AN HOUR AFTER I LEFT, WE BOTH STARTED SECOND-
guessing what went down in her bedroom. I texted her saying
that maybe it wasn't the best idea to complicate things so soon
after we'd finally started talking again for the first time in years.
Minutes later, she texted that she agreed. The ensuing text conversation lasted no more than five minutes, but two things were
made perfectly clear: (1) what we did could never happen again
and (2) things between us would stay exactly the same.

Admittedly, things aren't *exactly* the same. Just now, for
instance. When we first saw each other this morning, I tried
to dap her up, but Mickey came in, arms wide, for a hug. I
fidgeted, she flinched, and we ended up doing this awkward
side hug/handshake/back-pat move that probably looked like
the world's worst tango.

And even beyond that, I've noticed I'm not *seeing* her the
same way. She looked *great* this morning. Like really beautiful,
in that double-take kind of way that dries your throat or makes
you stutter. And when soccer star Brady Polis came up to her

locker and started flirting, I could feel myself tensing, teeth grinding, as she laughed and touched his forearm. Eventually Brady, in true Neanderthal form, made some stupid sexual comment to ruin the moment. Mickey's arms folded as she tried to end the conversation, and I stepped in with a firm "Yo, chill" because he just wasn't picking up on the vibe shift.

I'd expected a thank-you after he left, but instead Mickey seemed annoyed. According to her, I shouldn't have assumed she needed me to swoop in and save the day. This was the opposite of what Grandpa would try to teach me. Throughout his life, Papa Shades always said men were meant to protect women, and that a "true man" could use his brute strength, financial success, and inherent intelligence to make their lives easier. When I explained his doctrine to her, she just shrugged and muttered, "Grandpa knows best, I suppose," sarcasm bleeding through each word.

As bad as that was, things could've been a lot worse. I spent the entire weekend wrestling with my nerves thinking about the *Hollywood Hangout* story. Saturday, idle speculation was scattered on the WestlakeWhispers hashtag like buckshot, with a smattering of people opining on what the reveal could be. By Sunday morning, genuine curiosity by a few online had devolved into warring factions over the believability of my story. While the vast majority was still #TeamLionheart, a small but vocal group decamped to #TeamLyinel. Odds were booked and bets were taken. When 6:30 p.m. arrived and the show's opening jingle played, it seemed as if all of Westlake had swarmed onto a hastily made Slack channel for a virtual watch party.

And then what happened was . . . nothing.

No snitches. No narcs. Not a word on the pet store fire.

The chat on Slack exploded as soon as the credits rolled. If anything, once #TeamLyinel had been driven off the channel, I'd become that much more popular. An unassuming hero whose name had been unjustly dragged through the mud. Theo was the first to use the word "martyr," offering up the descriptor with the smug awareness of a fisherman hooking bait to a reel. By the time the chat wound down, I was being favorably compared to Joan of Arc.

That night, out of curiosity, I snooped the *Hangout* website to see what happened. Why all this buildup for nothing? The promo was gone, and there was no hidden online interview. It's like they'd scrubbed any insinuation that my story wasn't true.

Monday comes, and I'm distracted in my classes, doing mental gymnastics to solve this mystery. I'm still trying to figure it out as Mickey and I stand beside the B hallway entrance waiting for Jimmy at the end of the day. We're supposed to meet him here under the guise of me giving him tips on how to be more popular, but we'll really just be pumping him for more information on whether he was the one who contacted *Hollywood Hangout*. Neither of us is prepared for the state in which he arrives.

The first thing we notice is Jimmy's hair is all wet. It's matted to his forehead, and his shirt is soaked down to the shoulders. He's red in the face, his countenance even parts anger and embarrassment.

I get into his path, slouching to his eye level, willing his eyes to meet mine. But he won't look up. "Jimmy, who—"

"Chase," he mumbles, fists clenched. "It's always him."

Mickey and I flank Jimmy as we walk away from the school. Sympathy swells within me. I feel terrible for what's been happening to him. Chase's cruelty and relentlessness know no bounds.

As Jimmy looks ahead, I glance behind his shoulder and mouth *3-C* to Mickey as a reminder. Despite my sympathy, I still need to get to the truth, and we've preplanned how to do it: candy, compliment, and casual info request.

Mickey nods and asks, "Hey, Jimmy, would you like some gum?" He stops, thinking about it as he dries his ears with the hem of his shirt. Instead of turning down an obviously empty nicety, he says yes. Mickey and I glance at each other, perplexed. Mickey then says, "Lionel, go ahead."

"Me? You're the one who asked!" I shoot back. I check my pockets, but nothing's there.

"You chew gum like a damn cow eats grass, but *today* you're out?" she says.

Jimmy must think we're the oddest couple on the planet. He's trading looks between us but saying nothing. Fortunately, I remember the Warheads I won last week. I take my book bag off and pluck out the bag. There are three left. I hand them all to Jimmy.

The smile he gives is one of quiet elation. He says, "Thanks," and tells me they're his favorite, adding, "Back in Yonkers, we used to put as many as we could in our mouths, with a cayenne pepper and a tablespoon of vinegar."

Not the best advertisement for the community, but I manage to bury my revulsion behind an awkward nod.

Mickey isn't so subtle. "Seriously?" she asks.

"Dead ass," Jimmy says.

"Dead ass is right," she quips. I reach around Jimmy's back to flick her shoulder, and she's quick with a "Sorry." She then eyes his outfit. A green-and-white football jersey with "New York" written in bold at the top, athletic shorts, and a thin silver chain ringing his neck. "Cool threads, man," she says. Good. *Compliment.* She goes on to add, "Giants looking pretty solid this year, huh?"

Not good. My eyes burn a path right to her. "This is a *Jets* outfit," I say through clenched teeth.

"Wait, they have two football teams?" she asks, all too seriously.

"Yes," I shoot back.

"Oh, I thought that was just a basketball thing. Like Knicks, Globetrotters."

The sports fan in me just about explodes. I look over at Jimmy, whose eyes are squinted at Mickey. I can't risk her blowing our cover, so I quickly wrap an arm around him, leading him away.

"She wouldn't be able to spot a charge unless it showed up on her Visa bill."

"Sexist much?" Mickey calls out. I ignore her as she slows to take a phone call.

"You know, Jimmy, I'm actually glad to get you out of there. I'd been wanting to talk to you. Make sure everything's on the up and up. So other than Chase, everything good? Everything a hun-ned?" I ask, doing my best impression of a New Yorker.

"All right, I guess," he says. Not the most cheerful answer, but once I get him to open up some, I find out that not everything is bad. He tells me about a couple new freshman friends he made. Phineas and Treyvion. How he took charge and asserted himself like I would've done. I pat his shoulder like a proud dad at Little League.

We head onto the concrete walkway leading down to a chain-link fence that marks the school's boundary. A stiff fall breeze brushes up to us and carries the leaves past our feet. A train rumbles in the distance, and I wait for the sound to pass before speaking again. "Jimmy, you gotta be real with me."

After some cajoling, Jimmy admits to not just having a slow go at it socially, but also academically. He says Math I with Mrs. Laramie has been kicking his butt. In fact, the only class he really likes so far is PE, but he always gets picked near last during free-play basketball games. All because his classmates see a small kid with twiggy arms.

I wish I could tell him it'll get better, but I can't. I was never "the new kid." I'm a Westlake lifer. Know just about every street name and corner store in town, and almost every shop owner knows me. "Little Lionel Honeycutt," they'd always say when

I'd come around. "Show me that Hollywood smile that made your gramps so famous." If I did, Mrs. Howard of Treats and Trinkets would give me a free pecan square, and Big Walter Jarvis at Walt's Hot Dogs would supersize my drink cup, free of charge. Fame has always had its benefits for me, even if the fame wasn't necessarily mine.

Jimmy's situation is different. No connects. No companions. As Grandpa used to say, "Having no one to love you—well, that life's as empty as a piss pot on an ocean raft." The guilt welling up within me gets worse just thinking about it. As much as I'm needling Jimmy for info, I should spend an equal amount of time and energy giving back, too. I could really help him. If he follows in my footsteps, there's no telling how far he could go.

I stop walking, a foot teetering on an uneven crack where a tree root has pushed up the concrete. Jimmy stumbles a bit, but I'm right there to catch him. I imagine that being a metaphor for our budding friendship. Him, the bumbling nobody. Me, the steady hand guiding him through this crazy hormonal menagerie we call high school.

"Jimmy," I say. "You know I got you, right?" His nod is reluctant, so I go on. "You can come to me for anything. You wanna hoop sometime? Just ask. You see a girl you like—I can help lay the groundwork. Even if you only wanna sit down somewhere and chop it up, you got a listening ear in me. All I ask is that you be completely honest with me."

He opens his mouth but hesitates. I get in front of him. I put my hands to his shoulders, an earnest look in my eyes.

This could be the moment I get answers. This world of constant pomp and praise could be validated by what Jimmy reveals, or it could all come crashing down. But either way, at least I'll know.

"Could you help me deal with Chase?" he asks in what I'm coming to know as his demure, soft-spoken way. I've always had an impression of New Yorkers as being brash and loud and sending more birds flying in a day than all of the Westlake Conservation Aviary. Jimmy's decidedly not that.

I nod. "Tell you what. Let's go out by the train tracks where there's some open space. I can show you a few moves."

"Really?! Like what?"

"The Ghost Chop, maybe? And if you get that, we can try the reverse Hoodlock."

These were the moves Grandpa used to finish off supervillain Jamarcus "Jigga" Tate in *Hood Chronicles 2*, a cult classic.

"You know how to do the Hoodlock?" Jimmy asks, his eyes wide and unbelieving.

"I was taught by the best," I say.

"You were taught by . . ." He stops mid-sentence, as if the question rattling around in his head is so ludicrous that it doesn't merit asking. But when I nod, something sparks to life in his eyes.

Jimmy's "Wow" stretches on for at least three seconds. I grin. Maybe even blush a little. Something about having an admirer buoys a person. I think about that. For all the inconveniences fame can bring, it's the quiet moments like these that make it all worthwhile. It's the art that matters, of course, but also the inspiration. The chance to create magic on the big screen and dreams in little minds like Jimmy's. It's right then, looking into his eyes filled with childlike wonderment, that I curse ever having suspected Jimmy of going to *Hollywood Hangout* with footage that may have contradicted my hero status. There's no way he would've done that, and I'll believe that till I'm six feet under.

I bend slightly at the knees. "Matter of fact, why don't we make this official? You really wanna be somebody, huh?" I ask. Jimmy nods. "Then there's this philosophy I go by."

"Philosophy?"

"You heard of it?"

"They don't teach you that till college, right?" he asks.

"Yeah, but you can *learn* philosophy before that. They just don't call it that. Like, the Golden Rule is philosophy."

Jimmy's head lifts as Mickey wanders nearby, still on the phone. He looks off across the school parking lot as if he's studying the distant mountains. Slowly, he nods. "I guess you're right."

"Well, my late grandpa had this philosophy," I continue. "It's called Knights and Damsels."

"Your grandpa came up with his *very own* philosophy?"

"Yeah, it's not that big of a deal. I do it sometimes, too, ya know. Like, I'm in my room just sitting there thinking and, *boom*, new philosophy just drops." A low whistling sound comes from Jimmy's rounded lips. "Well, basically, the philosophy is that some people—the knights—are meant to be the badasses

146

in this world. The go-getters. The ones who swoop in at the last minute to save the day. You and me, Jimmy? We're knights."

He looks at me, and I can see the earnestness in the deep brown of his eyes. He's hanging on to my every word like they're gold. Rich enough to change the arc of his life. "I'm a . . . knight?" he carefully asks.

I chuckle. "Don't be so surprised."

"Wait," Jimmy says, perking up. "My last name. *Palladino.* My nonna told me a long time ago that it literally means 'protector.' Like a knight protects damsels."

I clasp my hands together. "Well, there you have it."

"But . . . how'd I get to be a knight?"

"You were born into it."

His eyes go wide. "You can be *born* into it?"

"Of course. Just like you're born Black or born gay. Not that those things are mutually exclusive or anything. I mean, I'm sure there's some Black gay knights out there."

Watching his demeanor change is like watching a sunrise. Bright. Uplifting. A spectacle that breathes life into you, too. "I'm a knight," he says again. Not as a question, though. As an affirmation.

"Now you're getting it."

"Wait. Who are the damsels, then?"

I point. "Take Mickey over there. Least heroic person I know. I mean, she couldn't save a seat in an empty movie theater."

Mickey cups her hand over the phone and says, "Heard that." I chuckle to myself. She's hearing all of this and not even calling me out on it. She's letting me give Jimmy a TED Talk on heroism when she should be the one behind the lectern. That's what I love about her. How we just get each other.

I notice Jimmy's looking a little too hard at Mickey. I even see him mouthing *Whoa* as she stretches an arm and arches her back for a yawn. I get annoyed again, just like this morning with Brady Polis. I'm not possessive or anything, but Mickey's *Mickey*. I nudge his shoulder. I whisper, "Don't bother. Out of your league."

Jimmy looks all kinds of sheepish as his attention returns to me. We walk farther, Jimmy's feet kicking rocks along the pavement. Eventually, he asks, "So if I'm a knight, how can I let everybody know?"

"I can teach you. Like a sort of mentor-mentee thing?"

"You'd do that?"

"Sure. I mean, we've both survived trauma. We both love sports, obviously. And we're both hella cool, even if the school doesn't totally see it yet." He makes a face, and I replay my words. "Y'all say 'hella,' right?"

"Might be a West Coast thing," he says.

"*Hecka* cool," I correct, nodding confidently.

I decide to train Jimmy down at the old railroad tracks behind the school. It's an out-of-the-way spot, like the wooded cabin area Rocky Balboa secluded himself in to prepare leading up to his second fight with the Russian guy. In the backdrop is a picturesque view of Mount Trembley, so I figure Jimmy could get some inspiration from the wilderness. You know, roughing it, getting in touch with your inner caveman, that kind of stuff. Theo ends up tagging along with the three of us for emotional support. *And* to shoot some B-roll footage for an upcoming campaign ad.

"Jimmy, you *are* the mountain," I say. "Be *one* with the mountain. Immovable."

He's balancing on a rail of the track as we throw rocks at him. Every time he gets hit, he gets wobbly and lets out a sharp yelp, but all in all, he's doing well. Mickey pelts him at the waist. Jimmy couples a pronounced "Ouch" with a half pirouette.

I look at her. "Why are you throwing so hard?"

Mickey shrugs. "Reparations," she mutters, bending down to pick up a handful more rocks.

"Well, *stop*. We trying to get him fit, not injured."

"Can I get down now?" Jimmy asks.

"Not yet, Jimmy," Theo says, surprising us both. He holds up his iPhone and switches on his camera. "Repeat something for me right quick. Ready?" Jimmy shoots me a quizzical stare. I nod hesitantly, and Jimmy nods, too. Theo speaks as if he's doing an infomercial: "Are you sick of a bickering, corrupt, do-nothing Council? Yes? Well, it's time for a change. Join me in voting for Theo James, and let's get this school back on track!"

Jimmy parrots Theo's monologue but gets no further than "do-nothing Council" before Theo yells "Cut!" Theo then instructs Jimmy to stiffen his spine, annunciate his vowels, and flash a thumbs-up the very moment he says "Theo."

Jimmy's just about to start over when I yell "Cut" this time. I target my irritation directly at my best friend. "What are you doing?" I ask.

"Making a campaign commercial," Theo answers. He points down to Jimmy's feet. "'Back on track.' Train tracks. It fits. Hey, do you think having him end with 'Make Westlake Great Again' might wrangle some conservative votes?"

"*Theo,*" Mickey says, staring blankly.

Then his mouth opens to form an O, like he just got a big idea. He pats my back. "You should get up there with Jimmy. It'll add some gravitas."

At this point, I've about had it. I love the guy, but it's so annoying the way he tries to make a lot of things about himself. I wave off Theo's suggestion to his dismay and say, "Jimmy, take a lap. When you get back, I'll teach you how to do the Honeycutter."

"From *Space Invasion 3*?" Jimmy asks.

I shake my head. "Two, actually. You're thinking about the Galaxy Punch. But we'll get to that, too."

Jimmy pairs a "*Yesss*" with a fist pump as he jogs off.

I watch as he goes, happy that he's engaged with the training but still concerned he's not built for this kind of pressure cooker. Theo hops on a track rail, teetering. Mickey joins him.

"The kid's got grit," Theo says. "Reminds me of myself when I was little. Driven. Tenacious."

"Yeah, but Chase can be brutal, and Jimmy's never encountered someone like him before," I respond. "I mean, I *want* him to be ready if things keep escalating, but my mind's just flashing this big red sign saying 'Too Young.'"

"*Ohh*, and you're so much more mature at your big ass age of what? Sixteen?" Mickey adds, the sarcasm evident in her tone and eye roll.

I'm about to respond when I notice a change in her demeanor. She squints, looking past my shoulder. "The fuck?" she says.

I turn. In the distance, Jo is hustling toward us. She's smiling like she's reuniting with loved ones after returning from war.

"Who invited her?" Mickey says.

When I say that I *may* have mentioned this little after-school field trip to Jo at lunch earlier, Mickey's face flashes with an expression I can't quite pin down. But I'm pretty sure it's not a positive one. I wasn't planning to ask her along—it all sorta happened after Jo delivered some not-great news about needing to cancel our Fall Ball date this Saturday. Turns out, she'd forgotten she'd already promised some of her girlfriends she'd go with them. It was a gut punch, especially considering the fact that our ball proposal video got two million views. And while her explanation didn't quite sound believable, what was I supposed to do? And besides, she swore she'd save me plenty of dances.

Jo slows as she nears us.

"You ready?" Jo asks.

Mickey's "For what?" is terse and unwelcoming.

"For the shoot?"

Mickey and Theo both look confused, so I fill them in: "We thought it'd be cool for me to do some TikToks to build my brand."

Jo points behind us. "Who's the middle schooler?"

"Oh, that's Jimmy," I say. "He's a freshman." I look at Jimmy a ways down the track. He's squatting, repeatedly touching the railing with his hand before recoiling like it's a hot stove.

"We're trying to help him with some bullying," Theo adds.

"Oh my God, I can totally help with that. I'm soooo against bullying! I see it all the time online. I literally kick out any member of the FinaFam who's credibly accused of cyberbullying. I abhor it."

"Really?"

"Yeah, I've even made TikToks about it," she says, getting out her phone. "After Megan broke up with Riley, instead of just taking the L, he totally tried to slut-shame her online. So, we egged his house, and then I thought this could be a learning opportunity for my fellows. So I posted this."

The three of us gather around her phone as the video starts. In it, Jo dances to some Bieber song for a few seconds before making the heart shape with her hands and breaking it apart afterward. She then closes in on the camera and says, "Remember, ladies, any time someone calls you a 'slut,' switch those letters around until they spell L-U-S-T '*lust*.' That way you'll remember to always want more from yourself."

Once the video goes off, Jo pockets her phone and gives a self-satisfied grin. I smile at the witticism, and Theo nods approvingly. Mickey, however, simply cannot leave well enough alone.

"Umm, what?" she says. It's less a question than a critique.

"So, slut and lust are like anagrams," Jo begins to explain, but Mickey cuts her off.

"People are actually . . . *influenced* by that advice?"

"Seems like it to me," Theo says, pointing at the 80K likes. Right beside it, I see it's got one million views. I stare at Jo's face, absolutely floored by her. Not only is she great at marketing. She also seems like a great person.

"Actually, now that I think about it," she says, "we can make this a whole thing. Lionel, this could be the hook for your brand. Defender of the little guy. We can do a whole series. You training Jimmy and giving advice on how to stand up for yourself."

"And my campaign could piggyback right off that," Theo adds. "The underdog taking on the entrenched system." While I'm annoyed he's inserting himself into this again, Jo's enthusiastic approval beats back my polite refusal before it leaves my lips.

Jo gestures toward Mount Trembley. "Why don't we start now? We're already at the perfect shoot location. This place is so beautiful. Reminds me of when Ida von Trapp invited me to the Hype Cabin."

Lines come to Mickey's brow. "You mean 'Hype House'?" she asks.

"Close," Jo corrects. "The Hype House guys own this cabin up near Tahoe. A place for content creators to get off the grid and unplug a little. Focus on their craft."

"Who's Ida von Trapp?" I ask.

"Bikini Mozart Girl," Jo answers. She says it in a matter-of-fact way that leads me to think I should've known already.

Theo lifts his eyebrows, clearly impressed. "Jo, you are a genius," he says just as Jimmy returns. "How do you think we should weave the campaign into it?" Jo drapes her arm around Theo as they walk off and she downloads her thoughts. He nods at everything she says, clearly on board with her vision. The only person who doesn't seem impressed is Mickey. In fact, she's no longer in the conversation at all. She's walking a tight-rope along a rail line. Just quietly shrinking into the distance like a long-passed train.

I sit down at the slope of the track, and Jimmy sits beside me. I realize this is a grand opportunity to pry for the full story about what happened, but Jimmy gives me the truth with one single, simple revelation.

He caresses his palm and says, "Boy, those rails were as hot as the shelf."

"What shelf?" I ask.

"The shelf we lifted at the pet store." I glare at him so quickly, my neck hurts from the snapping motion. Jimmy looks at me, confused at first. Then he must see the question in my eyes because he demurely adds, "Well, tried to lift, at least."

"*You* . . . were lifting the shelf?" I ask haltingly, pronouncing every syllable carefully, as if my words are as fragile as glass.

"Yeah, I came over and tried to help you. Or at least I

thought it was you." He shakes his head. "It was so smoky, I couldn't really see anybody. And then with the passing out, my memory's kinda spotty anyway. Honestly, everything kind of goes blank after I started lifting."

A question creaks out of me, whisper soft. "And you're *sure* someone was lifting while you were?"

Jimmy nods. "You know when you're lifting something heavy and you can just feel it getting easier when someone helps. It was like that."

I sit there in quiet, world-shattering unease as he regales me with the details of my own heroics. Fabrications stitched from faulty memory and Marvel-worthy imagination. In his mind, I did what he couldn't. In my mind, I piece together the truth.

I grabbed the shelf and then my cramp forced me to let it go.

Nobody witnessed—and the camera never actually caught—*me* picking the shelf back up.

Jimmy and Mickey were lifting the shelf at the same time, even though they couldn't see each other.

The camera never caught Jimmy stepping in where I failed. It didn't catch Mickey, either. If it had, the world would know there were two heroes that day. And neither one was me.

12

I DIDN'T THINK MY STAR COULD GET ANY BRIGHTER. BUT then again, I hadn't yet gotten to know the supernova named Josefina Ramos. After Jimmy's revelation, all I wanted to do was go home and disappear under my bedcovers. I sucked it up and stayed, though, not wanting to punk out in front of Jo. But you could tell my heart wasn't in the training.

Somehow, Jo's edits made me look like I was some CGI action hero. She made fifteen videos total of me instructing Jimmy on different moves from Papa Shades's films, the last eight of which have gone viral. They have this whole superhero-protégé theme. With around fifteen million views each, the Icy City Eye Gouge and Southside Slam tutorials are the most popular, but the Three-Finger Death Slap is on pace to surpass both by day's end. It's got this amazing slo-mo filter that has us looking like we're in *The Matrix*.

All are captioned and hashtagged with anti-bullying messaging, and the comments are blowing up with stories of kids inspired to join support groups or confront their own nemeses.

The fervor is even more intense on the local level. I have to admit, Theo really came through with a revamped campaign. On Tuesday of this week, he'd begun plastering the school with "Cancel Bullying" posters with me and him wearing what Papa Shades would call a "Kick Ass and Carry On" face. By Wednesday, swarms were coming to him telling him he had their vote come spring elections. The WestlakeWhispers hashtag even took an unofficial Twitter poll which had Theo within two points of Lori, all because of the videos of me mentoring Jimmy. Seeing them over and over, I can't help but to think maybe Jimmy or Mickey are the ones who should be teaching me. I don't even know why I haven't told them yet. Embarrassment? Shame? It's like every time I've gotten the inkling to come clean, a new worry arises.

Will the whole school think I'm a liar? Will the PetWorld sponsorship dry up? Will my family be ashamed?

The other person not reveling in the hoopla of this week has been Mickey. For the past three evenings we'd spent time at the pond doing different takes of the eagle's migratory habitat. Being there with her was like taking an express ride on a time machine. I caught nostalgic vibes like they were mosquito bites, all over the place. But she was just so out of it each day. Quiet. Sullen. Like our escapades were more business transactions than trips down memory lane. She even blew me off when I tried to play Two Truths and a Lie.

This morning wasn't much different. Theo literally had to yell across the hallway to get her attention before first period.

She's been ignoring my texts. And she's nowhere to be found during lunch. I guess it's for the best. I keep getting a weird vibe between her and Jo, so probably good to keep them separate.

Today, Jo, Theo, and I are filming a series of shorts titled *Straight Talk About Bullying*. I can't help but think continuing to coast on my fame is the same as playing along with the lie that I'm a hero. But I reason that worry away by saying I'm not *technically* even lying—the pet store incident and helping Jimmy with Chase are two totally different things. I don't like bullying, and that's the 100 percent truth.

The series is pretty elegant in its simplicity, actually. I'm just sitting on a stool spouting these eye-popping facts about the detriments of bullying.

I cock an eyebrow as Theo holds up his phone across the table from me and mouths the word "Action."

"Fact," I say. "Bullies are a hundred times more likely than the broader population to acquire tapeworms and other parasites."

"Cut, cut," Theo says. He lowers his phone. "Ten times. *Ten*."

"I thought you said a hundred," I reply. We both look at Jo, and she dutifully scrolls through her phone. A few seconds pass before she blurts out, "Reddit says thirty-five." After a spirited debate, we decide to average the three. Theo holds up his phone again and mouths, "Action."

"Fact: Bullies are *forty-eight point three* times more likely than the broader population to acquire tapeworms and other parasites. If you're thinking about bullying someone, think again."

"Cut," Theo says, smiling. "I think we've got a winner."

We congratulate each other on a productive lunch sesh before Jo splits to find her crew and Theo leaves to hang more posters. Despite the overall ick I feel, I do get a small amount of satisfaction knowing I'm really making a difference here. Yesterday after school, I saw a group of freshmen in the back parking lot drilling each other on the Hoodlock. I could see the gleam in their eyes. A spark of confidence. Life, which had been snuffed out by overbearing teachers and obnoxious jocks, slowly returning to them like an ember in the ashes. When they noticed me, they stood still in quiet acknowledgment, like military grunts saluting a ranking officer. It was just a moment, but it was so much more.

I use incidents like this to lift my mood, and it actually works. By midweek, the pep's back in my step as I'm walking the halls. I resume high-fiving and nodding at my fans, and I even autograph someone's copy of To Kill a Mockingbird. Unfortunately, the pep dies out later that day. Dad kills it.

When I get home that afternoon, he's out in the garage doing some tune-up work on his '69 Camaro sports car. It's been drivable for months, but he just can't stop tinkering with the damn thing. The car is in the garage, lifted on a jack and two supporting stands, with Dad's legs sticking out underneath the passenger side. I walk lightly, hoping I can slip past him without him roping me into helping. I've got my hand on the front door handle, when I hear, "Get me that adjustable ratchet on top of that toolbox, will you, son?"

Reluctantly, I take my hand away from the doorknob and turn around. I even drop my book bag to the concrete, knowing this is gonna take a while. It's never just one tool. I grab the ratchet and lower it where he can see it. His oil-stained hand sticks out and takes it from me. Seconds later, I hear the clanking of metal against metal. "How was your day?" he asks.

"Good," I answer.

"Excited about homecoming this weekend?"

"Yeah," I say, praying my one-syllable answers will ward off further conversation. Apparently, I didn't pray hard enough, because Dad rolls out from underneath the car and sits up on the flat part of his "creeper," the four-wheeled board he uses to roll under the car. He looks at me as he wipes grease across his already-stained white T-shirt.

"You got this dance, too, right?" I nod. "Mom said you had a date."

"To the premiere," I correct. "Next Saturday." I would've had a date this weekend had Jo not flaked out, but Dad doesn't need to know that.

"You need a ride?" he asks.

I decide to take a chance and say, "Not if I could borrow this car."

The look he gives tells me he's none too sure. But instead of saying no outright, he says, "This baby is still in its cradle. Might not want to disturb it just yet."

"But you drive it sometimes."

"Because I know it. I built it. And I'm an adult."

My shoulders slump. Nowadays, "adult" is Dad's language that basically means whatever age I've yet to reach. Annoyed, I see if I can try to throw off.

"Grandpa let me get behind the wheel of his Impala once," I say. It's not technically a lie. Papa Shades allowed me to get in the driver's side, in the driveway, before abruptly kicking me back out when I said the leather seats were uncomfortable. I can see the half-truth has done its job by the way Dad purses his lips.

"Dad did a lot of things I wouldn't advise," he says.

The diplomatic tone of his response pisses me off even more. Even with Papa Shades dead and buried, Dad still has trouble saying what he really feels about his father. If you can't stand up to a dead man, who can you stand up to?

My eyes narrow as I say almost plaintively, "Grandpa had *fun* in life."

"Fun isn't everything."

"But it's *something*," I spout back. "Face it. Grandpa had fun in life. He made the most of it." I don't say it, but the implication is clear to the both of us. Dad doesn't make the most of his life.

I can see Dad's even keel souring as he stands. He grabs a dingy old towel from the hood of the Camaro and wipes the grease from his hands. I can see the sweat beads streaking lines through the soot caked onto his face as he nears me. I realize he's annoyed. And not just that. He's angry.

I'm surprised by the nod he gives. It's curt and quick, but it affirms what I said, and not in a positive way. "He made the most of it, all right. And he gave his family the least." The towel drops from his hand, landing at my feet. He walks past me and goes inside.

13

THE REST OF THE WEEK FLOATS BY IN A HAZE OF BIG moments undergirded by *meh* emotions. Two more e-news gossip shows request to interview me in the lead-up to the movie premiere. Mom fields a call from the Hallmark Channel inquiring about film rights to my story, and Cheetos contacts me to ask about a possible deal to advertise their Flamin' Hot flavor.

But in all honesty, even with the positive press, I just haven't felt that great knowing that I'm not the hero. Mickey and Jimmy should be the ones getting all the attention. But how do I break that to everybody? How do I rein in a lie that the entire world believes? The sponsorship offers will disappear, the school will shun me, and everybody else will drop me like a bad habit. As of right now, I can't even come clean to Mickey. I've tried texting with her several times to test the waters, but her responses have been one or two words at most, like I'm conversing with a toddler.

Hey, lady.

What's up?

What's going on with you?

Not much.

Documentary shoot tomorrow morning?

Naw, got homework.

Got another sponsorship offer.

Good stuff.

Tonight's the night of the homecoming dance—the Fall Ball—and I'm hopeful for two big reasons. First, I hope Mickey will be there. I figure I can come clean to her, and she can help me game-plan how to tell the world what really happened at the pet store.

The second big reason is Jo. Even though she decommitted from going to the dance with me, we've still been growing a lot closer through our texts these past few days. We've only been out once since McSweeney's. It was the Saturday after our ice cream excursion. Jo hit me up because she was bored, and her friends were out of town or doing family stuff. She said she needed someone to go with her to see the new *Bloodsuckers III* vampire movie. Obviously, I jumped at the opportunity. It was decent. Well, not the movie. It sucked, both literally and figuratively. But being there with Jo was great. We barely talked, of course, because *duh*, it's a movie. But during three scary scenes she leaned into me and hugged my arm. So all in all, a win.

Even if I had to wrestle down my thoughts of Mickey. . . .

Otherwise, we'd planned more dates, but they didn't end up happening. There was our Hector's Pupuseria date, which got derailed when Jo had to do an emergency promo reshoot for Cassie's Curl Cream. And then we must've miscommunicated ahead of our library study date, because she ended up bringing along three of her friends. It's all good, though. I get it. With the internet and people's busy schedules these days, you've gotta stay flexible. And most relationships are basically virtual anyway. Since she's usually too busy to talk on the phone or FaceTime, text is our preferred mode of communication. And if a woman's interest is measured by the number of heart eyes emojis she sends, Jo just might be ready for a proposal.

And that's what I plan on doing, sort of. I think a few weeks of hanging out is plenty of time to make it official. I know nothing's for certain, but this is as close to a layup as you can get. We're both popular, we look great together, and we have tons of other similarities.

When I told Theo of my plan, he could barely mask his skepticism, saying maybe I was going too fast. I countered that Granddad always claimed that fast was the best way to live. My only hesitation is that I'll eventually have to come clean that I'm not the pet store hero she thinks I was. But I'm confident she can see beyond that to the good person I actually am.

I'm excited as Dad pulls up to the school for the dance. We actually arrived fifteen minutes ago, but I made him wait in a nearby parking lot so I could be fashionably late. There are a few cliques chattering as they stream past our parked car, but

165

a lot of people seem to have already entered. Even from the lot, I can feel the faint thumps of stereo bass in my ears. I open the car door to frigid air, wishing I'd worn one of those cool trench coats Grandpa so famously donned early in his career, during his *Guardians of the Block* trilogy.

I get out and Dad does, too, admiring his only child as he rises from the car.

He smiles. "My son. Debonair as usual."

Actually, this is far from usual. I'm in a seersucker sports jacket and faded jeans with regular white sneakers. I'm going for something that screams "looking good without trying too hard."

"Thanks, Dad."

"So Ms. Josefina's already in there?"

My nod is paired with a modest "Yeah," and I can't help smiling at the thought of seeing her. She refused to coordinate outfits, saying hers was a surprise. I spent nearly the entire drive imagining how regal she'd look.

Dad makes an extravagant production of walking to the passenger's side of the car and squaring up to me. With both hands, he brushes the padding of my shoulders.

"Just make sure to take it slow with her," Dad admonishes.

"I know."

"And great relationships are built on mutual understanding. Make sure she's in it for *all* of you. Not just the hero."

My eyes narrow. I don't know whether it's the irritating cold or the smug way he spouts his advice, or the fact that I might soon find out she's not in it for all of me. But the moment hits me wrong from all sides. It's as if only he and Mom could have an organically reciprocal relationship. "What's that supposed to mean?" I ask.

Dad's smile wrenches downward ever so slightly. "I didn't mean anything."

"Why *wouldn't* she like me for all of me?"

He fumbles through the beginning of his response before coming out with "I'm just saying that because you've recently acquired newfound fame, you . . ."

"So *what*, Dad? She likes me for me," I spit back. I feel like someone's wrapped their hands around my neck. I don't even know why I'm getting so angry. It's just that I *want* to be angry. At him. "I'm basically a man now," I continue. "I'll figure these things out for myself."

"Everybody needs *somebody*, Lionel," he spits back at me, his tone more aggressive than he's comfortable with. He quickly moderates it, clearing his throat before continuing: "Lord knows I don't want you thinking the people closest to you are your biggest enemies like—" He catches himself, but I immediately autofill the last word. There's only one word possible.

"Like Grandpa?" I ask. It's a question but also an indictment. An unspoken acknowledgment that he—or how we see him—has been a wedge that's divided us these past few years. I nod, my face tightening with rage. "Your own blood, the man who made you, who you then went and humiliated."

Between the three of us, I don't know whether it was me,

Papa Shades, or Dad who felt the most shame the day of the incident. But I know that Grandpa became a different man after it. An embittered old shell of the person he once was. A ghost or relic of the heroes he played on the big screen.

I had wanted to join a soccer team. One of the good club ones like Theo had joined the year prior. Theo had been training me, or rather *patiently enduring* me, as I gasped and wheezed well behind him during our daily runs around town. This particular weekend, Grandpa was visiting from California and Theo happened to be away. No matter. Papa Shades would take over. He teetered at that precarious age in which longtime wear on the body hadn't yet imposed its will on a spry and stubborn mind. And plus, it'd be a chance to exorcise some of those weaker habits that Theo and "men like him" might have rubbed off on me.

He had me running the school's stadium steps toting Dad's small barbells. Doing crunches by the pond as he threw pebbles at me—"Because rocks are hard, and so is life," he said. Finally, I was huffing through wind sprints along the hot asphalt of our busy neighborhood street. It was all to make me better. Stronger, faster, tougher. By my twentieth sprint in ten minutes, I thought I'd failed at becoming any of those things. Papa Shades apparently agreed. He was so disgusted with my effort after I collapsed, face down on the road, that he jogged toward me, planting his shoe on my back and ordering me to do push-ups.

There's something about being exhausted and desperate that jump-starts the nervous system. It's almost survivalist, the way the adrenaline ratcheted up my basest senses. I could see the heat waves lifting from the ground, and I could smell the acrid and oily scent of the asphalt. I could hear every car pass by—and even my front door opening—as I felt Grandpa's boot pressing me down, harder and harder. Through vision blurred by sweat and tears, I could also see Mickey and Mrs. Kyle step outside their house and pause, bewildered and concerned.

But the thing I remember most is the yelling. My dad's voice frantic, rising well above the roar of an approaching car. I remember the pressure of Grandpa's boot releasing and then coming right back just before I blacked out. When I woke up seconds later, an SUV was at a stoplight, taking a left before disappearing. But there was no turning the corner for Dad and Grandpa's relationship after that. No repair shop could fix the damage done on that street.

Papa Shades suffered a broken collarbone. Worse—I think Dad's push broke his spirit. Grandpa moaned and cried and cursed as people rendered aid. He demanded they let him up, that he could go it alone. But for the first time in a long time, nobody listened to him. I saw the man that day, not the Hollywood star. I knew he'd rather be dead than in that position. And he was there because of me.

His collarbone healed up soon enough, but the memory lapses rolled in like a morning fog soon after. The dementia was officially diagnosed two years later. A year after that, he was home with us.

To Grandpa, connecting the incident to his mental decline

was like doing simple arithmetic. In fact, this was the only deduction his pride would allow. He was weak only because someone else's ineptitude *made* him weak.

I knew what Papa Shades was trying to do with me that day. And I knew why. Ironically, he never wanted me to end up how he did on that street. Vulnerable and enfeebled, at the mercy of others.

"I wasn't trying to say . . ."

"I don't care what you were trying to say," I tell him. "I just care that you're trying to sabotage me like you did him." I huff, looking straight at Dad, eyes heavy with the weight of tears not yet falling. Instead of denying, he stands in front of me speechless, every breath a silent cloud at his lips. He's looking at me like he doesn't even recognize me, and I think maybe that's the natural result of him never truly taking the time to understand who his son really was. Or rather, who his son *could* be. After a long silence, I just say, "Admit it. You never really saw my true potential. Always underestimated me. Always thought I'd be just a run-of-the-mill person."

"Lionel, that was the furthest thought from my mind."

My head shakes at what I know to be a lie. I sidestep him, my shoulder brushing his as I push past and head to the door. "You always thought I'd be average like you."

14

GUILT SWIRLS AROUND ME LIKE THE BITTER FALL WIND AS I walk away. But I manage to shake that feeling off with the cold as I enter the gymnasium. The music pulses through me, every bass note like a shock from a defibrillator. Red and blue lights cut across the room at random angles. A large platform in center court has been raised for the dance floor. It all has the disorienting feel of being drunk off vibes and sounds.

Lucy Timmons grabs my shoulder, slouching off it like she's a wet towel on a rack. I flinch at the smell of perfume and alcohol.

"Yo, Lionheart!" she yells. Her fist pumps repeatedly as she starts a solo chant of "Lion*heart*, Lion*heart!*" Pacey Frampton calmly walks over and coaxes her off me, indulging her girl-friend's slurred protestations of "But he wa*ss* all *ss*et for a *ssss*peech. I wanna hear it."

I politely wave as they disappear into the throng of students. I stand there awkwardly for a moment orienting myself to the chaos. Even among the tumult, I can clearly hear the whisper at my ear. "Humoring your adoring fans?"

I smile and turn to see Jo smiling right back at me. I'm awestruck by her outfit. A beautiful turquoise dress with a flowing fabric hemline. It's so light and airy that it seems a stiff breeze might blow her away. I'm blown away just looking at her.

"You look—"

"Beautiful, I know," she interrupts, pinching the sides of her dress as she does a curtsy. "Isn't it lovely? It's a Jean-Luc DeClerc. Vivian Warner wore one to last year's Oscars. She just seems so well put together and nice."

"She is," I agree.

"Oh, you know her?" Jo clutches both my hands as if trying to read my palms. "Please tell me you do."

I nod stiffly. She doesn't have to know that the collective sum of me "knowing her" was my family watching a video recording of her singing a Marilyn Monroe–style "Happy Birthday" to Grandpa at his party ten years ago. While Papa Shades was appreciative, I remember J-Maw was none too happy about that little performance.

"Oh my God! I would absolutely love to rob her closet," Jo says. I glance past her shoulder to see four other girls approaching. Kelsey Howard drapes a pasty arm around Jo. "Lionel's family is tight with Vivian Warner," Jo announces.

The girls are arrayed and dressed like a foundation makeup color line. Taupe to toffee to Creamsicle. But nobody can hold a candle to Jo, and perhaps that's why they're almost deferential, none daring to take up Jo's center. They gush about how Jo is *this close* to being a star herself, so it's fitting that we linked up. Since I actually "know" Vivian Warner, they're careful to include me in the conversation, asking about movies of hers I've seen and whether she and my grandfather ever hung out off set. But it's quite easy to see who's the star here, and I quickly get a lonely, third-wheelish feeling.

Jo pulls out her phone and points the camera right at me. "Hey, how about that speech?" she says, and Kelsey echoes, "Speeeeeech." I shake my head, refusing even despite her pleas. But I do tell Jo I want to speak with her about something important later. She obliges, but "only if you promise to dance with me." I agree, which worries me seeing as how the rhythm gene in the family seems to have abruptly ended with my mom and dad.

I pull away from the clique with the flimsy excuse of needing to use the bathroom. I exit into the darkened hallway and head straight to the water fountain. I close my eyes, envisioning Jo in her beautiful dress, how great it'd be to dance with her, and how this night could be the beginning of something truly special. I'm so wrapped up in my fantasy that I don't hear the footsteps approaching from behind me. The large hand grasping my shoulder like a harness is what wrenches me back to the real world. I startle, nearly bumping my head against the top of the fountain. When I turn, my body goes rigid at the sight of Lovey and Big, the wrestlers. They're dressed in finely tailored suits, which has the effect of making them look that much more intimidating.

They don't say anything. Lovey just nods toward his right shoulder, gesturing for me to come with. I gulp and follow. They escort me down an unlit hallway, to the Council's meeting room and post up at the door again. I slink under the threshold and take in the same dark, Cosa Nostra setting, coupled with the same *Cake Boss* scent.

Lori Chen still sits at the end of the long table, with VP Paige Wellington backstopping her. Kelly Isengard, Sarah Wake, and Mason Vance are there, as well, along with a host of others I don't know. Only Mason is smiling. They're dressed for the dance, but it's obvious that at this moment, they're just here for business. There's a noticeable downshift in tone from the last time. Whereas previously, idle whispers blanketed the room, all I hear today is the dispassionate hum of computer hard drives.

An array of pastries is plated at the center again. I couldn't name any of them, save the strawberry muffins, which look as tasty as they smell.

Paige announces that "This emergency Council meeting has been called to order," and explains the speaking rules. Lori just sits there, her face a mix of boredom and mild displeasure. There's a long spell of silence where everybody's staring at me, but I have no idea what to say. Finally, Lori makes her move. But instead of outright speaking, she simply holds up her hand, palm facing up. The attendees do the same ritual as before, grabbing a pastry and taking a bite. Nods without words. Even Paige takes a muffin, pecking at the side before placing it beside Lori and standing right behind the girl. Noticeably, though, Lori doesn't offer me one. Mild disappointment mixes in with my anxiety.

Paige walks over and fetches a red felt case from a desk that lines the back wall. She places it in Lori's palm. Lori opens it.

"Lionel, I'll get straight to the point. I wouldn't be the strong-willed, no-nonsense overachiever I am today if I hadn't had a chance encounter with your grandfather several years ago, when I was in the third grade."

Huh? This is quite the unexpected opening. I blink, caught by surprise, not knowing how to react. I try to brush away the reveal with a hand wave and a laugh, but it quickly dies out among the crowd of blank faces. I narrow my eyes as I look at Lori. Whether it's out of suspicion that she's lying or curiosity of how this reveal will play out, I don't know. But I'm all ears.

"When I was but an innocent little cha-bó gín-á of nine years, I'd just moved to this small southern town. During the first few months living here, I'd suffered through near-daily racial invectives targeting everything from the shape of my eyelids to the supposed allegiance of my parents to totalitarian Far East countries. I came dejected to that year's Westlake Holiday Parade, thinking I'd never quite fit in."

"Your grandfather was the grand marshal that year," Mason interrupts, his words so enthusiastic that pastry crumbs fly out.

Lori quickly gavels him down, seemingly producing the tool from nowhere. Paige restates the rules about not speaking unless recognized, impatience edging into her voice. Lori continues: "Toward the end of the parade route, your grandfather happened to notice a sad little Asian girl in the midst of a crowd. Do you know what he did?" She leans into the table as I shake my head, curiosity eclipsing my suspicions: "He beckoned the float to stop, got off, and walked right to me, crouching to my level." She begins feathering her fingers over the head of the gavel, studying it. "Upon his prodding, I tearfully revealed the racist taunts I'd received. And he told me this: 'Baby girl, your inner strength shines through. Ain't nothing gonna stop you from fulfilling your destiny.' He went on to say that I have a kamikaze spirit, which in and of itself was vaguely racist since I'm *Taiwanese* and not Japanese. But I got the point."

In spite of my reservations, I can feel myself lean into the table, too. It's like I'm being sucked in. Hesitantly, I glance at Paige before speaking.

"Thus recognized," she whispers, with a smile and a wink.

I look back at Lori. "His words inspired you all these years?"

She opens the box before her. "His words and . . . *these*."

My breath catches as I take in its contents. My eyes go wide at the sight of the sunglasses. The words stammer out of me. "Tha—those are . . ."

She nods. "He said I needed them more than him that day. Told me he could always get a new pair."

The shock overwhelms me, hemming the words in my throat. Papa Shades never even let *me* touch his glasses. And he just up and gave a pair to Lori?

"Lionel, your anti-bullying campaign has stirred something

deep within me. A feeling my iron resolve long ago suppressed like a recalcitrant population."

"It has?" I ask.

"Yes," she says. "Compassion. Humans—even those as underdeveloped as high school students—deserve compassion. I want to give that to them, and you can help me."

"How can I help?"

"By ascending to the platform you deserve: student body president."

Wait, what? I do a double take, thinking I didn't hear her correctly. I then look around the room at the others, examining them for any hint of insincerity. All except Mason are donning nervous smiles. Mason looks absolutely giddy, basically bursting at the seams.

"I . . . I don't understand," I say, shaking my head.

"Lionel, have you heard of the Putin model of governance?" *Do I even want to?* I don't answer, which Lori sees as license to continue her explanation. "In 2008, Vladimir Putin, term limited as Russia's president, stepped aside to allow for long-time deputy Dmitry Medvedev to rule the country. Putin then became Medvedev's omnipotent prime minister, in what would come to be termed by scholars as a tandemocracy."

Lines form at my brow. "So you want me to be . . ."

"Lori's Medvedev," Mason excitedly chimes. "An inspiring, compassionate figurehead of sor—"

Right then, Lori's arms make two distinct moves in one fluid blur of a motion. There's a loud clacking sound as the gavel whacks the table, its top breaking from the handle and skittering to the floor. I also hear a muted puff, like a boxing glove hitting a bag. I see Mason's neck bend so acutely that his face twists at an angle. Muffin bits break apart at his cheek in what looks like a small whole-grain explosion. Bits of Paige's muffin scatter across the makeshift table, including a big chunk just a foot in front of me. I'd be tempted to eat it if I wasn't scared shitless to move.

I gasp as Mason keels over to the floor, coughing and choking on his own dessert. Without emotion, Paige drones, "Meeting participants are kindly reminded not to speak unless recognized."

My heartbeat quickens as someone gets up and walks to the door, opening it. Lovey and Big enter, lift a shocked Mason up by the armpits as if he were a rack of ribs on a meat hook. Eyes wide open, I watch in barely disguised distress as they escort Mason out. "You were warned, Mason," Paige says flatly as the door shuts behind him. If anything, his protests get louder once he's out of sight. I swear, by the time Sarah Wake rises and shuts the door, I hear screaming. *What are they doing to him?*

"Lionel?" I jump at Lori's voice, turning back to face her. She's calmly readjusting the cuff of her dress suit. Setting the gavel handle next to the red box, she says, "Now, where were we?"

I let out a breath I didn't know I was holding. "Medvedev," I say, almost gasping out the word.

"Ah, yes, Medvedev. I've come to realize my leadership style can be somewhat grating to those of lesser stock. I'm hoping your presence on the Council will smooth over those rough edges. So, here's my new proposal: I resign the presidency. You then assume the position via special election. I would still be doing the day-to-day governing, of course. I'll be the decision maker. You'd just be the face of it all." Without warning, she stands.

"Is this even legal?" I ask.

Paige recites, "The student body constitution states that special elections are triggered in the event of either presidential or vice presidential resignations, to be conducted within two weeks' time of such an event." She looks left, then right. "All in favor?"

Lori holds up a hand, but not as an aye vote. Rather, it's to freeze the room. She plucks the sunglasses from the box, rotating them in her hand as she says, "Lionel Honeycutt Sr. would take what he deserves. Will you do the same?" She lets the question rest like a freshly baked pie in a windowsill. I think about it. No. I couldn't possibly. But something still holds me back from saying that.

Lori sighs deeply and says, "Nevertheless, to ease your concerns . . ."

In turn, she eyes each person in the room. They all raise their hands. Some immediately, some hesitantly, but every single one except me.

Once I'm permitted to leave the room, I run down the hallway so quickly, I'm nearly breathless by the time I get back to the gym. I feel out of place among all the happy faces. People smile and wave when they spot me, but I simply stare awkwardly back at them. *What did Lori just propose I do? Undercut my best friend? And was it actually a proposal . . . or an ultimatum?*

Harriet Meyerson and Paxton Johnson come up and ask if I'll make a TikTok with them, but I fumble through a flimsy excuse and walk away. I can't be around all these people right now. I need some time to process what just happened.

I head straight to the dessert bar in a sparsely trafficked corner of the gym. Here, I can finally calm down. Once my heart rate settles, seeing all the desserts makes me realize how hungry I am. I get a brownie and a blondie, while also picking up a round, hard mystery dessert whose name placard must've fallen off some time ago. I'm about to put it back when I see Mickey at the other end of the table. She's gone all chipmunk with what looks like at least three lemon squares tucked into her cheeks. Additionally, she's holding two cups filled to the brim with red punch.

I walk over, getting within five steps of her before she notices me. In half a second, her expressions range from shocked to embarrassed to finally settling somewhere in the vicinity of bemused.

"Hi," I say, genuinely happy to see her.

A muted "Hey" works its way through a mass of lemony sweetness.

"How's the lemon squares?"

She chews and swallows before answering. "They're magically delicious."

"That's Lucky Charms."

She points a finger gun at me. "That's why you're the brand expert."

I take her in. She's wearing a sleek, sleeveless black dress. It fits her perfectly. For a moment, I'm simply awestruck by how pretty she is. It's like that night in her room, where I'm seeing her for the first time again. Except it's not the first time. Or the second or the third. It's Mickey. My neighbor. The girl who only months ago I would've been inclined to name zits or cold sores after. She's . . . different. Or maybe just the way I'm seeing her is different.

"You look great," I admit. At this, her smile grows wide. She does the most ungracious, clumsy half pirouette imaginable.

"Thanks," she says modestly. "Been going to the gym with my dad. He won this raffle a while back. Three months free with a personal trainer. Jax says when I started, my core was as loose as a Slinky." Her eyes descend into a contemplative navel-gaze as she presses both hands to her stomach. "Yesterday, he called it a pipe cleaner. So . . . improvement."

"That's awesome. You should celebrate when you achieve wire-hanger status."

She nods and stuffs one of those cookies dusted with confectioners' sugar in her mouth but gets some of the white stuff in the space below her nose, making her look faintly like she just did a line of coke. When I let her know, she laughs, embarrassed, getting all bashful as I take the cuff of my sleeve and gently wipe it off.

Slowly, we both sidestep our way down the rest of the dessert table, surveying each offering like we're art inspectors.

Mickey picks up a green rock-looking construction that might pass for a cloudy emerald. She brings it to her nose, sniffs, and eyes it disapprovingly. "Needs mascarpone," she says.

"How do you know? You haven't even tasted it."

She drops it back into a pile of similarly unattractive rock-cookie thingies. "That's what the judges in all those baking shows always say. That and, 'This tart looks fabulous up top, but firm up that sagging bottom.' Which, incidentally, is *also* what my trainer says."

We spend a couple more minutes taste-testing desserts and eventually make our way to a corner of the gym that's somewhat quieter. Not like the volume kind of quiet, but less trafficked and removed from the action. We stand there for a while, head-nodding and swaying to the music as we eat our food. I spot Jo sitting on the far bleachers with her friends. I wave when she looks our way, but she doesn't wave back. She just pushes hair from her face and keeps bantering with the girls around her.

Mickey's shoulder leans into mine. "Why aren't you dancing with her?"

"We will," I answer. "Just waiting for the slow songs." I guess. After a while, I add, "I think we're gonna be a thing."

Mickey's eyes pinch as she looks toward Jo. Then she turns her skeptical stare my way. "It's a done deal?"

I shake my head. "Not yet. Could be soon, though."

There's a long silence as the song changes from a hip-hop

beat to a more subtle pop ballad. She folds her arms as she blankly looks toward the banners above the gym doors. I can tell she's considering her words carefully.

Finally, she comes out with "You think you really know her that well?" Not carefully enough.

"What do you mean by that?" I ask.

Mickey shrugs. "Like, is she trustworthy? Is she nice?"

Anger rises from the depths of me, snaking up my chest and crowding my throat. This conversation is starting to resemble the blowup I had with Dad outside a half hour ago. She's been my mortal enemy for years. And now that we're semi cool with each other, she wants to govern my life?

My own arms cross as I mutter, "Nicer than you've ever been."

She squares up to me, eyes wide open with incredulity. "Wait. *You're* mad that I'm looking out for you?"

I shrug. "I'm mad that you're micromanaging me."

"Oh, bullshit!" Mickey spouts. She turns to walk away, but I'm not letting her get off that easy. I fall in step with her.

"You can't just be happy for me?"

"Not when you're diving into something stupid like a kid who can't swim at the deep end of the pool."

"You know when I said you look great?" I sneer.

She stops and turns toward me. "Yeah."

"Well, I take it back. Envy doesn't look so good on you."

With that, I break away, making a beeline toward the exit. I even walk right past Jo and her crew. I can see Jo trying to get my attention, but her entreaties are just white noise. I don't even know where I'm going as I barrel out of the gym door and into the hallway. I spot Jimmy in my periphery, flanked by two boys. They're walking arm in arm up the dimly lit hallway. When Jimmy sees me, he breaks free, shoes squeaking against tile as he approaches me at a jog.

He stops, nearly breathless, boyhood trepidation swimming in his eyes. When the light hits him, I can see the dark outlines of water ringing his blue shirt at the collar. His hair's wet, too, and his face is flushed. At first, I think he's just sweaty from the dancing, but the party hasn't even been on that long.

I hear laughter far down the hallway and see him seize up with some barely veiled emotion. Anger? Fear? Another thought hits me. My eyes narrow on him. "Chase did this to you? *Again?*"

Jimmy nods. "Must've seen me leave to get water. He caught me in the Arts hallway bathroom."

I look at his friends as they come up to me. "Did you try to stop him?" I ask.

"We weren't there," one answers. "Jimmy just called us afterward. Said he wants to get back at . . ." The kid glances over his shoulder before saying "Chase," as if uttering the word would be akin to summoning a ghost.

"Can you help us?" Jimmy asks, pointing to the other kid. "Treyvion's seen his car before, so we're gonna sneak out to the parking lot and . . ."

I hold up a hand. "Jimmy, stop." Just great. This night's

already gone halfway to hell. The last thing I need is to incur the wrath of my former bully.

Jimmy looks at me earnestly, eyes brimming with confusion, faint hope for revenge draining from his face. "You got something better?" he asks.

I shake my head no. And I know at that moment that I never will. I never will have something better for this freshman. Even if the truth is revealed that he was the pet store hero, there's no way he'd be able to capitalize on that clout. He'll always be a lowly freshman.

"Bu—*why not?*" His voice rises, the question almost pleading.

"Because it's not feasible," I reply.

"But it's like you said: When life punches you, you just gotta punch back! And besides, you haven't even heard the whole idea."

"I don't need to!" I snap. Sound spills out of the gym as a door opens behind me, but it quickly tapers back into silence as the door draws shut again. I don't turn. I need to get this off my chest. "Whatever it is, it won't work. You'll never be able to top Chase because that's not the way the world works."

"But that's not what you taught me," he says, jamming a finger to his sternum.

For a moment, I can sense the fire burning through his insides. The searing desire to rise above his station and make something better of his life. Just like Grandpa did. Just like I did. But there's no other path for him. I see the same shortcomings

185

in him that Grandpa must've seen in me all those years ago.

I bend lightly, getting to his level. I imagine tears forming in his eyes after I say what I have to say. But they'll be good tears. Needed tears.

"Yeah, Jimmy, I *taught* you. And that was a mistake."

He forms his lips like he's about to speak but says nothing at first, as if his brain is a checkpoint, deciding which words should get through. "What are you saying?" he asks, his voice cracking.

I don't answer. Instead, I just shake my head. Then I rise and turn to walk down the hallway, not looking back. I hear the whispers of his friends, quietly cajoling as they walk toward the opposite exit. Soon after, the clack of heels fills the hallway.

"Hey!" I turn and it's a five-foot-five active, lava-spewing volcano inhabiting the form of my longtime neighbor. "What the fuck is wrong with you?"

"Mickey, leave me alone," I say.

"Not until you tell me why you've been acting like you have." I simply lift my chin as if I'm inspecting a spot on the ceiling. She huffs, but I ignore her. Seconds pass. Then a resigned "You're such an asshole."

I mutter, "If I'm an asshole, why are you so jealous?"

Her heels clack against the tiles, and within seconds she's next to me. "Whether that's true or not, it doesn't absolve you from treating everyone else around you like trash." I try to ignore her, but she grabs my arm and yanks me around to face her. "I saw the way you treated Jimmy back there. He looked devastated after you left. Whatever you said to him, he didn't deserve it. And what's with you and your dad? He's only been supporting you throughout this whole thing, and *this* is how you repay him?"

My brow furrows. "What about him?"

"I saw you two out in the parking lot. He spotted me after you went inside. Waved for me to come over and talk."

"And what did you say to him?"

Her eyes flit toward the locker. She's still angry, but her shoulders loosen. "I wasn't gonna say anything. I *never* say anything! I didn't when you started getting all the attention from the video. I didn't that night after we were on my bed. I didn't the night of—"

She trails off, but I catch the implication. My chest tightens as my mind tries to fill in the blank. Only one thing comes to mind, but I want her to say it. I *need* her to say it. So I ask, "The night of what?"

"It's nothing."

She angles away from me, but I don't have to look into her eyes to know she's keeping something from me. The tell is in her hand. She lifts it to the nape of her neck, her nails scratching skin as if she's just gotten a rash. Ever since elementary school, this has been her tell for whenever there's something she's hiding.

My voice is softer as I say, "The newscast. Was it you?"

Mickey looks me in the eye but can't bring herself to speak. Then she turns and walks wordlessly down the hall. I follow without prodding, a few steps behind. Everything tells me I should be angry, erupting with a string of invectives at a girl who planned to expose me before millions of viewers. But the only sentiment I can latch onto is concern. I'm concerned that she doesn't seem okay.

The sound fades as we descend the steps and go into a lower-level gym hallway, where they keep the weight lifting and wrestling rooms. It's quiet enough down here that I can make out her sniffles. She stops in front of a drink machine and studies the selection, the warm glow of light hitting her face in a way that illuminates shiny streaks along her cheek. I creep closer, expecting some thoughtful explication, or at least something emo enough to put into a Taylor Swift song. But all she says is "They don't have Sprite anymore?" in the voice-quivering way of a kid who's just been told there's no Santa.

I step closer, inspecting the display. "They, umm, switched all the sugary drinks out a year back. Federal law, I think. Some new health initiative."

Her eyes shut tight. I can see Mickey's grasp on her emotions slipping away like a wet bar of soap. Suddenly, there's a loud bang as she kicks the base of the drink machine and shouts, "We used to be a proper country!"

Then it's like a dam breaks somewhere within her soul, because the sobs really start flowing. The stomach-crunching, convulsive cries you'd more likely see at funerals than in a gym hallway.

I rub her shoulder and whisper sweet sentiments and even

promise to run to Rite Aid across the street to buy her one. After a while, as the heaves largely dissipate and the river of tears dries up into a stream, she wipes her eyes and begins to gather herself.

"It's not the Sprite," she finally admits, still sniffling.

"Then what is it?" I ask.

Instead of answering, she simply holds up her iPhone, thumbing through her gallery as I position myself behind her right shoulder. Once she finds the video she's looking for, she looks back at me, frowning almost mournfully, as if she knows life will dramatically change once she hits the play button. When I don't shrink away, she plays it. I immediately recognize the setting. The pet store, right as smoke begins drifting down from the ceiling.

But how? How is this possible?

I take the phone from her, bringing it closer to my nose, needing to make sure what I'm seeing is real. This is a totally different angle than the security footage. No frame cuts. Just one continuous clip, streaming the entire incident.

"It's from my phone," she says. "My *old* phone. The one that got destroyed." But that's impossible. There's no way she could've salvaged that from the carnage. It's as if she's reading my mind, because she says, "I was recording the fish for comparison. I'd forgotten that my default setting was to automatically upload to the cloud."

I continue watching as the first screams ring out. An alarm sounds. Ash floats onto the screen. In the video, Mickey rushes down an aisle, her body clipping the corner of the row. The screen goes shaky before it's clear again. It must've fallen from a shelf. It now sits at the base of an aisle, recording the trapped man struggling to wrest his leg free under the weight of a collapsed shelf. Mickey, his girlfriend, and I all crowd around him. We almost lift the shelf enough, but it's just too hot. The man groans loudly as it falls. Smoke descends like a falling parachute, but it still hasn't touched the floor. I stagger out of the frame. A moment after that, a hand comes back in. A hand that isn't mine, not even close. Pale. White but streaked with black ash. Not stronger but strong enough.

In the video, Jimmy bends down and with Herculean effort helps Mickey lift the shelf, as the girlfriend pulls like her own life depends on it. The only evidence of my presence is my hand grasping at my leg in a lower corner of the screen.

"How long have you known?" I ask quietly, not sure whether I really want to know the answer.

Demurely, she says, "A few days," as if trying to downplay the gravity of this new information.

"Mickey? How long exactly?" I ask.

"The day before you came over to my house. I found the video that morning," she admits. A new tear forms at the well of her left eye, shining like a diamond. "And then the next day you were talking about your ice cream date with Jo and people were calling you Lionheart and I guess I just got . . ."

"You could've come clean," I interrupt. "That evening, in your bedroom. You could've admitted it, but you denied it."

Her eyes blink shut as the tear slides down. They reopen just as quickly. "I'd decided before then I wasn't gonna go through with it. I didn't know how to tell you."

I back away from her, like I've just touched a hot stove. She faces me, shocked at the abruptness of the motion.

"I trusted you." She opens her mouth to speak, but I cut her off again. "I *trusted* you."

I press both hands to my head, as if trying to squeeze out this new revelation. I can understand her thinking about squealing to a news station in a fit of anger. But lying about it? Implying it could've been Jimmy? I pace back and forth. My steps are angry. I feel betrayed. I stop pacing and square up to her. "Guess you're mad your plan didn't work. Is that why you're telling me this now?"

She slaps her hands against her waist. "What *plan*?"

"You wanted to see my downfall."

"Yeah, for like a *second*! And I regret that. Honestly, I do."

"Then why come clean about this now?"

"Because you *asked*, dumbass!"

"I didn't ask to be manipulated."

"You asked for the truth, Lionel!" she shouts.

"So why didn't you give it to me that night?" I say, my words rising to meet hers. "Or any time since then?!"

"Because I liked you!"

I stop. Look at her curiously. No, the word "curious" doesn't actually meet the moment. I'm absolutely gobsmacked that Mickey would actually *like* me. Yeah, we made out. But we agreed right afterward that it'd never happen again. And besides, no amount of attraction can overcome years of being bitter enemies. She glances past my left shoulder and makes a noise like she's about to speak again, but there's no way I'm gonna pull my punches now.

"If you liked me, why would you want to embarrass me?"

"Just stop, Lionel," she insists, blankly looking into the space behind me. But I can't stop. She deserves every bit of the steam I'm about to blow off. The Mickey I knew during childhood was loyal above all. This girl's the opposite of that. She shakes her head like she wants me to stop, but I won't. She needs to hear every word.

I point to the phone in her hand. "You had everything to prove to the world that I didn't save that guy. That I'm a fraud. Why didn't you? Are you even sorry?"

"*Of course* I'm sorry," she answers.

Mickey looks off to the side and huffs as a new tear forms. She gathers herself, taking a deep breath and closing her eyes. For a moment, I feel the beginnings of something deep inside me. That dull, pulsing pain you get when you see a friend realize the magnitude of a mistake they've made. Everything about her—from the way her lips tremble to the restless scrape of fingernail against fingernail—demands I feel sorry for her. But I press my sympathy down like I'm packing an overstuffed suitcase.

I point to my chest, my voice wavering as I say, "Well, 'sorry' isn't gonna cut it. You weren't truthful with me. You could've made a fool out of me. And all because you *like* me?"

Something changes in her eyes at that moment, like a fire went out, letting the coldness set in. Her eyes zero in on the space just above my shoulder, like she's not looking at me but past me again. It gives me goose bumps. The rest of her face hardens. At that moment, all I hear are the low hum of the vending machine and the sharp sound of her heels against concrete as she walks toward me. When she's right in front of me, she jabs her finger into my chest.

"*Like* you?! You really don't listen, do you? I said I *liked* you. Because pretty much every decision you've made these past few weeks has painted you as one of the biggest egomaniacal pricks this school has ever seen. And for what it's worth, *you've* made a fool out of yourself." As she walks past, I bring a hand to my chest, rubbing the spot where her nail dug into me. She pats my shoulder. Her parting words are "But honestly, it runs in the family. Papa Shades would be proud."

I turn to watch her walk away, but instead I see what she must've noticed seconds ago. Why she tried to keep me from speaking. Jo is standing there. She's wearing this coy smile that doesn't quite reach her eyes. She's also holding her phone in front of her, recording everything.

15

THE ENTIRE SCHOOL IS BUZZING THIS PARTICULAR FRIDAY
morning. Our homecoming win put us at 7-0 and first in con-
ference, so we're having a pep rally to celebrate. Everybody's
dressed for the occasion, too. I see football jerseys dotting the
crowd. Cheerleaders in uniform. Way more students festooned
with our school's colors, blue and gold.

I'm in the hallway when Theo rushes over for a quick hey
before leaving to tell his flutist boyfriend good luck at the rally.
I cut left as the drum line passes and enters another hallway,
and I head to the gym as the pep rally begins. It takes some
time and effort and good balance as I nimbly wade through an
unforgiving crowd. I arrive at the entrance at the same time as
Mickey. She gives an uncomfortable, deer-in-headlights look
before trying to split away, but the crowd is so tight and herded,
we have to stay packed together. When we reach the bleachers,
she ends up sitting by herself only a couple rows down from
where I sit. Theo joins me about a minute later. He's absolutely
engrossed in the spectacle. "Can you imagine me up there?" he

asks, all starry-eyed as he gazes at center court.

I look down, seeing what he sees. The same platform that was made for the Fall Ball dance floor is back at the half-court line. At least two dozen people are up there. The entire homecoming court. A few cheerleaders. Jersey-wearing athletes. And in a huddle that tightly orbits Lori Chen is "the Council." Several members take turns whispering in her ear, one at a time. With each new person, she stiffly nods, points, or shakes her head, causing them to back away, having received their marching orders. Lastly, in a back corner of the stage stands Weyrich, keeping a watchful eye out like he's a one-man Secret Service.

The festivities surrounding the stage are manic. Cheerleaders tumbling, football players shouting into megaphones, students whooping and cheering, all under the deafening blanket of house techno booming through the gym speaker system. Even with all this liveliness, there's an eerie vibe hanging over everything. For example, when Mickey and I first entered, the cheerleaders greeting people at the entrance got cagey with us—hands behind their backs, standing right in front of the huge box of flyers they were handing out to others. When Mickey tried to reach for one, Susie Perkins literally blocked her hand and snapped, "Fresh out."

The weird overtones continued in the stands. Once we'd sat down, I soon realized that even though the bleachers were packed, nobody else was sitting within a two-seat radius of us. Not talking to us. Not looking our way. Nothing.

There are a few more team recognitions and group cheers

before Sarah Wake, the head cheerleader and StuGov treasurer, steps up to the microphone.

"Good morning, Westlake High!" she yells, her voice a weird mix of irritating glee and nervous energy. "How ya doing?" she asks.

The crowd erupts. Oddly, Sarah glances back at Lori, her smile misting away like vapor, before speaking again. It's like she's looking for permission or a green light. Lori's nod is almost imperceptible. Sarah pastes her smile back on as if it were a well-worn accessory. Then she turns back to the crowd. "We have a couple more teams to introduce, but before we get to that, we need to welcome a special honoree."

We all cast curious glances toward the exit doors. *Since when does Westlake do honorary guests?* Must be big-time if they're being lauded right around homecoming.

"This person's deeds have altered the course of so many lives." Theo and I look at each other, mentally sussing who it could be. *A doctor or something? Politician? Silicon Valley bro?* "He represents humility, bravery, and grit. All qualities that Westlake seeks to instill in its student body."

This person sounds amazing. I look back toward the exits as Sarah begins recounting the biblical story of David and Goliath. Westlake isn't exactly a launchpad for famous people, Papa Shades being the notable exception. For the life of me, I can't think of any recent grad who would merit this honor. The crowd quiets down as a drumroll sounds from the far bleachers, soft at first but crescendoing into a crashing finale.

"Ladies and gentlemen, please welcome to the stage, a man for our times. A man for *all* times." Wow, she's really good at building suspense. Everybody's attentive, waiting for the big reveal. "Welcome our hometown hero, Lionel Honeycutt III!"

My heart stops, and maybe so does time. I look around, not sure I heard correctly. But everybody's turning and looking right back at me. Amid the groundswell of noise, I hear a discordant "You've gotta be fucking kidding me." I look to my right as Theo bear-hugs me sideways. As I rise, I see students, all holding up those mysterious flyers the cheerleaders refused to give Mickey and me. But they're not flyers. They're life-sized pictures of my smiling face with a photoshopped crown atop my head.

As I squeeze past others toward the row of steps, I catch a glimpse of Mickey, disbelief crowding out all her other emotions.

Several hands reach out for me, and I'm pulled up and prodded down to the hardwood with the ease of someone being floated around a mosh pit. I walk toward the stage, absorbing the energy of the entire student body as I go. As I make it to the stage apron, the noise is rapturous and chaotic, but it quickly congeals into a steady chant that makes me smile wider than I could've ever imagined.

"Lion*heart*! Lion*heart*! Lion*heart*!"

It takes a full minute of Principal Weyrich calmly cajoling, then insistently imploring, then threateningly gesticulating for the crowd's chants to die down. I'm riding a wave of adulation as Sarah Wake approaches me with the microphone.

"So, Lionheart," she says, "would you mind answering some questions for a curious audience?"

Hesitantly, I take the mic. The crowd stills and quiets, as if their collective energy is at the whim of whatever words I say. "Yes," I answer. The crowd cheers again, as if I'd just recited Cicero.

This must be how Grandpa felt on all those red-carpet nights, with everyone's excitement directed at him. On top of the world. I remember years ago Dad saying that Papa Shades was addicted to fame. I'm sorry, but who *wouldn't* want to chase this high?

Sarah's interview is like a puff piece. No surprising questions. Softballs, really. We hit a road bump when she asks me to retell the events of that fateful afternoon. I can't help but glance up at Mickey. My throat gets dry and a sense of guilt coils around me all python-like. I think about shouting her out as the real hero, but something stops me. I then look at others in the crowd, leaning forward, elbows propped on knees and chins resting in their hands as if they're campers listening to a fireside ghost story.

My words are soft and quiet. "I don't wanna talk about it."

I can hear multiple "Awwwws," but Sarah quickly interjects with "*Trauma*, ladies and gentlemen. This guy's been through so much, you see?" The crowd applauds, as if my "trauma" was worthy of praise. But it's Sarah's next question that really riles them up again.

198

"You've saved one human and countless pets' lives. You've started a popular anti-bullying campaign. You have the entire universe at your fingertips. So let me ask, Lionel Honeycutt: What's your encore?"

A few students in the gymnasium start an impromptu chant of "Encore! Encore!" but it doesn't catch on. Most are too busy streaming the moment from their phones, broadcasting my words to the online world. A lump in my throat forms at this realization. I feel the nerves crawling over my entire body. I lean toward the microphone. The words "Just taking it one day at a time" eke out.

Sarah's first response is an awkward "Ummm . . . okay?" backstopped by a forced grin. The moment of silence that slides in between us is infinitesimally small but feels like an ocean. She glances back. My eyes go with her, trying to divine what's happening. I see Lori over Sarah's right shoulder. The Gavel's lips barely move, but I read the words clearly: *Do it.*

I don't get it. I don't need to, though. Sarah turns back, her grip tighter on the microphone, her confidence apparently steeled.

"There's been talk, Lionel, of you possibly being elevated to a position of school leadership."

Soft murmurs roll through the crowd. I don't understand what she's getting at, so the word "Principal?" flies from my lips before I can rein it in. Sarah laughs heartily, as do several others onstage. Seconds later, the laughter catches on in the audience like a virus, like everyone just thinks I told some scripted joke.

I even see Weyrich breaking out of his steely demeanor to chuckle. My laugh is wholeheartedly fake, like I want to be in on my own joke.

"No, silly!" Sarah responds. "You know what we're talking about." She turns to face the crowd. "Lionel, here, has been given an incredible opportunity, and we'd love to hear your thoughts on the matter."

I can hear the excited whispers build behind me. I glance at Sarah again, seeing Lori's eyes fixed on me. I notice something I've never seen on her. A smile. It's not big or anything, and it doesn't reach her eyes. But it's there, born not of warmth or joy but cold calculation.

Oh no.

"Some sad news." Sarah makes a pouty face before saying, "Lori Chen has decided to resign the student body presidency effective immediately." Scattered gasps come from the crowd. Sarah waits for silence to settle in again and says, "But . . . that means a special election will be triggered within two weeks. . . ."

No no no.

"And do you know who's been in serious talks about running?"

Sarah's doe eyes land right on me. The crowd's collective shock quickly morphs into unbridled excitement. Within seconds, they erupt in cheers. They stand just as I feel I'm about to sink beneath the stage. Serious talks? They set me up. They totally made it seem like I'd been actively plotting this.

I look for Mickey and then Theo in the bleachers, frantically searching for their reactions. I'm silent, but my eyes are pleading, wanting them to know I didn't plan for any of this. I didn't ask for this. No way I ever would have. But I can't see them. Everybody's standing and cheering. Sarah has to yell into the microphone to drag down the crowd's decibel level for anyone to make out what she's saying.

"Seems the crowd just took a poll, Lionel! And I'd say the answer is pretty overwhelming. So what do you say?" I start to shake my head as I look at her, wishing she'd take the hint. But she doesn't. In fact, nobody does. What I meant to be a polite denial, they mistake for modesty, and it only eggs them on. The chants build again like a tidal wave, first from a smattering of soccer players near the baseline and then slowly catching on with the entire home bleachers.

"Lion*heart*! Lion*heart*! Lion*heart*!"

I grab the microphone, but I'm unsure of what to say. I notice someone approach from behind Sarah. They tap her shoulder. Hand her a box.

A *red* box. Sarah opens it and holds it out to me like a platter. I stare at Papa Shade's sunglasses as the noise swells. I glance back toward the throngs of admirers. The sight makes me feel heady, the same way the air gets all wavy when it's really hot out. I can't think straight. The cheers soak into my very pores. I'm swooning and unbalanced, but in a good way. Like if I stumbled off this stage, I'm 100 percent sure someone would catch me. Or maybe I'd fall into a cloud.

One last time, I quickly look for Mickey and Theo.

Nowhere to be found. Maybe it's just an innocent oversight that I can't pick them out in a crowd. Deep down, however, I realize I don't actually *want* to see them.

I take the glasses, slowly, reverently fitting them onto my face as an eruption sounds out in my ears. They fit perfectly.

I don't hear the "Yes" when it first comes. I simply hear the crowd's reaction, which is tantamount to a shot of adrenaline. That, in turn, makes me repeat it, smiling now. For every "Yes," the crowd gets more animated, until I've said it so many times the student body threatens to turn into a rave or a riot. When Weyrich finally steps toward me, angling to wrestle away the microphone, I'm pumping my fists in the air like an engine piston while we all yell it as rhythmically and passionately as an incantation.

"Yes! Yes! Yes! Yes! Yes!"

Weyrich again attempts to grab the microphone, and I lurch to the side, doing a theatrical mic drop, at which the crowd explodes. I do this with the chest-thumping confidence of someone who knows they won't face consequences. After all, stars never do.

With that, the rally ends, and the crowd files out as Weyrich gives me a stern talking-to about respecting authority figures and avoiding impulsive decisions, but I'm barely listening. I simply nod away and "Uh-huh" all his admonishments until he's gone.

When the frenzy is all said and done, and the crowd is emptying out of the gym, I find myself alone. It's like I've been zapped of all the energy I had just seconds ago. A small line of freshmen approach the front of the stage, holding up their flyers along with red and green Sharpies. I do what Papa Shades did in his early days—before he got really famous and insisted on charging. I stick around and autograph each and every one. I try convincing myself I'm doing it to give back and encourage future generations. But honestly, I just don't know what else to do. Normally, I'd celebrate with Theo, but he's not here. Or I'd bury a laugh at one of Mickey's snide comments. But she's gone, too.

I wonder what Theo and Mickey are doing right now. Where they are. What they're thinking. It's like I don't want to see them . . . but I *do*?

I finally spot them when I exit the gym. Theo is leaning against a locker, looking straight up at the ceiling, the light of which makes plain the tear streak on his face. Mickey's beside him, her hand touching his shoulder. My thoughts nose-dive into regret. At that moment, I realize the severity of what I did. I destroyed his chance to be president.

I start walking over, but Mickey notices and her eyes laser into me as she moves to intercept. She plants her feet in front of me, blocking my path. Up close, I see that she's angrier even than that day at the pet store.

"*Don't*," she sneers.

"Is he okay?" I ask.

"His best friend stabs him in the back, and you're gonna ask if he's okay?!"

"It's not my fault!" I move to step around her, but her push to my chest stops me in my tracks.

"Screw you!"

I know enough about Mickey to know that I may as well be trying to get past a pit bull.

She protects those closest to her. And right now, that's Theo.

I remember the last time she was this angry. She was protecting another person dear to her. Her mother.

Our *first* fallout, four years ago, happened as quickly and explosively as lightning in a summer storm. I was waiting for Mickey at Loving Pond. I'd busied myself patrolling for lizards along the near bank when she stormed down the pathway toward the water. I knew she was hurt when I saw the tears streaming from her eyes. I knew she was angry by the way the thorns and brambles scraped her skin, but she kept right on walking. She got so close to me, I could feel the heat of her breath.

"Your grandfather is a slimeball!" she pronounced, as if she wanted the whole thicket to hear.

"Wha—" I stammered for a response. Mickey wasn't patient enough to wait.

"They were talking about some movie project, and they got into some argument and he made my mother cry, and, and . . . he's a *slimeball*! She said that right to his face."

"Why—"

"Because he's *slimy*," she said, her foot stomping the ground.

It was as if her mother's description for Papa Shades was an oak tree, big and authoritative enough that she felt no need to come out from behind it. But there was no way I was abandoning my allegiance to my idol over a single insult—a single word—no matter how intractable Mickey made it seem.

My jaw clenched as I gritted out, "But everybody loves him," a perfectly sensible defense in my twelve-year-old brain.

Mickey crossed her arms. "Well, I *don't* anymore. And neither does she."

I leaned my chin in. "Well, your mom's just jealous she's not famous like him."

Her kick to my shin punctuated the conversation. Audibly crying, she turned and hustled back down the path as I sank to the ground and grabbed my leg. I watched as she left the thicket—and my life.

"Theo?" I call out.

Something flickers in his eyes. They move from the ceiling to find me, the exuberance that usually emanates from him— gone. All I see is tearful coldness.

"I never meant for this to happen," I say. And it's true. I never intended to take his dream away.

He palm-wipes his right cheek. Slowly, he starts walking, my heart skipping a beat as he closes in on me and Mickey. But he only briefly stops when he gets to us, just long enough to hook his arm around Mickey's elbow. "But you didn't have to go along with it" is all he says as they both walk away.

16

I'M STANDING FIFTY FEET FROM WHAT'S BEEN A LONGTIME
dream, but my mind is running nightmare scenarios on a loop.
It's the night of the premiere. I'm in front of Jo's house. My steps
start out slow along the weed-pocked gravel path that passes as
the Ramos family driveway. The home is small and unimpos-
ing, tucked so far under the canopy of an oak tree that one could
mistake it for being shy.

I don't know what to think about this date with Jo, honestly. I can't even believe it's still on. Jo insisted. She smilingly,
shoulder-touchingly assured me right after Mickey had stormed
away at last week's dance that, and I quote, "Nothing's changed
between us. We can still do great things together." Jo's words
were so syrupy with sentiment that I actually blanked when it
came to grilling her about her intentions for the recording. Only
on the walk home did the idea of blackmail settle into my mind
like the first chill of fall.

Consequently, tonight I'm here, not sure I'm a willing par-
ticipant in one of the biggest events of my life.

To make matters more fraught, plenty of other mixed feelings are hitting me. I'll finally be seeing Grandpa's posthumous premiere of his critically acclaimed documentary. Our family is taking his place on the red carpet, and the media is treating it like some grand farewell tour. "Lionel Honeycutt's Last Ride," they're calling it. My throat tightens as I think about how *final* this all is. His last movie. His last reviews. His last celebration.

I'm kind of surprised Dad still let me take his '69 Camaro. This was always the plan, but after our blowup last week, I half expected to be Rikers Island level of grounded. But I wasn't. In fact, I got no punishment. Then, this evening, the first time we'd talked since the dance, he came to my room and said Mom showed him a TikTok of Jo's and complimented her beauty and creativity. Then he laid the keys on my desk.

He even offered an apology, saying he shouldn't have implied Jo might only be in it for the fame. At that, my face went rigid, lips settling into a thin line. What my dad must have seen as stubbornness was a gnawing sense of humiliation. Dad may have been right about Josefina Ramos. I may have been all wrong. A chill crawls up my spine just thinking about what she could do with that recording. What exactly she wants in exchange for not releasing it.

I walk up two steps to a concrete slab landing. I push an unlit doorbell, and no sound comes. I can hear both Dad's and Grandpa's voices in the back of my head insist I knock instead of just texting Jo that I've arrived, so that's what I do. When the door opens, two people are waiting to greet me, and I see exactly where Jo got her smile.

Jo's mom embraces me in a warm hug. She then steps back and brushes the shoulders of my suit like a proud parent. She's basically Jo's twin. Her dad holds out a leathery hand, which I shake, and they introduce themselves—Alejandro and Isabella—and invite me in.

I sit on a plush brown couch that reminds me of Papa Shades's old man-cave sofa at his Calabasas home. Grandma always harangued him about retiring the ratty old thing, only to be met with his adamant refusals, saying, "If I can still work, this couch can damn sure work, too."

I hear shuffling down a hallway, which they either don't notice or ignore. I think to call out for Jo, but Mrs. Ramos beats back my words with her own.

"So, Lionel. We heard what you did. Josefina's lucky to have found someone so considerate of others," she says, an accent playing hide-and-seek among the syllables.

"Thank you," I respond.

Mr. Ramos pulls a phone from his pocket, unlocks it, and hands it to me. "Jo showed us a, uh, *Twitter* of your heroics."

I watch another clip of the pet store video, one I hadn't seen before. Same footage, but in this one, Daddy Yankee's reggaeton classic "Gasolina" provides the soundtrack. I give a smile void of emotion as I hand it back. I suppose it's a good thing Jo hasn't told her parents the truth—that I'm a fraud and a liar. But it doesn't make me feel much better, because the question of *why* still hangs in the air like a rotting apple.

"I'm sure your parents are very proud of you," Jo's dad says. "As we are of her. You know, she said in elementary school she wanted to be a millionaire by the time she was twenty? And look where she's headed."

"That's awesome," I respond, genuinely impressed. I think the biggest goals I had back then involved later bedtimes and getting sweets before dinner.

"Yes. She was bullied back then, for her clothes," her mom says. "And I think her culture. The way we did things . . ." The words grow faint as Mrs. Ramos's lips list into a frown. "I think that motivated her."

"She's so lucky to have you to guide her the rest of the way," Mr. Ramos says. "Hollywood can be a rough business, we've heard. We were very concerned, to be honest. So you offering your experience and connections to smooth out her path was very reassuring. An absolute bendición de Dios." He makes a praying hands gesture as he looks toward the ceiling.

I nod absently as his words rattle around in my head. Jo casting me as her celebrity sherpa definitely wasn't on my radar. But then again, neither was her recording me.

Footsteps hurriedly pad along carpet as all our heads turn. Jo appears in the living room like an apparition. She looks both beautiful and frantic. She eyes her mother and says something I can't understand but what I take to be some kind of reprimand. Mrs. Ramos raises her hands. "All right, all right," she says. "We'll stop talking. But it's rude not to entertain a guest."

"Entertain," Jo responds. "Not interrogate."

"Just a friendly conversation," Mr. Ramos adds innocently.

Jo rolls her eyes before giving cheek kisses to both and grabbing my hand. I get up and we say rushed goodbyes. It's only when I open her car door that I really get a chance to take her in. She has on a red dress with a plunging neck and high side slits, almost up to her thighs. A choker necklace that looks like a heavy, sparkly mound of crystals. Her hair hangs over a shoulder like a pageantry sash. It's a look fit for a starlet.

I sputter through a compliment as she gets in, and I'm glad to turn the ignition and have the engine roar to life if only to allow me a few seconds to break the glamour she's seemingly put on me. Those seconds turn into five full minutes of silence, and it's not until we've pulled onto the interstate and passed the "35 miles to Charlotte" sign that I regain my nerve. Not only do I have the recording on my mind, but I'm aware that being in the car with Jo isn't *technically* legal, as I'm only allowed to have a non-adult in the car when driving to and from school. Dad knows this, of course, but I think letting me do this is his way giving me space.

It takes a few miles of highway for either of us to speak. We pass the off-ramp for Killian City when Jo suddenly stops snapping selfies on her phone, places it in her lap, and sighs.

"Sorry about the parentals," she says. "They can be just so *ugh* sometimes."

"They were, um, nice," I respond. Much the same as Jo but

different still. They're like the roots of a dogwood to Jo's flowering branches. Every part of the tree working, but only one part on display for the world to see.

"I can't hate too much, though. Their sacrifices got me here, you know? I'm going places thanks to them."

"Like Hollywood? They didn't seem like fans."

I glance at her as she twists her body toward the driver's side, eyes boring into me. But there's no threat in her body language. Just passion. "But they don't see the big picture. That's just how America is. Capitalism literally means 'use whatever you've got to get ahead.' Just like you and me."

My mouth twitches. I'm both annoyed and confused as to why she's roping me into whatever point she's trying to make. "You and me?" I ask.

"*Yes.* Your name. My content. They don't see that to get to the top, you've gotta be ruthless about exploiting your advantages."

I visualize her parents. Softspoken, warm, and proud. "Ruthless" seems about the furthest adjective from my mind.

"Maybe you should listen to them," I spit back. "Maybe they're just trying to protect you. After all, that's what parents do."

Jo sinks back into her seat, smiling as she crosses her arms. "You wouldn't say that if they were your parents."

Although she didn't mean it as a gotcha response, Jo's comment still catches me off guard. I realize right then that her parents *are* very much like mine. Kind, caring, overly protective.

"You know, they nag me all the time," Jo says, "but in all

honesty, I do everything for them. It's not about money or fame, really. Just family." I glance over again, and she's staring out at the road. Moonlight hits her like tinsel, bringing to life a thoughtful expression. "And I'd do anything *for* them. Like jump into a volcano. They've just done so much for me, ya know?"

I feel a twinge of guilt that I don't think I could say the same. I mean, sure, I love them and would be absolutely devastated if something were to happen to them. But "anything" is, well, *everything*. And I've seen several volcano YouTubes. Those things are *hot*.

"What about your friends?" I ask.

She takes a few seconds before she nods. "I'm pretty loyal there, too."

"Then why blackmail me? If I'm your, you know . . ."

I'm making it a point to keep my eyes forward, but I can still make out Jo's face in my periphery. Her cheeks suck in and her lips crater, as if she'd just sucked on a lemon. Finally, she comes out with it: "Lionel, I have no intention of blackmailing you. You're a true friend. And I was actually thinking we could be more."

"You mean like girlfriend-boyfriend?" I ask, the last words coming out squeaky as a bath toy.

"Some type of . . . *arrangement* like that. But on an even broader scale." My face must be riddled with skepticism, because she suddenly goes into sales mode. "It's not like I'm some gold digger. I've gone Dutch with literally all my past boyfriends, every single meal. And I get so uncomfortable when anyone buys me a gift that's more than thirty dollars. I'm like, spend it on something important." She looks at me, her eyes probing. I still say nothing, so she shifts gears to flattery. "Face it, even without the name, you're special. We both are. Think about how we could propel ourselves to new heights. Honestly, I have big plans for us. We could do social collabs, joint brand management. . . ." She pairs her smile with a wink and a shrug. "And no better way to boost the brand than some dating speculation."

My hands tighten at the wheel as I focus on the road ahead. Not even the road, really. I'm just looking out into the dark distance, vaguely scanning for what's to come. It all sounds so easy. And yet, so artificial.

"I don't think I'm comfortable with that." My declaration comes out so quietly that for a moment, I'm not sure whether I've spoken the words or simply thought them. However, Jo's reaction tells me she heard all too well. She picks up the phone from her lap and thumbs to the app she wants. The sound of my gym hallway conversation with Mickey floods the car.

"Every plan needs an insurance policy" is all she says.

She pauses the video and places the phone back in her lap. The rest of the ride to Charlotte is in silence.

17

THE THREAT IS UNSPOKEN, BUT AS CLEAR AS A MOUNTAIN stream. I am not to deviate from the plan, which Jo excitedly fills me in on as we arrive in Charlotte. I'd been told to park five blocks away at the staging hotel so that the whole family could ride in a black stretch SUV to the red carpet. Jo and I are to put on a show fit for Hollywood as an upstart power couple and dynamic social media juggernaut. One crooked smile or off-kilter post and my confession will be out there for the world to see.

When we exit the car, Jo acts totally unbothered. As we walk, she latches onto my arm and even leans her head into my shoulder, as if we're a regular couple and not a hostage situation. Most of me wants to recoil. However, a small part of me leans into the fanciful idea that this is the end goal. This is what I always wanted. Fame. Popularity. A pretty girl on my arm. Grandpa didn't really smile all that much, but I find myself thinking that if he saw me now, he just might. In spite of my misgivings, I find myself leaning into her.

My family is already piled into the SUV when Jo and I arrive. The car ride consists of Mom and Dad peppering Jo with inconsequential questions and compliments. When J-Maw finds out Jo's grandparents emigrated from Colombia, she absently rhapsodizes about "that time I met Pablo Escobar at a Medellín coffee shop," but otherwise stays weirdly quiet in a seat beside a window. I'm noticeably absent from all the chatter, looking out at skyscrapers that line the city like rows of dominoes.

Jo sidles up to me, gripping my hand and letting out a quiet squeal. The SUV stops at the Grand Station Theater, the brightness of the marquee above and the mounted industrial lights just beyond spilling through the windows. We're both shaking as the murmurs of the crowd filter in. Her from excitement, me from nerves. We wait there an impossibly long time as a woman in the front passenger seat barks directions into a phone. She then turns around and reviews the protocols: who'll exit first, where to stop along the carpet, how we shouldn't try to cover or shield our eyes, no matter how overwhelmed we get by the flashes. Then a white-gloved man comes up and opens the door. One by one, we exit to a festive kind of chaos.

People are everywhere, most waving and yelling directly at us. It's disorienting, walking past a gauntlet of camera flashes using only a red carpet and rope line as our guide. Someone calmly but sternly instructs us to stop and pose, and we do. And that's when I realize most of the yells are for me.

"Hey, hero, look over here!"

"Lionheart, smile!"

"Who's the lucky lady, young man?"

I'm speechless. I open my mouth, but words won't come. Then I see Jo stepping forward, her hand releasing mine. I had offered it to her to help her from the car. Sensing opportunity in the small gesture of kindness, Jo simply never let it go.

"My name is Josefina Ramos. I am a social media influencer, and I also happen to be Lionel's friend from school. Find me at JoTheRamost on all social platforms."

Someone yells, *"Friend* friend, or something more?" to which Jo just responds, "I guess you'll have to settle for a cliff-hanger," and the paparazzi laugh.

She banters with a captive audience for two whole minutes, volleying back witty rejoinders to their intrusive questions like she's a star at Wimbledon. They ask about how we came to be friends, what she's wearing, whether she wants to act "because you've sure got the charisma for it." The sheer volume of camera flashes seems like a tidal wave of light, but Jo doesn't even flinch. She's a natural at this. The only person I've seen more smoothly navigate the limelight was my grandfather, and that's because he'd been doing it for decades.

I'm more relieved than I should be when someone official-looking instructs us to head toward the door. We all wave politely, with the exception of Jo, who blows kisses toward those just past the rope line. The photographers eat it up, with one even comparing her grace to that of Lupita Nyong'o. My family gets inside, where we have to wait a few more seconds for Jo to catch up. Dad jokes that she's the actual star of the show, which grinds at me, even though I laugh with everybody else. But as we head to the appetizer table, Jo directs her bubbly joy toward me, and I can't help but lighten up. It's so uncanny how charming she can be. How I know none of this is real, but a part of me wants to believe it could be.

Eventually, we file into the theater full of those fancy plush reclining seats. We all sit in a middle row, with J-Maw and Jo flanking me. About a minute later, the lights dim.

Instead of movie trailers, they're scheduled to show this fifteen-minute highlight reel of Lionel Sr. on set. Candids, mostly, along with some interview outtakes. The first few are bloopers, scenes where he flubbed his lines and a laugh-out-loud moment where a boom microphone fell, hitting his head. If Papa Shades were alive, he likely would've stood up and told the film operator to "cut the damn show." He had this thing about imperfection. This has always been one of Dad's major gripes about him, at least dating back to Dad's first ever high school wrestling match. As the story goes, Dad got pinned during the first period. Papa Shades was so incensed that he actually stormed down the bleachers as Dad was about to get up and pressed his palm into Dad's back, forcing his entire body to return to the mat. In front of both teams and the crowd, Grandpa made Dad kiss the mat, saying, "You gonna stay right here till you *hate* it."

People cover their eyes and wince at the famous "bear attack" footage where Grandpa actually slipped on a rock and got pinned down by an Alaskan grizzly on the set of *Death on Denali*. Legend has it, when the OR doctors said a full recovery would take up to six months, Grandpa ripped out his IV and said, "*Shit.* Alls I need is a BC Powder and my damn bill." Three weeks later, he was back at work.

The next clips are some of his most death-defying stunts, set to a soaring, *Rocky*-esque track. The rhino ride, the skiing ahead of an avalanche, and him piloting a jet through a narrow canyon get the most applause.

Then the music gets notably softer as the clips transition once again. This time, they feature his costars. Stills of people on set with him as their voice-overs extol his virtues. I can't help but notice there are way more female costars speaking kindly about him than male. Ariel Sharpe cries as she proclaims him the "sweetheart of all sweethearts." Roxy Devine notes how he's "so affable and carefree," and Jackie Wright calls him "the most giving person in the world," telling the story about how he literally gave her the shirt off his back when she spilled red wine all over hers. None of these quotes bear even passing resemblance to the Grandpa I knew, but it's really profound hearing about this newer, softer side of him. Who says heroes can't be warmhearted, too? By the time we get to footage of Papa Shades and Alana Noel both nuzzling a baby elephant, there isn't a dry set of eyes in the theater. Well, except for one, curiously. J-Maw's.

Honestly, I can understand the unease Grandma must be enduring. Her spouse is sharing beachside daiquiris, gallivanting under the Arc de Triomphe, and riding horseback with all these fawned-over women, none of whom are her. Come to think of it, not one person in our family is in any of this footage. It's like he had an entire life cordoned off from us.

I glance at Jo, and she's enthralled. Like most others, caught up in the lore and lure of a man she never met. It's ironic that she's excited while the woman on my other side—who knew him the most—seems like she couldn't be more over it.

I lean over to ask if J-Maw's feeling well, but the reel's ending interrupts me. The lights get bright. Audience members shoot out of their seats for a standing ovation. Mom and Dad slowly follow, their claps obviously less uproarious than those of people surrounding us. Jo and I stand as well. It's only Grandma who keeps sitting. Everybody directs their applause toward us, wanting to show the family their appreciation for the departed. Nobody seems to mind Grandma remaining seated, probably because they think she can't stand for too long. But I know better. Something about those clips got to her.

A petite white lady in an elegant black dress meanders in front of the stage. I recognize her face from one of Grandpa's movies. It's Wendy Grace Benton, a starlet who made it big doing a lot of late '90s teen rom-coms. In an effort to avoid being typecast, she started taking on more serious roles later in life. *The Sparrow and the Spy* with Grandpa was one of those. An international espionage thriller set in the Philippines, it was supposed to usher in a "new, Black Bond franchise," according to reviews. Although it received moderate box-office success, the series really took off after Papa Shades was booted as protagonist in favor of the younger, more muscular Malachi Jenkins for the sequel and beyond.

Wendy begins talking about their first day shooting the film. How, when setting up equipment near a cave, a production assistant found a litter of orphaned kittens near the beach. There were five of them. They were alone. When Grandpa saw how heartbroken Wendy was, he insisted on having the staff conduct an all-out search in and around the cave for the mother. He'd even refused to do a take until the mother was found, dead or alive. Filming was delayed for two days, but miraculously, they found the mom, shivering and stranded in a nook about a quarter mile into the cave.

"That was Lionel," Wendy says, her eyes shiny with tears. "A kind, gentle soul to the core. A star burning bright in an impossibly dim galaxy. The kind of man we all want our husbands, brothers, and sons to be."

It's right then that Grandma audibly groans. I look at her, and she's rubbing her eyes. I wonder if she has a headache or motion sickness from the highlight reel. She doesn't get out to the movies too often. Or maybe this spectacle is just overwhelming her. I lean in and whisper, "Are you okay? I know this memorial is probably a lot to take."

She doesn't speak. Instead, she rises from her seat and starts jockeying through the aisle for the exit. The lights dim again, and the movie starts without her. It's a devastatingly beautiful documentary. Everything from the interviews with the marsh people to the twilight shots from the sand dunes is exquisite.

220

Toward the end, a guy in the row in front of us even murmurs something to his wife about how this has been nothing short of "a reawakening of my soul."

As the credits roll and the ovation begins, I stand and look around. I see that everybody's moved, awed, inspired.

Everybody except J-Maw, who missed every second.

18

AS PEOPLE FILE OUT OF THE THEATER, I LOOK TOWARD MOM and Dad. Both are checking their phones, neither even bothering to feign interest in the applause. It's Grandma's opinion I really want, though, and she's nowhere to be found.

We graft ourselves onto the back of the line and head out, with Jo excusing herself for the bathroom the moment we step out of the theater. Mom and Dad make their way to the reception room, so I just sit on a lobby bench and wait.

I get bored people watching, and my thoughts settle on Mickey. I entertain myself imagining the snide remarks she'd have muttered during the theatrical scenes, or the random movie factoids she'd serve like Mike and Ikes at the most inopportune times.

Eventually, throwing caution to the wind, I pull out my phone and text her. **How's it going?** Immediately, I jam the phone into my pocket, exhaling deeply as I try to wrap my head around why I did that. It'd be a damn-near miracle if she answered back this year, if at all, I think. So, I'm surprised when the phone buzzes at my hip. I pull it out again and see that she's written me back.

Good. How'd it go with you at the premiere?

My thumbs can't work the keys fast enough. Went great. A bit off balance and melodramatic at the end, but enjoyable for the most part.

I see dots on the screen. Seconds later: The movie, not Jo???

I respond with a simple lol. And then a question drifts light as a feather into my mind. I type: How'd you know I took her?

Her reply is as simple as it is obvious: She posted. And then, Seems like a great time. And seconds later, she sends a picture of Jo's Instagram post. An all-smiles selfie we took huddled together in the crowded theater right before the show began. Something about Mickey knowing I'm here with her guts me. Mickey witnessed Jo's betrayal—her businesslike willingness to trade in my hero's journey for her own viral moment. Mickey would never do that. And yet, somehow she's the one at home watching the Jo and Lionel show like it's Netflix's next best thing.

Oh, I text.

I shove the phone back into my pocket and stand up. Jo walks out of the bathroom. Together, we walk toward the reception. I scan the room for J-Maw, but she isn't there. When I ask my parents of her whereabouts, they don't know, either, so Jo and I head to the catering tables. We're two lemon squares and a Shirley Temple deep when the lady giving orders from the

SUV taps my shoulder.

"They want to interview you" is all she says. *They?* She must read my expression, because she follows up with "EGTV." When it doesn't click for me, she says, "Entertainment Global. They've got this whole segment planned where they're talking about you stepping into the family legacy. Taking the torch, that sort of thing."

I look at Mom and Dad, who are two tables over talking with one of Grandpa's past actor friends. "Not my dad?"

The lady looks as if the answer wasn't obvious. "You're telling me he saved a person in a pet store, too?" She smirks at her own joke. I give a fake laugh, not because it's funny but because I don't know what else to do. "Taping starts in twenty. Can you be there?"

I just shrug, while at the same time Jo answers, "Yes!" She then drags me over to my parents to tell them about it. Mom and Dad look wary but they don't stop me, so Jo and I exit the reception and go down two hallways into a much quieter area. I peek into the setup room and notice the boom mics and stage cameras that dominate Hollywood sets. I stop, my nerves suddenly making a playground of my body. A production assistant walks up to us and tries to introduce herself. I say nothing, frozen in the moment. Jo sees my discomfort, apologizes with the excuse that "He needs some fresh air. You know, side effects from the smoke inhalation and all." And with that, she whisks me away to an outside alley.

I can breathe easier here. No questions. No fans. Just the

distant sounds of car engines and fire sirens. I even manage a soft smile. In some ways, the escape from that interview was more fraught than the pet store inferno. I look over at Jo to thank her for giving me an out, but she no longer seems concerned. She's just staring down at her phone.

"Can you believe that?" I ask.

"Yeah, crazy, right?" she answers, in a decidedly unexcited tone. I step closer. She doesn't notice. I peek to look at what's got her so fixated on the screen, but I can't see.

"What are you looking at?" I ask.

"Sharing a video clip I took at the reception hall." She looks up at me. "How many reposts do you think we could get if we stitched this?"

I don't know, and my blank expression says as much. She puts the phone to her mouth and voice dictates, "Share the link to the group chat with hashtags LionelandJo and Dynamic-Duo."

Someone FaceTimes her. I hear excited screams from the other end of the line as she scurries deeper into the alley to chat. I'm left alone wondering what to do with myself. I get out my phone and go back to my text thread with Mickey.

I text: FYI, I'm interviewing with EGTV in a few.

There's no response. I call. It rings for a while before going to voicemail. So, I'm left there, waiting for Jo and quietly whittling away the awkwardness of this moment.

I hear someone's throat clear somewhere near the street. When I turn, I see J-Maw, purse in hand, laboring away from the theater. She looks out of place alone out here, headed toward the darkness. Her face is grim with her eyes affixed to the ground. I hustle toward her, but she doesn't even notice me until I'm at her shoulder.

"Grandma."

The word wrests her out of her fixed stare. Her fists clench as she looks at me, but they relax right as recognition sparks in her eyes. "Now, you know not to go jumping out on old folks like that. Liable to land both of us in the hospital. 'Bout to give me a heart attack."

"Why're you walking alone out here?" I ask. "It's not safe."

"Damn right it ain't safe. *I'm* out here. Got my cane." She jabs her cane at the cement. "Taser." She pats her pocket. "Spiked my punch cup with some Red Bull I snuck into the theater, too. Hell, *you* slowin' *me* down."

I keep pace with her as we walk along the sidewalk.

"Still think I'll stick around you," I say. "Safety in numbers."

She groans but doesn't protest. We head toward the brilliant glow of tall buildings and angled cityscape a few blocks away, feeling the chilly breeze of a fall evening with each car that passes us by. We start to cross a long bridge spanning a river shimmering with lamplight and reflections of skyscrapers. I look back toward the theater. I wonder if Jo's noticed I'm gone. I check my phone. No texts from her yet. Mickey hasn't written me back, either. I guess this sojourn with Grandma could stand to last a bit longer.

Just about every time someone passes us, I get nervous, and

I brace myself when a guy in tattered clothing blocks our path. Grandma barely even raises an eyebrow. I feel slightly guilty when he simply asks for change. That sentiment is quickly overtaken by awe as Grandma fishes a twenty-dollar bill from her purse to give him. By looking at the man, you'd think he just won the lottery. After profusely thanking us, he carries on his now-merry way.

"Why'd you give him that money?" I ask, genuinely curious.

Grandpa made it his mantra never to give to the homeless, always saying, "Ain't nobody gave me nothing in my life. Why should I give anybody a handout?"

"What am I gonna do with it?" J-Maw says. "Save it for retirement?" She laughs at her own joke.

"Give it to charity maybe?" She gives me a suspicious look, like she knows exactly what I'm not saying. So, I decide to come out with it. "You think Grandpa would want his money going to . . ." I nod over my shoulder instead of finishing the sentence. Shame emanates from within me as I see the guy in the distance. Honestly, I don't mind giving an extra dollar or two to the down-and-out, but I'm pretty certain Papa Shades would. I feel a weird need to protect his legacy.

Grandma stops suddenly. "I earned every damn cent of this money. My job was every bit as hard as his."

I scrunch my brow. "You had a job?" slips out well before I've even considered how those words would play.

"Hell yeah, I had a job. Puttin' up with his trifling ass." My eyes go wide. She glares at me for a long while before letting out a frustrated sigh. She mutters, "Jesus, boy, smart as you are, you as dense as a rock when it comes to him." I flinch at her barb. What's that all about? I'm not some Papa Shades groupie. I just recognize and celebrate his accomplishments. The real question is *why doesn't she?*

Slowly, she makes her way to a bench set against the railing. She makes a big production of sitting down—taking a white kerchief from her purse and wiping the seat. I sit next to her, the back of my pants getting damp from rain droplets. "You've always taken a shine to your grandpa, huh?" she says.

I nod. "We're basically benefitting from his legacy."

"His legacy ain't just what you see on the big screen," she replies.

"But that's most of it," I say. My tone is more defensive than I want it to be. I glance at her. She's looking into the distance, her stare unmoved by the blur of passing cars. She looks tired, like she's ready to leave. Not just this event, but this whole exhausting part of her life.

"Why'd you go so soon?" I ask. "I mean from the premiere."

"Because I've seen it play out half my life."

"What do you mean?"

"You seen that tribute video at the beginning?" she asks.

Of course. Everyone did. How many other stars can say they have a highlight reel that large? "It's crazy how many other celebs he filmed alongside," I say.

"Crazy, huh."

"Were you ever starstruck by anyone?" I ask.

228

"Can't say I have been. Kind of easy to avoid it, though, when your husband won't allow you anywhere near the set."

I bat an eye her way. "He *never* took you to the set?"

"Sometimes," she admits. "The buddy comedies usually. That movie where he nursed the abandoned puppy back to health. What's the one?" she says, snapping her fingers.

"*A Paw for Pauly*," I say.

"Right," she agrees. "Some of the action stuff, too . . . Never would take me to the dramas and romances, though." Her gaze goes skyward. "Figured out that pattern a few years into the marriage."

My eyes follow hers. "You saying that to me or to him?" I ask.

"Oh, if I was talking to him, I don't reckon I'd be looking up," she deadpans.

I give an awkward laugh.

"Your grandfather was one of the finest actors of his time. Blessed us with some iconic performances and personas. And a big part of me is honored to have witnessed such talent up close. But boy, don't you ever mistake characters for *character*."

"But everybody loved him," I say.

"You just saw the highlight reel. You didn't see how he yelled at stagehands or cussed out B-listers when they flubbed lines. There's enough footage of that for a full-length movie."

My nod isn't one of agreement, but rather deference. I know he could be combative at times, but that was his nature, right? It's who he was. Grandpa was always about creating the perfect product, whatever it took. If that included butting some heads or breaking fine china, so be it.

I feel a buzz in my pocket. I check, and it's a **Where are you? Interview in 10** text from Jo. I stare at the message for a long while as J-Maw fishes one of those candies in the strawberry wrappers from her purse.

I wonder if J-Maw ever had moments of starry excitement and anticipation with Grandpa like I originally had with Jo. A time where she was sure things were gonna happen, like the precious seconds between a firework being launched and setting the night's sky ablaze. Dad told me J-Maw played hard to get at first, but Grandpa eventually won her over. "Thousands of flowers and even more promises," Dad would always say.

I think back to the way Dad lingered in my room after he gave me the car keys. I noticed how he gulped as he looked at me, eyes heavy and red with a sentiment I could both see and feel.

"About tonight," he said. "I know your grandfather meant a lot to you. That man was larger than life. But don't ever forget that he's just that—a man." I nodded, afraid to talk lest a Pandora's box of mixed emotions escaped me. He continued: "*You'll be a man too someday.* And the marker for manhood isn't saving someone from a burning pet store or jumping out of a bullet train or even winning the affection of a pretty girl."

His words cut deep. I hadn't done any of those things. My life was a lie. Where I'd normally snark or roll my eyes, I simply swallowed Dad's words as the bitter pill they were. Dad patted my shoulder, offering up a tight smile. Voice breaking, I asked, "What *is* the marker?"

Dad's eyes floated upward as he considered the question. Then they settled back on me. "I'm certainly no definitive expert, but I suppose when you can be strong and be weak and be everything in between," he said. "I'd say that's true manhood."

There were so many words I wanted to say right then, many of them expressions of regret and shame. Those things Papa Shades told me real men didn't feel.

I unlock the screen on my phone and type out **On a walk with my grandma. Brb.** I look at the woman beside me. "J-Maw?"

"Hmm?"

"Did you ever feel head over heels for him? Like, just completely into him?"

"'Smitten,' us old folks used to call it." She nods. "And yes, I suppose there was a time. Way back. Probably around your age. Couple years older."

That makes sense. I'd always figured the strong emotions so ubiquitous in those swoony romances thinned with age, like worn spark plugs on an old car. The warmth had been noticeably absent in their latter years.

"Why'd y'all stay together?"

She shrugs, still watching the distance as if it were a mindless television show. "I suppose what I should say is 'for the family.' But honestly, I just thought he'd change eventually. I fell in love with a man who thought the sun rose for him. He was that confident. And that attracted me. But a woman soon learns what's attractive in the moment isn't necessarily what's best for a lifetime."

I feel a buzz and see another text from Jo. A simple **U out here??** Seconds later, **U can't miss this** paired with a frowny emoji pops up. Could be the temperature dipping or a draft of wind curling across the bridge, but I don't feel as warm inside. On a whim, I text Mickey one last time: **Kind of wish you were here.** I shove the phone back into my pocket and look at J-Maw.

"Did he? You know, change?" I ask.

"Not for a long while, but eventually. A little."

"What caused it?" I ask.

Her stare becomes more intent, as if the answer lies somewhere along the horizon. She says, "Time has a way of humbling even those not inclined toward humility."

Half joking, I say, "So let me get this straight: For most of his life, you really thought your husband was an egomaniac?"

She rises with the slow movements of someone not used to taking long strolls. She wipes the back of her dress as she straightens, looking down at me. Her expression is serious. "He ain't the only one I was talking about."

She starts walking off toward the theater without me. Why would she say it like that? She couldn't possibly be talking about me, could she? I'd always thought I was humble. I search my recollections for any instances that could prove this, and I'm quite unnerved that I can't think of any.

I feel the phone buzz once more as I stand. Finally, it's

Mickey. A jolt of anticipation shoots down my spine as I unlock the phone.

She responds to my last text, but in the worst of ways. An impossibly short I **don't** paired with a sad-face emoji. That's all I get.

19

J-MAW AND I HEAD BACK, AND JO'S WAITING FOR US UNDER a streetlight near the entrance to the building. The only words she says are "I think we might be late," but in the tone of a chastising parent rather than a worried significant other. As we enter, she hooks her arm into mine, her steps outpacing me to the point that I feel like I'm almost being dragged. Several turns and half a minute later we're back at the interview room.

A man and woman with microphones come up to us. I recognize them right away. Justine Carlson and Braxton Nance from EGTV's *Hollywood Hangout*. The ones set on outing me before Mickey yanked her scoop. In turn, they reach out to shake my hand. Justine seems nice enough, voice smooth and warm as cocoa on a winter evening. But Braxton's eyes are too searching and suspicious, his grip too firm, like he's trying to squeeze the truth right out of me. Jo loses it, bouncing on her tiptoes and getting all jittery as she shakes their hands. She barely manages to squeak out a "You two are sooooo good!"

A production assistant brings a stool from a corner and

beckons me to sit, but Jo is so effervescent that the duo openly muse about having her sit with me. The quickness with which she can point out the only other matching stool in the room makes me wonder if this was a part of her plan.

Even though we tell them we're just friends, Braxton and Justine talk about potential ship names, with "Lionina" as an immediate frontrunner. As the assistant retrieves Jo's stool, Justine briefs us on the interview. She tells us not to worry and how to sit for the best camera angles—easy stuff like that. But it's Braxton who drops the bombshell.

"And remember," he says, "even though it's gonna be live, just be yourself. The audience likes authenticity."

Live? As in, if I make a single mistake or I sneeze and snot shoots out my nose, untold millions will see? I nearly balk at the whole thing. Braxton's smile lingers in an inauthentic way that makes me not trust it, but Jo takes me aside and reassures me that the questions from these interviews tend to be softballs. "It makes them look good if you look good," she says.

I don't honestly know if she's telling the truth, but I'm too intimidated by the moment to interrogate her reasoning, so I just say, "Seriously?"

"Yeah. You think if they bombard celebs with tough questions, they'll keep getting A-lister interviews?"

Makes sense, I guess. And seeing Jo so unfazed helps me calm down, too.

Once the interview starts, the questions are easy. How I liked the movie. How I'm acclimating to social media fame.

Who's the lucky lady on my arm? Simple. Straightforward. Fat, slow softballs, every one of which I should be hitting out of the park. *Should.*

Turns out, the simplest question is the hardest. In reference to the pet store fire, Justine asks me to "walk us through that moment."

I talk about going with a friend to help her buy a goldfish, and then get to the part where we see the smoke, but then it's like my brain flickers out. *Ugh.* Why didn't I see this coming? The truth seems pinned to the back of my throat. I just can't admit it. Not in front of millions. The silence gets so awkward that Braxton makes a stilted joke about me falling asleep on air. I wish I had. At least narcolepsy might give me a valid excuse for not answering.

Calmly and firmly, Jo reaches over, interweaving her hand with mine as if I were a person who needed saving from drowning. She squeezes gently at first, but then tighter. Too tight, digging her nails into my skin. I snap out of my stupor and fight the urge to jerk my hand back. I notice her smile, steady as she looks at the camera. Then I brave the glare of the soft box lights to look at the interviewers. They're waiting. The camera behind them, too.

I feel my mouth open again. Words come slowly at first, like a trickle through a leaky dam. But then the flow of syllables gets heavier and levels out. Jo's grip loosens up, and so do I. Soon, I can hear myself speaking of smoke and ash and searing heat and lifting with all my might to free a guy's arm.

I leave out the part about me dropping the shelf on him. And, of course, any mention of Jimmy or Mickey. I simply let their imaginations fill in the gaps, like millions of others had in the weeks prior.

Judging by the interviewers' nods, I can tell they're intrigued. When I hear myself saying, "And then I just found myself alone at the fountain, and that's when the firefighters took over," I expectantly look toward Jo. She's gazing right at me, nodding and covering her mouth with a free hand as if she's witnessing a world wonder rather than a world-class liar. That's enough for me to think my recounting was a success, but instead of a *rah-rah* feeling, a queasiness curls in and around my stomach. It gets worse with the next question. I can see it in Braxton's eye, the spark of mischief you see in kids wondering what'll happen if they give the vase at the edge of the counter one last nudge. The amount of chaos they can cause with a single observation.

"I thought there were two people at the fountain," he says.

I flinch. Brows scrunching and eyes narrowing on him, I ask, "What?"

He clears his throat as if he thinks I didn't hear him correctly. "The official police report and even your past retellings have you sitting with a friend at the fountain."

"Oh, I, um . . ." My voice rises an octave higher than usual.

"I'm surprised you don't remember," he half laughs, and I wonder whether he's genuinely amused or just drawing attention to my mistake. My insecurity creeps in like oil spilled on fabric, leaving inky black spots of doubt on my narrative. If

Braxton's suspicious, wouldn't the online sleuths watching now be even more so? Could a few true-crimers band together and crowd-source my downfall?

In the corner of my eye, I catch Jo leaning forward. "I think he meant the opposite," she says, ending her statement there. She looks 100 percent self-assured, and seconds later I understand why.

The statement is bait, and Justine dutifully takes it. "Opposite of what?"

"He meant to say he was sitting with his friend. He just got mixed up."

"Seems like a pretty important detail to mix up," Braxton responds, scrambling to reel his scoop back in.

At this, Jo simply flicks her wrist as if batting his reply away like a pesky gnat. "Honestly, with PTSD, fog of war, and all that, he's lucky to get half of the details straight with any consistency," she says.

"Wait," Justine chimes, looking straight at me. "You've been diagnosed with PTSD?"

I open my mouth, but Jo cuts me off. "Severe," she says. "Like CIA black site level." Jo brazenly takes control of the interview like it's some midday car heist. I'm awed by how effortlessly she weaves in details of my recovery from a partially collapsed lung, my night terrors, and my random, uncontrollable bouts of sobbing over the pets I couldn't save. When she ends with "God rest those chinchillas' souls," Justine's mouth is wide open.

I used to think lying was an ugly thing, but Jo just spun the most beautiful, arresting fiction I've heard since we studied *The Kite Runner* last year in sophomore English.

Jo even manages to squeeze in how I saved Jimmy Palladino from an asthma attack and ratchets the sympathy level to a shade under a billion by claiming I've used my fame to start a charity for underprivileged kids. It's not until we leave the interview room and we're safely out of earshot that she admits the "charity" for "underprivileged kids" is just me taking Jimmy under my wing.

"And the PTSD thing?" I ask hesitantly.

"*Oh yeah.* You caught that?! The tabloids eat that shit up. I was gonna go with recurrent seizures resultant from your traumatic brain injury, but I thought that might be a little over the top. Wait, you're okay with this stuff, right?" I don't respond. She takes my silence as acceptance and adds, "*See?* With me around, you'll go places. Now, you'll want to rewatch the interview after it airs so you can memorize your ailments, because consistency is important."

She goes on to detail our meet-cute volunteering at the local Boys & Girls Club and riffs on our favorite dates, which include taking Jo's corgis to the local dog park and watching sunsets atop Mount Trembley. By the time she's done coaching me, she's the breathless kind of giddy. I honestly don't know how I feel about this. But I'll admit that Jo's lies saved me from being a trending topic in the worst of ways. And she seems so pleased with herself, like a kid who just learned to tie her shoes.

She grabs my hand, and we walk through the reception room like we're one of those Hollywood power couples. More than a few in the crowd stare and smile at us. I awkwardly smile back because I've been taught it's impolite not to. But Jo's smile is so big and bright you'd need an eclipse to dim it. As I pass famed director Klaus Kristofsenn, he grips my shoulder and says, "Bang-up job. Your granddaddy would be proud."

"Thanks," I mutter, not really knowing what I'm thanking him for.

One of Papa Shades's costars comes up and literally blocks our way, jutting his hand out. As I shake, he says, "You are such an inspiration."

It's only when I see my parents that I catch on to why everybody's acting so weird. Turns out, someone cast our interview onto the TV mounted over the dessert table. What started as a smattering of people aimlessly watching as they grazed brownies and sugar cookies quickly became a throng hanging on to my every word. To hear Dad tell it, by the end of the interview, folks were asking him for info on how they could donate to my charity.

Again, Jo fields most of the questions the curious celebrities ask with the poise of a seasoned movie star. And again, I stand there like a bystander in my own story.

20

I SHOULD FEEL ON TOP OF THE WORLD RIGHT NOW. MY social media follow counts are skyrocketing, that cool new *Tiny Tot Superstars* show asked me to be a guest judge, and Weyrich even invited me to come down to detention Friday to talk to some of the "at-risk" kids, to see if I could inspire them to turn their lives around.

All great developments. It just doesn't seem right, though. It seems unearned. On the outside, I'm high-fiving and smiling and autographing forearms with Sharpies, but on the inside, I'm sleepwalking. Wishing for something to wake me up from this fame hangover.

On midday Wednesday, I get just that.

I'm walking down the hallway when I see Jimmy in the Foreign Language wing. I freeze, suffering through a prick of regret for how I spoke to him at the dance. He's ambling my way, looking like he's struggling under the weight of the world with that massive book bag on his shoulders. When he notices me, his eyes flash with . . . irritation? Or anger? Maybe even contempt. Whatever he feels, I can't process it for too long, because he quickly redirects his gaze toward the ground.

"Jimmy, wait!" I say as he walks past. But he doesn't, and I find myself in the unenviable position of chasing down a freshman, practically begging for his attention. Once I've caught up to him, I press a hand to his shoulder, but he shrugs it off. "Jimmy, at the dance, I was just angry. I didn't mean what I said. . . ."

"You meant every word," he mutters, not breaking his stride. We weave past a gaggle of seniors returning to school from their lunch breaks, most still with fast-food cups in their hands. Jimmy picks up his pace, and it's all I can do to stay with him. I end up doing a weird sideways gallop as I try to get him to listen.

"You think I'm just a putz. Well, I'm *not*," he says.

"Jimmy, you're not a putz. You're a *hero*." He flinches at the statement, like he just got tongue-tied. Eventually, he stops and looks dead at me, so I add, "I can prove it." I pull my phone from my pocket and thumb through my video gallery before remembering that, although Mickey showed me her video, she never actually sent it. "I can't right now, but *later*."

Jimmy's look is one of incredulity and anger. He just shakes his head in disbelief and resumes his walk, muttering, "Don't bother."

He pivots and starts walking again, and I'm left standing there. I watch him walk away, guilt riddling my conscience. It's only when Jimmy abruptly freezes that I notice he's glaring at something. When his fists clench, I figure out what that something is.

Chase is walking down the hallway, flanked by two of his lackeys. They're all looking at his phone and laughing as they stride toward us. I whisper, "Don't do anything stupid," to Jimmy, but really to no one, since he's well out of earshot. I hurry up to him, rounding his body to face him. He's got the same look in his eyes he had at the dance. Cold. Ravenous. Vengeful. He sidesteps me and goes directly toward a group of senior girls. Before anyone can react, he grabs Melissa Mitchell's soda and pops off the lid as he heads straight for Chase.

Something knotty and dreadful settles in my stomach. I know if I don't prevent Jimmy's ambush, it'll be a disaster.

It's like instinct takes over. I sprint toward Jimmy. He's barely ten feet away from Chase when the upperclassman and his friends take notice. But they're not even looking at him. All they see is me, hastily wresting the soda from Jimmy, with liquid accidently flying in all directions. Chase never even witnesses the stream of soda coming. He lurches back as it hits his face and drenches his shirt. The two guys beside him recoil at the droplets landing on their sleeves as if they're blood splatters.

First come the gasps from the seniors, loud and low, like they've just witnessed a war crime. This is quickly followed by a chorus of laughter.

Instead of doing the practical and imminently understandable thing and running like hell, I simply stand there. Jimmy stands there, too, mouth open in awe. The cup drops to my feet as I ball up my fists, ready for what neither myself nor any bystander thinks will be anything resembling a fight. It'll be a massacre.

Once the initial shock wears off, you can see the rage building in Chase like the blowing of a steam pipe. He makes this wince-inducing, guttural sound as all his muscles flex, even in places I didn't know a person could have muscles. Both Jimmy and I, sensing what's coming, finally turn to run. Chase lunges as we take off, his feet making a loud screech as he slips to the floor. Consequently, we get a ten-foot head start as Chase tries to steady himself. That's enough—but just barely. He's nearly caught us as we reach the staircase. To avoid his outstretched hands, we jump down the entire flight, almost breaking our ankles as our feet hit the landing. Chase does the same, but with an objectively less fortunate outcome. I can't tell whether it was Chase's desperate reach for our collars that did him in or his shoes, still slicked with Sprite. Jimmy and I are anguished but standing, fists clenched. Chase lies right before us on the floor, semiconscious, a bruise blooming at his cheek from where it smacked the tile. With Chase too dazed to protest, a swashbuckling underdog story is born of faulty assumptions of onlookers who arrive and our own deliberate silence.

Chase stays wobbly for minutes afterward—more than enough time for Jimmy and me to make our quiet retreat from the scene. Once we escape to the shabby awning outside the science hall's double-doored exits, Jimmy stands straight, putting his hands behind his head to catch his breath. I double over and take a deep breath. Then I hold out a fist for Jimmy to dap. It takes a few seconds for him to see it. He stares at my gesture for a moment before walking away.

I get word in fifth period that Chase went home with a probable concussion, so that makes this tough day a bit easier. The lament from Chase's camp is that he just "slipped" since it'd be too embarrassing to admit he got taken out by a freshman. And to be fair, that's the truth. But #WestlakeWhispers was never good on fact-checking.

Jo texts me in seventh period asking about going to the Marin County Fair together this weekend, figuring an appearance there would drive the narrative with the Hallmark Channel crowd, a new demo she wants to make inroads with. Small Town Couple Makes Big Splash, she texts, mimicking a news headline. Then, They'll eat that shit up, punctuated with a winking emoji.

I think about it for a long time, envisioning how great it would look to have Jo by my side for the town to see. But after much consideration, I do what would've been unthinkable just weeks ago. I ignore her. I don't simply wanna be the hot, angsty teen like they have in those fake-dating YA novels. I'm worth more than that. Even if I'm not a hero. Even if I feel like trash.

I head to my locker and shove my textbooks inside.

"Hey, Mr. Big Star."

I look left and flinch at the sight of Kelly Isengard, smiling right at me. It's still a bit jarring whenever I see her now.

She was at the StuGov meeting where Lori Chen propositioned me. I guess everything associated with that incident still freaks me out.

"Hi, Kelly," I say, not able to disguise the discomfort of my greeting.

"Hi," she says, her voice all bubbles and rainbows. "Long time no see. So how are things on your side of the world?"

Hesitantly, I say, "But we're . . . locker neighbors."

"Oh . . . right." She opens her locker, tosses in a single pen, shuts it, and immediately goes back to staring at me. My brows knit in confusion at her chilling smile.

"Is there something you want?" I ask.

"No. Just to say hi. Oh, and that the Council's thinking about you."

I've spent the last few days trying *not* to think about the Council. But since she's brought them up, I venture to ask a question that's been stuck like a sticky note to the back of my brain.

"How's Mason doing? I haven't seen him around."

"Good," she says. "Just got his finger brace off on Tuesday. Still can't type, though."

"Wait, he hurt his finger?" I distinctly remember his *face* getting hit by the muffin. Nowhere near his fingers. Unless . . . Mason's scream from the hallway that night echoes in my mind.

She makes a *tsk* sound. "So unfortunate, getting his hand caught in the elevator right after the meeting. But I did want to bring up another issue."

The way she says it, I'd rather not hear what this other issue is. But I have a nagging sense of dread that if I don't stick around, that I'll somehow end up worse. I squeak out a "Yeah?"

"The interview, with EGTV. Lori requested to view the clip at her Presidential Daily Briefing. While I thought you did fine, Lori has more . . . shall we say 'exacting' expectations. Specifically, she remarked that you looked skittish. Duplicitous. Like you had something to hide." I gulp as Kelly leans in. "*Do you have something to hide?*"

"No," I reply hoarsely. My heart drums at my rib cage.

Kelly's smile returns, her eyebrows going up just a twinge. "Good. Because the Council needs a figurehead who won't wilt under the limelight. These are turbulent times for StuGov, and we want someone who can land this plane, so to speak. So can you? Land the plane?" My nod is stiff, unassured. Kelly doesn't seem to mind in the least. "Awesome," she says. "But please sharpen your public speaking skills. Lori's not big on second chances. 'Kay?"

"Yeah."

She gives my chest a soft pat. I shiver at the touch. "All right. I'm gonna go now. After-school tutoring. Where're you off to?"

"Home."

She squints, studying me. "You look pale. You okay?" I nod, but she looks less than convinced. "Well, try not to overexert yourself. Maybe take the elevator."

She sidesteps past me. When I turn to track her exit, I notice Lovey and Big, who she's walking toward. Their eyes are burning right into my soul. Kelly splits the two like turnstiles, and they follow.

21

I LEAVE SCHOOL DEFLATED. IT'S LIKE ALL MY ACTIONS OVER the past few weeks have been digging a huge grave and the events of this afternoon have just completely buried me. Neither Jimmy nor Theo wants anything to do with me, I may have burned my bridge with Jo, and I now have the nausea-inducing feeling that I'll be under Lori's thumb for the rest of my high school career. So, I reach out to the one person who has a knack for dragging me out of the depths of my emotions.

I text Mickey as I walk into the school's back lot, and her response is almost immediate: Loving Pond in 15?

Sounds good.

I get there first and settle into our usual spot, a grassy knoll along the near bank. It's quiet except for birdsong and wind rustling tree branches. I crane my neck until my eyes are settled on the clouds above. I think about the cloud-naming game we used to play. The recollection brings one of the rare grins I've had today. We've created memories as numerous and splendid as the crackly maple and hickory leaves drifting down from fall branches. Some funny and whimsical. Many others on the more serious side, which I suspect this one will be.

I hear her footsteps before I see her. Wordlessly, she sits down in the grass beside me. I lie down, feeling hundreds of blades edge up against my skin. Mickey's flicking pebbles into the pond, absently looking out as rippled waters return to still.

Another memory comes to mind. A favorite.

"Two Truths and a Lie," I say.

Mickey perks up, laughter bubbling and spilling out from her lips. "Whoa, blast from the past."

"You scared?"

"Hell no. Shoot."

I think long and hard about my three things. She knows me too well to just blurt out some childhood factoids, so I settle my thoughts on the past couple years, the time when we weren't together. Finally, I come up with a perfect three.

"I caught pneumonia this past January, I'm helping Dad fix his carburetor, and I went skinny-dipping at the pond with JoAnn Wellsbury this summer."

"Easy, JoAnn Wellsbury."

"Why?"

"Because JoAnn's a germaphobe."

"The pond isn't that dirty," I protest. "And you're wrong. That one's true."

"So what was your lie?" she asks.

"Carburetor. Your turn."

Her eyes travel skyward as she brings a finger to her jawline.

I catch myself soaking in her features and have to force a blink to keep from gawking. She doesn't notice, thankfully.

"Okay," she says. "I thought I was gonna die in that fire. I knew we'd eventually make up. And ever since Jo, I can't think about butterscotch ice cream without laughing anymore."

I shake my head. "I hate you for that last one."

"But also, you love me," she quips.

"Okay, so it's either one or two." The statements rattle around in my mind. I trade glances between her and the sky above, with neither giving up their secrets. "Okay, I'm gonna go with two as the lie."

She says nothing, neither confirming nor denying, but something about the way her smile somehow changes from airy to pensive without moving tells me I'm wrong. Not only that. I'm wrong in a way that's dispiriting, too. She'd always had hope for us.

"One was the lie, actually."

"Oh."

She turns to me, eyes drifting cloudlike until they meet mine. "You never thought we'd make up?" she asks.

I can't say I did. When friendships that close end, it's almost like you have to bury them. Because the thought of holding on to a hope that may never come true would be too unbearable. But I don't say that to her. I simply say, "Anything can happen, I suppose." I listen as squirrels walk on branches somewhere up above. It's her lie that eventually draws me back. Back to the fire. The danger. The escape.

"You ever think about that day in the store?" I ask Mickey. "Like, really think about how close we came to almost not—how close that guy came to dying?"

"I try not to," she says. I listen as birds call above. Another pebble plunks the water's surface.

"I'm just saying, if you weren't in there, doing what you did, this isn't a feel-good story."

She shrugs. "I don't think you're allowed many feel-good stories in this life. Best to soak them up while you can."

Something about her tone makes me think she's not just talking about the fire at the store. I think back to why we were there in the first place. Not the cat-ate-my-goldfish obvious reason. But the *less* obvious precursor. Mickey bought the original fish to honor her mother. This documentary we're doing is a way to do the same.

I don't think you're allowed many feel-good stories in this life.

I wonder how many feel-good stories these past few years have been drowned out by the sadness of a loved one's death. I wonder how many days Mickey actually *feels good*. About the ways things are. About life in general. Or even when she does, does she feel guilty or lonely experiencing that without the woman who was her closest confidante?

"Do you think your mom saw you save that guy's life?" I ask.

"I'm sure she's got better things to do than watch me."

"Like what?"

She shrugs. "Iron Jesus's tunic, I don't know. Wait, that

sounds kinda sexist." She rethinks it and says, "Maybe just a stroll around Eden."

My gaze toward her is sheathed in mischief. "You think she'd rather chill in paradise than watch you almost die of smoke inhalation?"

"Well, when you put it that way . . ."

Mickey throws one last rock into the pond before lying down right next to me. We both look skyward. We spend a few minutes just lying there, our bodies grafted onto the scenery as our minds untether like lost balloons. It's lovely here, with her, thinking about nothing and everything.

An ant crawls up her white shirt and veers left for her midriff. I brush it away. She bends from me, thinking I'm poking her like I always used to.

"I think both your mom and my grandpa were watching," I say. "Rooting for us."

Offhandedly, she says, "Can't imagine Mr. H wanting to watch a show he wasn't the star of."

I can't help but cut my eyes at her, wondering why she refuses to let the past go. "Mickey, was Grandpa that bad?" Her nod is barely perceptible in my periphery, but it's there. "Then why all the awards?" I ask, almost plaintively. "Why the accolades? Why do people think he's the best man this town has ever seen?" I say, wanting to believe it. The aching desperation in my tone lingers well after the words are spoken. I have to believe I've been idolizing someone with a legacy beyond bad memories and ill feelings. Someone who didn't walk tall all his life without giving a thought to look back at all the people he stomped over.

Mickey turns toward me, wrapping an arm around my torso and waist. In a warm, bracing way. Her words are quiet, soft, respectful of the dead. "He was a good actor. That's what they do. But that didn't make him a good person."

The sadness pushes up my throat as I finally take stock of what I didn't want to believe. Who my grandpa really was. It feels like I'm having a funeral for a person who only existed in my own mind. "Is that why you didn't want to be at the premiere?"

"You could say that."

"But you loved my grandfather for the longest time. You enjoyed his movies, his visits. Why not enjoy his final farewell?"

Mickey's eyes lilt downward. I can tell she's thinking long and hard about what she'll say next. Finally, she comes out with it: "Because it should've been my mom's."

Her words gut-punch me. Various conversations and recollections over the past few days have dragged me into the reality where Grandpa wasn't one of the best of us. But an out-and-out thief? No way. But why would Mickey lie? A month ago, I could manufacture a million reasons. But now? Absolutely none. I shift my body to face her.

"Four years ago," I say, "they were friends." Mickey nods. "They bonded over film," I continue hesitantly, as if each new clause were a puzzle piece. Her eyebrows lift in acknowledgment as I put it all together. Very quietly, I add, "And—what?

Did your *mom* tell him about the marsh people? Was it her idea to film them?"

She nods. She never speaks to affirm what we both now know, as if allowing me the space to process my grief in silence.

"Is there proof of this?" I ask. The question is instinctual, but guilt still coils around me from the sheer fact that I asked.

"Pitch proposals. Draft production schedules. Dated email correspondence. But do you really need all that?"

She's right. I don't need those things. I don't need anything, really, to believe it's perfectly within Papa Shades's capacity to have stolen someone else's idea. I don't need anything to believe my best friend.

My heart tears apart for Mickey and Serena at that moment. To live for years knowing someone else would get the accolades for something you thought of. To lack both the means and resources to do something about it.

"Mickey, I . . . I honestly didn't know he was like that."

She eyes me skeptically for a moment, but her demeanor softens as a realization hits her.

"You don't know what happened that day in the street when Papa Shades was training you, do you?" she asks.

I nod, confused. "I do remember."

"Not all of it. Your dad mentioned you going unconscious."

"Because it was too hot," I respond. I replay the scene. The way he had his boot on my back to force me to do better push-ups. How I couldn't take it in the end.

She shakes her head. Her next words shatter the fiction

I'd made Papa Shades out to be. "You blacked out because he *stomped* you. He raised his boot and stomped down so hard that your head hit the asphalt."

I stare out at the pond, my stomach knotting as she tells me what she witnessed in those precious seconds I was out. How she saw Grandpa's body rocket toward the asphalt as Dad pushed him off me, the man's famed sunglasses breaking against his face. How Dad then yanked me up, basically flinging me to the curb. The shock she felt at hearing my grandfather's shoulder crunch when it hit the road, just as the speeding SUV passed between me and him, leaving the angry whine of a car horn in its wake.

When she finishes recounting, I shake my head as an intense sadness wells up in me. "I'm so sorry," I croak out.

"About what?"

"About everything," I say.

She waves my apology away. "Why? You didn't do it." But it's not enough for me. I feel the need to atone somehow because, up until a few weeks ago, I'd have chosen my version of the story—where he was just trying to get me to become a better soccer player—over hers and Mrs. Kyle's a hundred times out of a hundred.

"What can I do, Mickey?" I ask. "How can I make this right?"

She shakes her head. "You can't. Their story is done. But . . . I suppose you can with ours."

The implication clicks into place like a last puzzle piece. I could atone by coming clean. By relinquishing the credit I stole. It hits me that I'm doing the same thing Papa Shades did to Mrs. Kyle. If I continue living and profiting from what I know to be a lie, I'm no better than him. And honestly, I might be worse, because I've been taking advantage of those people closest to me.

But could it be that simple? Could I really just tell the truth? Could I just go back to being regular old Lionel?

Weirdly enough, it's Mickey who has to console me. And she does it with a question and then a story. Her arm moves down to my hand, coupling it with hers. They fit together like that's where they were always meant to be.

"Did I ever tell you about the time Mr. Honeycutt *was* a hero?" she asks.

I take a brief pause from my lamenting and eye her skeptically. "What?"

I can see the beginnings of a smile play across her face. "Yeah. He saved me from drowning in the pond. When we were, like, eight or something. That summer."

"And I wasn't there?" Mickey and I were thick as thieves back then. Did everything together. It doesn't make sense that I'd have no recollection of this.

"You were but your mom called you back. Said you forgot to clean your room. I remember you getting all huffy about it, stomping away."

"But why would he even be out there if I wasn't?" Mickey's eyelids pinch. Seriousness and skepticism color her eyes, as if she's not sure I can handle what she's about to say.

"He wasn't, actually. At least not initially. I was dangling out on that big oak limb that juts out over the water."

"On the far side?" I ask, surprised. That was a no-go zone for even the most daring kids. There was a steep underwater ridge there we called Dead Man's Drop.

Mickey nods. "I guess I went out too far, because suddenly I just heard this *crack* and then like a millisecond later my head was underwater." *Jesus.* I wince at the visual. I can't imagine what it must've been like being alone out there in such a dire situation. "I got all panicky and couldn't get my bearings. The most salient things I remember were my arms burning as I flailed, and the water starting to rush up my nostrils. And then hearing a splash. It was him jumping in the water, pulling me out onto the bank."

I flash back to one of my favorite movies of Grandpa's, a Cold War Soviet submarine spy thriller titled *The Boys of Bering Strait.* He told me once that the high-stakes water rescue was one of the most dangerous stunts he'd ever done. Apparently, something went wrong during the stunt. A harness broke, causing him to slip from atop the submarine hull and into the freezing seas below. He barely made it out alive and had an acute fear of water ever since. To just up and run toward danger after a trauma like that would really test a person's mettle.

The memory is like throwing kindling on the dying embers of a fire. Where there was once nothing, now there's something. Hope. Confidence, even, that Grandpa might yet have some redeeming qualities. That the legend I've made him out to be exists. That the elementary-age kid who walked the red carpet his first time for the *Bering Strait* premiere actually walked with a bona fide hero.

Wait.

I turn toward Mickey, shaking my head. "That can't be right," I say. "I was nine when that movie came out."

Mickey breaks her gaze to look at me. "Why can't it? What movie? What are you talking about?"

"He was away off the coast of Siberia all summer filming the previous year," I explain. "When I was eight. He couldn't have been at the pond."

Slowly, her head shakes. "I . . . wasn't talking about your grandpa," she says. "I was talking about your father."

It's like a synapse misfires in my brain, because it takes ten full seconds for her sentence to fully compute.

My dad?

As if by instinct, I say, "Why did I never hear about this?"

"I made him promise not to tell," Mickey quickly adds. "I was afraid my dad would never let me go back if he knew. And I guess I was a little embarrassed. I was surprised your dad went along with it. But he said he knew what it was like to get on a parent's bad side."

Mickey's revelation grips me like a vise, squeezing every bit of regret to the surface. My face flushes, and my eyes burn. My dad. The person I'd so long ago cast as the antagonist in my story turns out to be the hero.

I get up and slip off my shoes. I quickly step down to the sandy patch that stands in for a beach. I'm trying to hide the tears, but my sniffles give it away. I hear the crickets call. Smell smoke in the distance. Someone burning fall leaves. Mickey gets up behind me. I stiffen as a hand rounds my shoulder.

Her words are a whisper: "The real hero isn't six feet under. He's two doors down."

Her hand slips from me with the ease of an idle thought. She then goes toward a large maple at the water's edge. She puts a foot to the trunk and pulls hard at a thick branch above her, testing out the sturdiness for a climb. She scales the tree. I watch for a while until she invites me.

I join, and it's nice. In that moment, it's like I can reach out through the grieving and sadness and grasp a sense of childhood joy like it's a firefly in the evening. The kind of joy that comes around as often as comets or eclipses once you reach a certain age. This feeling I've experienced with Mickey so many times past. I look at her, smiling, wondering if she's feeling it, too.

22

IN MANY RESPECTS, I SEE THE MARIN COUNTY FAIR IN
much the same way as Grandpa's haters saw him: loud, tacky,
and at times completely overwhelming. It's a wonder that I
spent my childhood adoring Papa Shades but hating the fair. I
can remember coming here throughout my younger years even
though I'd get motion sickness by simply walking the promenade. Too much movement. Way too much noise. The only
reason I'd ever go was so Mickey would have someone to go on
rides with. Someone to split funnel cakes and cotton candy and
whatever new deep-fried malformation vendors could come up
with year after year.

Ironically, tonight, the only reason *Mickey* is going is
because of me.

Well, me and Theo.

She's dragging herself out of the house to support us in our
big moments. Theo's performing with the Norse Club. This
is my chance to apologize and hopefully repair our friendship.
Mickey stated she wanted to be there not only to watch him, but

to make sure I didn't fuck things up.

And later tonight, I'm also in line to receive the town's Order of the Eagle Award, as both a recognition of my courage under fire and a fitting bookend to my grandfather's life. Decades back, he won the award for his inspiring performance in the epic war film *Saving Lieutenant Jamal*. It was total Oscar bait. Scored by Hans Zimmer, most of the film shot was in that artsy, low-key lighting that looks almost black and white. Action-packed, but in a cerebral, thinking-man's way. Grandpa said it could appeal to "both the jocks *and* the nerds—like you."

In the end, he got a Best Actor nod. No trophy, though. Perpetually complained about the snub.

Everybody thinks it's pretty cool that I'm being given this award for saving that guy and the animals at the pet store. They see it as a full-circle sort of thing. I thought it'd be great, too, until I learned I didn't deserve it.

To this day, it's still only Mickey, Jo, Jimmy, and me who know the truth. I've been too ashamed to tell my parents. My mood swings from hopeful to dire as competing thoughts of consequences swirl in my mind. Will the school think I'm a fraud? Will social media make me a pariah? Whatever happens, it feels like once word gets out, my life will change drastically, and not for the better.

Mickey and I walk toward the canopied stage near the haunted house at the end of the main drag. There's a crowd already there for some country singing act. I'm scheduled to go up at 8 p.m., but the city officials told me to be here by 7:15.

It's 7:13 now. Mayor Harvey Kirk, a heavyset guy in a suit who looks every bit the part of a used car salesman, doesn't notice us as we drift into a clearing of dirt and gravel. He's at the side of the stage talking in an annoyed tone to two roadies about the lights. Suddenly, his head turns, as if set off by a motion detector. He sees me and waves, beckoning me over. I respond in the dodgiest way possible—by turning and walking the opposite way, nerves kicking in. Mickey catches up to me a few steps down the main drag.

Across the walkway I spot Jordy Walston, Theo's boyfriend. He's holding a cone of blue cotton candy as big as his head. When he notices us, he smiles, his hand coming up halfway for a wave before stopping midair. The smile fades, like it's just clicked for him that our fight isn't some abstraction but a real thing, with real sides and real boundaries. Theo enters my field of vision, kissing Jordy's cheek, plucking a piece of cotton candy as he turns to see what his boyfriend sees. When his eyes catch us, he looks away, like he can't bear to see me.

Just about every time Grandpa came to visit, he'd make some utterance about Theo, often in the context of asking if I'd still hung out with him. When I'd say yes, Papa Shades would always smirk and make some joke about him being "soft." I was always so confused about that. When I was young, I never really associated the word with much more than the feel of fabrics. But even as I grew older and learned its connotation, the confusion never left. Theo was the opposite of "soft," as Grandpa meant it. He was the toughest kid I knew. He stuck up for me,

263

for Mickey, and for himself when we were nothing more than middle school pinballs for the popular kids to knock around. He grew up as a gay Black boy in a small southern town. He *existed* in a world full of Papa Shades.

No doubt Grandpa would feel justified in his assumptions. But he'd be wrong. And I guess that's what makes me angry. The way Grandpa felt about Theo was absolutely terrible. Only jerks think that way. But I guess that's what Papa Shades was.

We watch as Theo and Jordy walk away. Once they round a corner past the dunk tank, I drift a few paces from Mickey, wanting to sulk on my own. I go to a makeshift sitting area near the sno-cone stand and drop down in a chair, elbows to knees, chin rested in palms. I stare out at the flashing lights and excited pedestrians for a long time, but it's all just a blur.

Eventually, Mickey comes and sits next to me, her hand touching my thigh. I let the moment play itself out before saying anything. Finally, she speaks: "You know *Saving Lieutenant Jamal* was one of my mom's all-time favorite movies."

"Seriously?"

"Seriously." I see her nod in my periphery. "During snow days when Mom and I would be stuck at home, she'd force me to curl up on the couch with her while she streamed it. I'd always doze after the first hour, but it was . . . nice. Just being with her. Like, just totally chill." I shift my head to see more of her. The soft smile she wears like a comfy sweater. The sad, daydreamy look in her eyes. The sparkles of water at the corners. She sniffles and presses her lips into a thin line. She adds,

"We can get great things from not-great people, you know."

I look out at the promenade without actually seeing much of anything.

Great things from not-great people. To me, that seems the perfect distillation of my grandfather. Very good, inspiring even, in one outsized way, while monstrously deficient in just about every other. I can appreciate the good while acknowledging the bad. I think of the Shade Wall, my shrine to him. The way I never actually saw Papa Shades beyond the 2D mythical figures on posters taped up in my room. The way Mickey and Dad made me see the truth.

I once heard someone say you should never meet your heroes. I don't like that advice. Meet them. Love them. Hell, share a surname with them. Just be real about who they actually are. That's what I resolve to do, somehow years late but not a moment too soon.

My thoughts settle on the one person who I've had a simmering resentment for during the past few years. My dad, the nerdy scientist who wouldn't know swagger if it stomped across the toes of his Sperrys. My dad, the person who saved one of my best friends' lives. The man whose extraordinary act of bravery was never put to film or honored at any awards ceremony.

My eyes meet Mickey's. My words are incredulous and near breathless. "My dad. I can't believe he actually saved your life."

"Not all heroes wear capes," Mickey quietly mutters. "Some wear glasses and ill-fitting sweatpants."

For the first time since I can remember, I don't want to be

just like Papa Shades. In fact, I want to be the opposite. Kind, compassionate, loyal to those who've always stuck around. And I want to be those things to the girl right next to me, who's somehow *still* here after all the times I've ignored her. Shoved her to the side in favor of something as fleeting and fickle as popularity or the interest of a longtime crush.

I want to be those things for Theo, the one constant source of unending hype and positivity throughout my formative years. The person who relied on me for one big thing this year. A thing that I cast away once I saw a better opportunity.

My hand slides down my thigh until it finds Mickey's hand. She flinches, caught off guard, but her hand doesn't recoil. Quite the opposite—it curls into mine as if fitting into a glove.

"I truly am sorry for the way I've treated you. For these last several years, but especially the last couple months." In true Mickey fashion, she tries to make light of my apology. I hold her hand tighter. "I'm serious. I know I don't deserve it, but I'd like another chance at a real friendship."

She angles her body toward mine. "That's what we've been doing, isn't it?"

"Yeah, but this needed to be said." I take her other hand. "And I also want to say something else."

Mickey opens her mouth to speak. It's as if she's instinctually loaded another funny reply and is ready to fire away. But whatever words she was about to speak remain unsaid. She simply closes her mouth, clears her throat, and nods. The vulnerability so often shielded by her dry wit is present and perceptible. "And that is?" she says, her voice noticeably higher than usual.

"I wanted to ask if we could be more than friends."

At first, I don't think she's heard me, because she takes an impossibly long time to answer. Our breaths cloud at the lips as we face each other in complete, desperate silence. At least it's desperate for me. She seems implausibly content just existing in the moment, wrestling with a thought she can't yet say. Eventually, she answers.

"Not right now. And I'm sorry for that." I nod, but my pleading look must give away my confusion, because she explains: "As much as I would like to, I need to trust you won't let me fall by the wayside again."

It aches to hear this, but I know it's true. I've given her little reason to trust me with her heart. I'll have to earn that in time. We spend the next few minutes talking about Theo, how I'll have to apologize to him, and how it'll probably be a lot harder than it was with Mickey. Sitting here with her, I'm reminded of how our conversations would always be as easy and smooth as water running downhill. Fame was never easy. This is. Honestly, I like this better.

Finally, we get up and make our way to the row of fair games, where I begin a Herculean—but in a way easy—task of winning her over. I figure since I hooped in middle school, the best place to start would be the ball-toss booth. After spending twenty dollars on four tries, I manage to win one of those big stuffed rabbits they always have. While losing my last two weeks' allowance stings, seeing the smile on her face when I hand her the prize is more than worth it.

I also drop some more money and win her one of those *Star Wars*–esque lightsabers from the shooting gallery, and we swing by the haunted house just for kicks. I can't help but revel in the fact that even though I hate the fair, I like being here with her. It's like we're in an orbit all our own, divorced from the cacophony of loud vendors and tinny fair music. There's only one thing bothering me: accepting the award, and the speech I have to make in front of the town. Mickey somehow senses that and takes my hand. Both our hands warm quickly, as if we're making our own heat. Soon enough, my nerves settle. She's good like that. We just work together. Always been that way. It's a shame it took me this long to realize.

Mickey knows that the moment I step onstage to confess my fraud to the world, all hell will break loose, so she suggests we take some photographs on the Ferris wheel as sort of a symbolic culmination of my journey—taking the ups and the downs in stride.

When we get to the operating booth, the conductor barely even acknowledges our existence. He's too busy texting. "No spitting or throwing things at any point during the ride. Please stay in your seats. Hands inside the ride at all times. Weight limit four hundred pounds," he says without looking up. My eyes survey the ride. There's nobody else on it.

I notice a stretch of caution tape tied to a platform pillar, fluttering with the chilly night air. "What's with that?"

The operator stops texting and glances over his shoulder.

Shrugging, he says, "Idiot kids broke in last night, graffitied the side. Tried to ride the damn thing. Had to shut it down and do a spot check."

"And you're sure it's safe?" Mickey asks.

"Happens more than you think," he answers, as if it were more nuisance than felony.

Surprisingly, the operator won't allow Mickey and me and the giant stuffed rabbit in one seat. And the platform is too dirty and damp for the bunny, so reluctantly we decide to sit in adjacent seats. She gets in first, with the stuffed rabbit and lightsaber beside her. I get on the next one.

It's the kind of ride with those facing bucket seats, so we'll see each other. The guy secures us with those ill-fitting metal latch belts. My stomach drops when we go up, and I feel squeamish at the top. While I don't have a phobia of heights, I'm not a fan.

Cresting the top for the fourth time, I get comfortable enough to actually enjoy the view. I spot the promenade to my left, lit up like Westlake's own Vegas Strip. Behind me, people scream as they swirl and dip on the cluster of random thrill rides. And ahead of me is Mickey, first brushing her windblown hair back as she looks to the side, and then smiling shyly as she notices me noticing her. I can't stop staring because, of all the views at the fair, I have the absolute best.

Finally, Mickey shouts, "What are you looking at?"

I point to my lips. "Something in your teeth."

The smile that had been edging into her cheeks and eyes

disappears, and she shoots me a death stare. She can't hold it, though. She laughs weakly, trying to hide the fact that she's back to smiling.

As we descend again, she crosses her arms and says, "Soooo cold."

I spread mine. "I'm feeling great!" And I am. I'm not with her right now, but I'm *near* her. And that's enough.

"Show-off," she jeers.

"What? Just a little cold weather. Nice night. Beautiful sights. What more could a girl want?"

"A good fucking picture!" she shouts. I get my phone out and take several as she smiles wide, makes air kisses and even mimics that *Titanic* boat pose.

Suddenly, I jerk forward as the Ferris wheel lurches to a stop. Metal joints creak as my bucket swings. A loud snap sounds out ahead of me, and my eyes immediately find Mickey's. She's unblinking, still, her seat at a gentle sway.

"What was that?" she asks.

Glancing down, I see the operator. His back is turned, his phone up to his ear. Another snap pierces the lull. A sense of dread courses through me as metal screeches against metal. Then one of the bolts attaching her seat to the outer rim pops. I see it fly off. The right side of her bucket slumps. Her safety bar pops free, and she spills from the seat.

A sharp scream follows the breaking of another cable. The stuffed animal and lightsaber fall. I look over, and Mickey's seat is slanted at a severe angle. She's huddled in the lower corner, held there more by gravity than fear. The seat sways. I spot the problem. A cable rounding the wheel is frayed to the point that it's literally hanging by threads.

It's like my brain turns off at that moment because, without thinking, I'm jerking at my own safety bar. Once I'm free, I grab on to the outer rim and pull myself out of my own seat. Mickey looks hysterical as I crawl up the narrow arc. I'm several feet out before I regain my good sense. Dizziness hits me as I glance down. Then body-crippling horror sets in as I realize this fall would be the death of me.

The operator is furiously pulling at a latch the size of a toilet plunger. The wheel jerks, nearly knocking me from the steel cable. "Damn thing is busted!" the guy yells.

Beyond him, I can see a crowd gathering, watching a disaster dawning right before their eyes. Several have phones out, but instead of scrambling for help, they're . . . taking video? Like it's fucking reality TV.

Why aren't they helping?!

I zero in on one person who's pushing his way from the back of the crowd. My heart drops as Jimmy bursts forth, launching himself onto the chassis of the ride. *What the hell is he doing?*

"Call for help!" I yell, but he's not listening. He just starts scaling the spoke like a damn rock climber. "What are you doing?!" I yell. He ignores me again.

Jesus Christ. This is a disaster. I give him twenty seconds before he's a splatter of blood and guts. I close my eyes and try to concentrate. *Think, Lionel, think.* If I don't save Mickey before Jimmy gets too high up, it might be curtains for all of us.

I open my eyes again and start inching my way forward, fear turning my stomach as I see what's below. Solid ground, concrete, and wide-eyed onlookers itching for a spectacle. I see kids pointing, flashes from phones. They look enthralled, as if this high drama is concocted for their pleasure.

Mickey gathers her voice just long enough to shout, "Dude, they'll rotate the wheel. Don't be a hero!"

"Kinda late for that," I say. I know it's a long shot, but if I could just reach her, I can pull her onto the one intact cable before the seat completely falls.

I hear Jimmy's labored breathing as he reaches the wheel's center spindle. He bends over the thick metal axle to catch his breath. God, he won't make it.

"Go back down!" I yell.

He looks up, and I can see the fatigue in his eyes, and how his forehead gleams under the harsh light. He shakes his head and huffs, "I'm gonna save her."

He can't, though. He's absolutely wiped. His face is twitching, and the muscles in his scrawny little arms strain with even the slightest movement. *Even if he does reach Mickey, what's he gonna do?* It's right then that I get what this is about. Jimmy feels he has to make his mark. To show the world he can be a savior.

Mickey screams as the Ferris wheel lurches forward. Her metal restraint bangs against the rim. I take a deep breath, hardening my resolve. Every inch of progress is slow, but I can't quit. If I can get *to* that bucket, I can get her *out* of it. If not, well . . . I don't even want to think about what could happen.

"Jimmy, stop!" I shout.

He grits out, "I gotta save her!"

"No you don't, Jimmy! I was wrong, okay? I shouldn't have treated you the way I did. I exploited your heroism because I could." His muscles relax just a bit, and he gets this weird, cross look on his face. But he says nothing, so I continue: "I could've told the world you and Mickey were the real heroes weeks ago, but I didn't. I think, deep down, I just wanted to be larger than life, like my gra—"

"Uh, a little help here!" Jimmy and I both look at Mickey. "Sorry to break up the therapy sesh, but let's prioritize, please!"

She screams again as the bucket dips down farther, now nearly vertical. Jimmy and I restart our mad scramble toward her.

An idea comes to me. I urge Jimmy to unfasten his belt. He does, wrapping one end around his wrist and the other around the spoke that he's climbing at my direction. As he does this, I see a spark of recognition in his eyes.

Only the real fans would know about Papa Shades's thriller *Terror at Crunkleton Tower.* Done early in his career, it had a low budget and nonexistent marketing. Reviews were terrible, with one stating that the scaffolding fight scene was "so cheesy that Honeycutt should quit acting and start a dairy farm." Ironically, from the ashes of mediocrity came a movie with a cult following.

When Jimmy begins swinging back and forth like a

pendulum, I start to doubt whether the Double Hoodflip would ever work in real life. It was *barely* believable on film. But as Jimmy's eyes turn cold as steel, I get the sense that something amazing is about to happen. At the last swing, he has enough momentum to propel himself upward to hook a foot around the bucket seat's crossbar. From there he's able to give the belt to Mickey, a fail-safe in case the bucket falls.

Slowly and methodically, I make my way to them and carefully latch onto Mickey's bucket. Mickey turtles up as I find my footing in a tight space near where she's sitting. I grab the cable as Jimmy steadies himself, too, and suddenly we're all bundled close, contorted to fit into an impossibly close space, like some high elevation game of Twister.

"I think we're good," I huff. "Now, let's wait here a sec. I gotta catch my breath."

Jimmy and I grin goofily at each other. Mickey's expression, however, is scrunched up in concentration. "You guys hear a noise?" she asks.

I pause and listen. In fact, I do. Below us, but distinct from the crowd. I look and see the ride operator, who's frantically waving to get our attention. We stare down, our looks quizzical. The operator takes a deep breath and belts out, "Wait!"

We look at each other, confused. Mickey even gives off a half-hearted laugh, trailed by "I mean, what else are we gonna do, am I right?"

The operator shouts it again even though we haven't moved an inch. Seconds pass in bemused silence. Finally, it's Mickey who solves the puzzle. Her nose scrunches as she asks, "You think he means '*weight*,' like how much we weigh?"

I point excitedly, like I've just guessed a word in charades. "Oh, like weight limit."

Mickey's face turns ashen. The bucket creaks, and suddenly I'm no longer excited.

Mickey screams as the left side of our life raft collapses, leaving the seat swinging. I'm left without a foothold, and the broken cable's snapback lashes Jimmy's shoulder. But Mickey gets the worst of it by far. The belt's slipped from her hands, and she's spilled out of the bucket like water from a pitcher, holding on with just her fingertips, her legs twisting in the air.

As I torque my body to regain footing, I hear another snap, this time from above. A second cable is starting to fray. If something doesn't change in seconds, we're all dead. Jimmy crouches, one of his hands clutching his opposite shoulder as the other reaches down to grab Mickey's wrist. I touch Jimmy's good shoulder.

"But we can save her," he insists.

"You've gotta save yourself, Jimmy." He opens his mouth to protest, but nothing comes. Two more snaps sound out from above. "Go. Now," I say firmly.

Reluctantly, he nods. It's just a short, labored climb for him to the stabler metal rim. Tension from the cable eases. Less weight equals more time. By bowing out, Jimmy may have just saved us all.

I hold the side as I crouch, trying my best not to reciprocate

Mickey's frightened look. Even though I'm a wreck inside, my face is steady, as are my words: "I got you."

I hook one arm around a spoke and grab her wrist as her fingers slip from the metal. The jolt of her body weight almost sends me down. But I soon figure out this isn't the hardest part. I can use one arm to hold her, but I'll need two to actually pull her to safety. And that's what I do. Carefully, I unhook my second arm from the spoke and double up my grip. And I pull like hell. Like she's the only person in the world who matters right now. Because she is.

Every muscle surges with adrenaline as I strain to lift her. Somehow, amid all the chaos and exhaustion and panic, she rises. First her elbows, then her torso slinking onto the seat, and finally her knees. When I finally let go, she's right on top of me, smashed against me and breathless.

I wish I could've done something sentimental at that moment, but all I can think about is the fact that I can't breathe.

"Could you please get off me?" I mutter. "Your chest is suffocating me."

In between ragged breaths, she says, "Congrats, pal, you're living the dream."

23

MICKEY AND I ARE SITTING TOGETHER ON A BENCH, WITH hordes of firemen milling about around us. We are huddled together, shivering from shock as much as the cold, with blankets draped over our shoulders. Just like at the pet store. It's one of those back-where-you-started moments so common as to be cliché by now, but somehow still weirdly satisfying for those blockbuster romance flicks. We started here. We end here.

But the good thing for me is that we actually *won't* end here. The credits to our story won't roll for a very long time, I hope.

"Lionel!"

I'm startled by the yell from behind. I turn and see Mom and Dad rushing toward me, dirt kicking up in their wake. Before I can even fully stand, they've swallowed me in an embrace. I feel the warmth of tears at my cheeks. But what surprises me the most is that *both* are crying. Mom hugs me the hardest and the longest because that's what moms do. But it's Dad whose eyes stay locked on me as my mom checks in on Mickey. Dad stares at me like I'm a distant mountain or a close friend returning from war. Something to be marveled, something worth remembering. I stare, too, because for the first time ever, I see him. I truly *see* him for the man he is, not the one I always thought he should be. That thought fills me with a chest-tightening, tear-inducing, all-consuming shame.

"I'm so sorry," I say. "I didn't save that guy. Mickey and my friend Jimmy did. And even after I found out the truth, I still lied—"

Dad shushes me, holding me close again, his body a buffer against the noisy fair buzz, nosy onlookers, and the cold world. He takes an old tissue from his pocket and wipes my tears away. He says, "It's okay," two words so simple yet powerful enough to set off a bomb in my heart.

There are no solemn quotes so often used to fill the climactic moments in Papa Shades's movies. All Dad gives is his unconditional love and support. It's funny how neither Papa Shades nor the characters he played knew what I've just figured out and what Dad must've known all along. That this is more than enough.

I suppose it's fitting, if somewhat morbidly ironic, that Theo's Norse group does a sea shanty a cappella version of "Love Will Keep Us Alive" by the Eagles as their outro. While others are swaying and dancing, Mickey and I are standing together at the side of the stage, trying but failing to keep straight faces. Our hands haven't separated since we left that ride, and that would continue to be the case if I didn't have to make this speech. I still don't know what to say, but at least I consider myself worthy of the moment. I'm a true hero now. I saved someone. Just like Mickey. Just like Jimmy.

I look back at Jimmy. He's behind us, his shoulder in a sling. He's tucked into the shadow of the stage scaffolding like a forgotten toy stashed in a closet. He refused an ambulance ride to the hospital, saying he couldn't miss my speech. Minutes ago, as people were lining up to congratulate me and ask me how exactly I'd done it again, I caught a glimpse of him off to the side. Smiling, trying to look happier than he was. Now he's not even trying anymore. His feet kick at gravel. His eyes wander. The air, the ground, anywhere but the places that would allow others to see the hurt in them.

I think about how amazing it is that he's a hero twice over, even if he's just a regular kid to everyone. Our spectacle was obscured enough that only us three know the true story. From what I gather from listening to the crowd, a narrative has formed that has Jimmy climbing the Ferris wheel like a crazed lunatic, breaking the cable as he tried to get onto the seat, and leaving the mess to Mickey and me as he scurried out at the end. In this story, Mickey and I are the triumphant party. He's the incompetent klutz clamoring for a shot at fame.

His fierce climb against all odds. His life-saving initial grip on Mickey. His pivotal decision to save us all by *not* being the hero. Nobody saw it, so to them it didn't happen.

They also didn't see everything that came before. The toilet dunks courtesy of Chase. The shelf-lifting heroics credited to someone else. The countless times he was overlooked.

The song ends, and the mayor introduces me as if he were announcing a heavyweight contender at a championship boxing match. By now, the entire fair has seen or heard of the miracle at the Ferris wheel, so there's a massive crowd throttled into a small area along the promenade and in front of the stage. Everybody's curious about what I have to say.

The mayor hands me the Order of the Eagle Award as I step onto the platform. I hold it up to raucous applause as he adjusts the microphone to my height. He leaves as the chatter subsides, and suddenly it's just me up there. Nothing written, nothing in mind. Thousands of eyes on me. Even though they don't know me, I can tell pride swells in most of them at the mere sight of me. Supposedly, I represent the best of what this town has to offer. I'm exactly who they saw in my grandfather.

I inch closer to the microphone, the cloud of my breath forming at my lips as I open them to speak. I can hear my own breathing. The nerves creep into my extremities. But then I see movement at the front of the crowd. Mickey and Jimmy squeezing toward the center. Stopping only when they're next to Dad.

He's smiling the same smile I've seen all my years. It's the same one I saw when I hit my first triple in Little League, and the same one when he consoled me after I fell off my bike the first time and skinned my knee. That smile predates most of my other memories of him.

I clear my throat first, and then there's silence, save for the fair-ride jingles in the distance. But even that fades away as I say my first words.

"I've learned a lot these past few weeks. I've learned that life is short," I say to expectant nods. "I've learned that kitty litter is flammable." People burst out laughing at that, as if it were a scripted joke instead of the would-be catalyst for my shortened life. I wait for the laughter to die out before I begin again with what I really want to say: "Most important, I've learned how *not* to be a hero."

I can see expressions changing in the crowd. The pleasant looks dissipating, consumed by more thoughtful countenances. I glance toward the Ferris wheel, still crawling with firefighters and first responders like ants near dropped food. Still wrapped in caution tape like a Christmas gift. This is where I saved someone. *Actually saved* someone. But it honestly doesn't feel that way.

I recenter my gaze on the crowd. "You know, everybody likes to think my grandfather was some great guy who lived his days surviving thrilling adventures and tackling the most dangerous feats known to mankind. But he wasn't," I say, my head shaking. I dry-gulp before saying something that part of me has always known but never wanted to admit. "In reality, he was a bitter, weak old coward who smiled brightly for the cameras but treated those closest to him like crap." As expected, cynical expressions and curt whispers follow. Suddenly, it's like the truth wants to spill out of me, the weightlessness of confession crashing down and washing out the risk of embarrassment.

Anger pushes out my words as I say, "You know the documentary? His prestige project? Well, he stole that idea from my best friend's mother. That's the kind of guy he was."

I point to myself. "And that's the kind of guy I am," I say. The crowd blurs as tears form in my eyes. Despite that fact, I still find Mickey. She's frowning, shaking her head no, as if she's willing me to stop. I can't, though. Everybody needs to know about my fraudulent legacy. "I'm *not* a hero." In the crowd, I hear someone spout *"But you just . . ."* before catching themselves. "Or at least I wasn't a hero back at the pet store."

Phones rise, with camera lenses trained on me. I know I'll go viral soon, in the worst of ways. But I'm relieved instead of afraid, because, somehow, I know it's for the best.

"Me and my childhood best friend used to go out to Loving Pond to just be in nature and joke around and play every game we could think of. One of those games was Two Truths and a Lie. And I want to play that with you today." Soft murmurs lift from the crowd. I hold up one finger, signaling the start. Slowly, I point it toward the two frigid bodies at the front of the horde. "Jimmy and Mickey were the true heroes at the pet store. They saved that guy. I mean, I tried but my leg cramped and the shelf was too hot for my hands and—"

The noise emanating from the audience gets perceptively louder. More cell phones rise. I hold up two fingers, doing my best not to let this unnerve me. "My dad is a thousand times the man you think my grandpa is." I read their expressions and quickly add, "And that came as a shock to me, too." My eyes catch those of my father. He's stern-faced, but his expression still has an intrinsic warmth to it that could thaw the coldest of nights. "My grandpa used to be my idol. But in time, I learned that's not who I want to be. I want to be more like *him*." I point straight at my dad.

The crowd sees who I'm staring at and wonders, *Who is this guy?* So I fill them in: "My dad. The person who's always been there for me, even though I've pretty much always overlooked him or taken him for granted. The person in our family who's a real-life hero. Who saved my best friend when she was drowning, without the aid of special effects or CGI technology."

As the crowd takes this all in, I return my gaze to Mickey and Jimmy, both wrapped in a huge blanket, their heads tilted toward each other's as their tired stares center on me. Right now, Jimmy is looking pensive, and I wonder what's going on inside that head of his. Is he thinking of all the attention and accolades that'll surely befall him now that I've just cast my hero's tale to the dustbin of history? I hope not. I hope he doesn't go down my path. I hope, after all is said and done, he's still the exact same Jimmy. Bright-eyed. Optimistic. Striving.

Mickey's traded her worried look for something more contented. I have no worries about her changing because, through it all, she never has. Never made a play for fame or got sucked into the pomp and circumstance of it all. She just wanted to live life on her own terms. To honor her mother. To see me become a better me. I recognize that now, and I'll always be grateful for it.

When the murmurs die down, I hold up my hand as if to quiet them all. It's then that I see a tall, skinny Black guy working his way through the crowd to witness a friend's atonement firsthand. Theo sidles up to Mickey, wrapping a long arm around both her and Jimmy.

I curl all my fingers, minus my index, into a fist, and slowly jab it right into my chest. "To spare you the guesswork, the lie is me. The life I've been living these past couple months. I've been lying to you. And lying to myself. I thought if I could do something amazing, then people would treat me as specially as they treated my grandpa. And they did, for a while. I was the kind of hero my grandfather had always played on the big screen.

"But I realize I don't want to be like him," I continue. "Instead, I want to be like Mickey and Jimmy and even Theo. The people who stuck with me as friends even though I didn't deserve to be theirs. Who somehow know that the most heroic thing we can ever do is see someone at their lowest and refuse to walk away."

I hold up my award. "They deserve this, more than me or my grandfather ever did."

The crowd is still for a long while because nobody is sure what to do. Drift away like leaves with a breeze? Applaud the speech delivered by a fraud?

It takes a while, but they figure it out. Suddenly, and without signal or word, the crowd morphs into something akin to the world's tamest mosh pit. Jimmy, Mickey, and my dad find themselves swept up in the collective movement, not so much moving as being moved. Pushed and encouraged and cajoled until they're right at the steps to the stage. Hesitantly, they walk up, looking around as if they don't quite believe what's happening. I hold out the award to make things clear. I'm facing them, so the microphone doesn't catch what I'm saying, but they can read my lips: "This is yours."

They raise the award together, and the crowd goes wild. Out of everybody, I cheer the loudest.

24

AS I LOOP A FINGER THROUGH THE WINDSOR KNOT OF MY tie, I realize it's the second time I've worn one in the past month—the other occasion being Papa Shades's premiere celebration. This afternoon, it's Mickey's.

This whole process, like kicking the tires on an old car, seems to have reinvigorated her love for filmmaking. I'm totally, 100 percent with her on this, happy to let her shine as I stand in her corner.

Jimmy, Theo, and I are screening her documentary in a reserved meeting room at the Westlake Municipal Library. It's just us three. We decided to surprise her by dressing up for the occasion.

Jimmy's suit is way too big, to the point that he looks like a *Boss Baby* remake. Theo, forever a politician, has an American flag lapel pin neatly positioned directly above a Black Lives Matter pin, which in turn is above an LGBTQ+ rainbow pin. There's nobody in the room he needs to convince to vote for him during next week's SBP special election, but I think he just likes playing the part. Five minutes before the ballot access deadline, I withdrew my name from consideration, and Theo entered his. When I was reinstated as his campaign manager, my first thought was to rein him in. But my second, *better* thought was to let Theo be. Theo. To just be happy to have witnessed this flaring meteor of a person take his place among the stars. He taught me how to do that. They all did.

Having Theo see my speech at the fair gave me the narrowest of lanes to apologize, and I gladly and grovelingly took it.

Sure, I've made an enemy of Lori and the Council. Lovey and Big have been staring me down in crowded hallways, and someone's been slipping pictures of a gavel through the slats of my locker. The threats are worth it, though. Any crushed hand or broken limb is a small price to pay for having Theo back on my side. Plus, they've got another scandal to deal with. Turns out, meeting minutes weren't the *only* thing StuGov secretary Mason Vance had been recording.

Jo. Well . . .

My county-fair confession basically neutered her blackmail video. But she didn't get mad. She got creative. That weekend, she cut and spliced the dark hallway conversation between Mickey and me to make it *seem* like a secret tryst between lovers. Her video hit the internet Sunday night with no caption—just a simple sad-face-single-teardrop emoji. Within seconds, the #FinaFam swarmed her with sympathy. Her clip and my "infidelity" went viral soon after. By Monday, Jo had begun vlogging her breakup journey in an *Eat, Pray, Love* wellness sort of way.

Her follower counts have exploded. I gotta say, the Machiavellian nature of it all makes me more impressed than offended.

As for me? I'm thinking of logging off social media. Permanently. For one thing, the #FinaFam can be very scary. But mainly, it's because I have all the friendship I need right here in this room.

I brought mini cupcakes, and Theo did a great job of controlling the projector and manning the dimmer switches. And when Serena Kyle's portrait appears over a translucent shot of a soaring eagle, we all stand and applaud as if we'd watched Spielberg or Scorsese. Mickey takes an appreciative bow as we line up to give her hugs. Mine is last, and Theo playfully harps that I got the longest embrace, saying he's jealous. Smiling, I simply respond, "I'd be jealous, too."

He says his goodbyes and daps me up last. We do the thing where at the end we pull each other in for a bro-hug with the fist to the back. As we do it this time, I whisper, "Thanks, man."

"For what?" he asks.

"For being you."

He pulls away, smiling. He's never been one to spout profound truths about the world or its intricacies. But his expression says it all. He's glad I'm back at his side. "Norse Club next week? It's Thor Thursday. Anders Jacobson is even gonna bring his papier-mâché hammer."

I nod. "Wouldn't miss it." Honestly, I *would* miss it. I'd be glad to miss it. But it's important to him, so I'll be there.

He nods, too. "Thanks."

After he leaves, Jimmy comes up, and I offer him the last of the cupcakes. He's overwhelmed with gratitude, greedily grabbing and smashing the first two into his face before I can even finish my sentence. It's good to see fame hasn't changed him. After my confession went viral, Mickey uploaded her pet store video—the one showing Jimmy lifting the shelf. Since then, his local celebrity has skyrocketed. He hasn't quite reached the fame I did, but he doesn't have the benefit of a celebrity forerunner. However, I don't think even giving him that would change him from the cupcake-pounding, New-York-accent-talking, diminutive kid I've grown to know and appreciate these last few weeks.

"Hey, me, Phineas, and Treyvion are gonna play *Final Earth* on the PS5 when I get home. Wanna come?" he asks.

Despite the urge to play one of my favorite role-playing games, I must decline. Mickey and I have plans. A date, actually.

I shake my head. "Love that game, but I'm good, man. Have fun, though."

"Aight," he says. Then, hesitantly, "Lionel?"

"Yeah, Jimmy?"

"I couldn't have done any of this without you."

"Yes, you could've," I answer.

He turns and goes. When he's reached the door, I call out, "Jimmy?" He pauses and looks back. "Watch out for that last boss. It's tough. You have to take it as a team."

"I will."

"Don't go trying to be a hero," I joke.

"Wouldn't even dream of it," he answers.

"Never change, Jimmy," I say to myself as he walks out the door.

After he's gone, I turn back to see Mickey standing there, smiling coolly as she watches me. The way her hands are clasped together and one leg twists in front of the other like a pretzel makes the nerves obvious. But then again, my lips suddenly feel chapped and my fingernails have somehow magnetized, involuntarily raking against each other. We're both hopelessly awkward at this. But it makes sense today, with us.

I go up to her, stopping just short.

I nod toward the projector, the end credits still showing on the stopped video. "How is it you're so good at this?"

Mickey shrugs. "Runs in the family, I guess."

"Well, it was Oscar-worthy. And I mean that."

"Thanks."

"In fact . . ." I reach a hand into my pocket and slowly pull out a plastic Oscar the Grouch *Sesame Street* figurine. I hand it to her. Mickey feigns shock, hands covering her mouth, willing her arms to shake as she grips it tight. Her acting chops draw me into the charade, because by the time she holds it high into the air, I'm chanting, "Speech, speech, speech!"

She clears her throat. "I would like to thank all the haters and losers who motivated me to do better." She pauses, watching as my eyes go wide. She holds her free hand daintily to her chest as if she's done something wrong. "What?!"

"No thanking friends and family?"

She waves the question away. "*Pssh*. You all were implied."
My face and posture straighten. Once my arms cross, she knows
I'm serious. Her eyes roll. "Okay, whatever."

She opens her mouth, and I expect an easy name-check of
people you're supposed to thank for these kinds of things. But
her words jam up just before they reach her lips, and I can tell
this isn't going to be a walk in the park for her. My posture
relaxes and my expression softens. It's not a joke anymore. She's
putting that shield of humor down for a moment, letting herself
really indulge in her feelings.

She stares at the wall behind me. As her eyes begin to water,
I step closer, taking Oscar away and setting it on the floor. Then
I hold her hands. I nod, reassuringly, and she does, too.

"I'd like to thank my mom, for giving me the talent and
drive. And my dad, for putting up with me. And you."

"Why me?" I ask, genuinely shocked.

A wry smile comes to her face. "It just wouldn't be right to
not thank your boyfriend."

My throat dries as I do a double take, mentally replaying
what I just heard.

Boyfriend?

It's the one word I wasn't expecting at all today. But it's
everything I didn't know I needed.

My lips part, and I make a noise that sounds suspiciously
like "Really?" and she nods. Really. My heart jumps, my even

keel obliterated. I break into a smile that could power a city.

She raises an eyebrow. "I mean, if you're cool with it."

"I'm *very* cool," I say.

Mickey puts her arms around my shoulders, and mine slide around her waist. We stand in the middle of the library meeting room, once enemies, now a couple with a history of childhood affinity and adolescent feuding. It all comes together in a kiss made for the big screen.

Our lips break apart. Her cheeks are flushed. She looks like a starlet.

"Guess I've tamed the Lionheart, huh?" she says.

"Lionel," I reply. "Just regular old Lionel."

And for once, I am perfectly fine with that.

ACKNOWLEDGMENTS

I never got to know either of my grandfathers. I always wondered what it would have been like to talk to the men who had a hand in molding my parents, who, in turn, molded me. So, it was both a pleasure and a revelation writing *Two Truths and a Lionel*, a story about a boy dealing with the fact that his famous grandfather isn't as gilded as Hollywood made him out to be. About how we too often look for heroes on the big screen while neglecting the ones in our own homes.

To the teen boys out there looking for heroes: I see you. And I hope you find them.

I thank Alyssa and Jon, my editor and my agent. You made Lionel shine. He grew up right before our eyes, in no small part because of you both. I also want to shout-out Erick Dávila and the design and copyediting teams, who've seen this book through to near perfection. You are much appreciated.

Thank you, God. I am living a dream, and I owe it to you.

To Mom and Dad. You got the best out of me. I hope you see that.

To Heather and Shannon. Thanks for being my big sisters.

I couldn't have had better footsteps to follow.

Thank you to my grandmothers. You two gave a lot of people a solid foundation upon which to build. Somehow, somewhere, I know you see that.

To Ashly, my love. Again, I couldn't have done this without your unwavering support. I couldn't have asked for a more wonderful, caring, and considerate person to be by my side this past decade.

To Channing and London. I hope you two grow to be as humble, kind, and compassionate as adults as you are now. I love you both.

To Zahara. Welcome to the world, little girl. You are a true bright spot in all our lives now. Keep being you.

To the teachers, the librarians, and the readers. You are always in my heart. Thanks.